OBSOLETE THEOREM

ACROSS HORIZONS - BOOK 1

STAN C. SMITH

A Skyra Publication

Copyright © 2020 by Stan C. Smith

All rights reserved.

No part of this book may be reproduced in any form or by any electronic or mechanical means, including information storage and retrieval systems, without written permission from the author, except for the use of brief quotations in a book review.

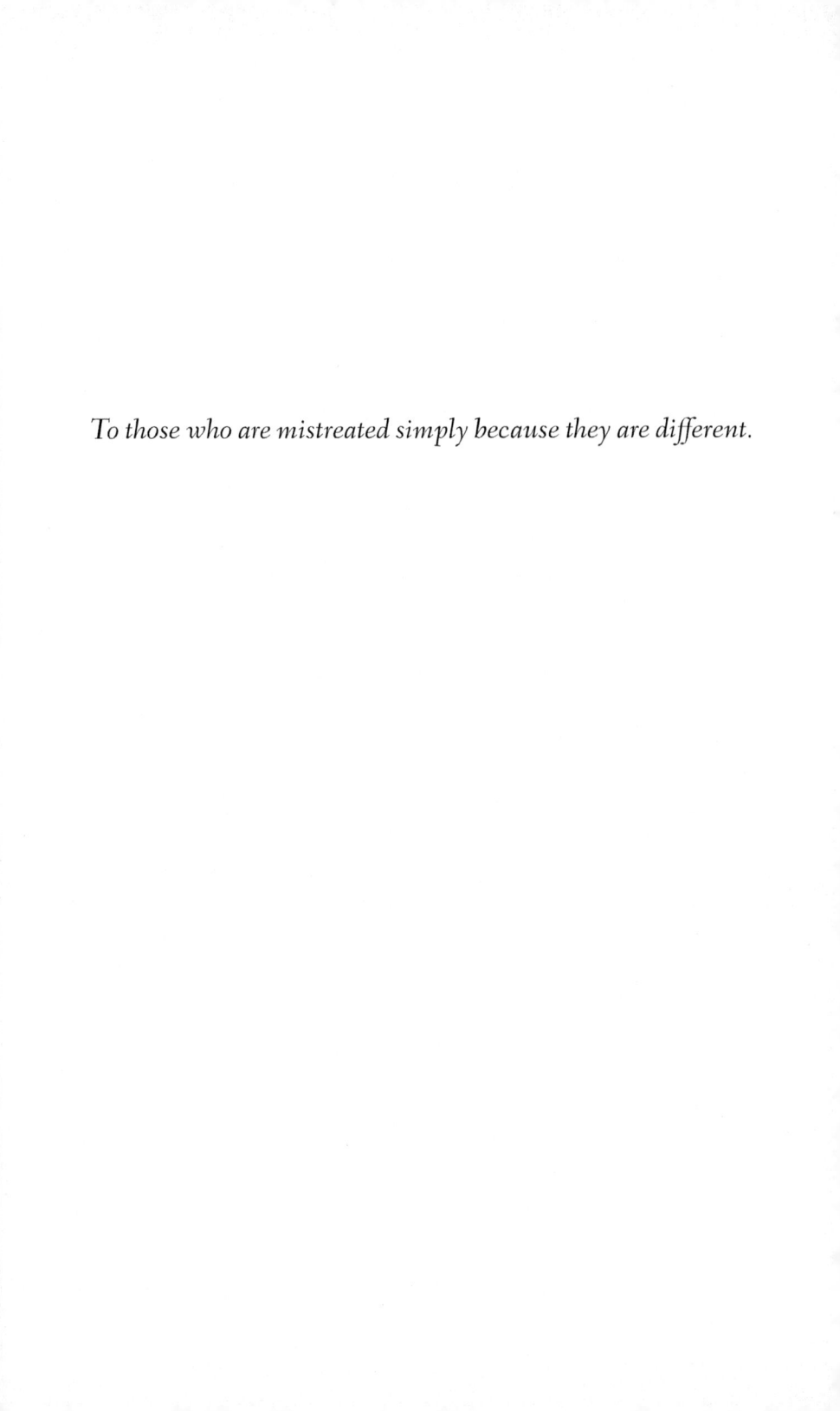

To those who are mistreated simply because they are different.

OBSOLETE THEOREM

Listen to me speak, bolup men. I will not submit to you, and I will take your strength.

SKYRA-UNA-LOTO

1

SKYRA

47,659 years ago - Zaragoza Province of Spain

Skyra-Una-Loto wasn't fond of hedgehog meat—a shame since this meal would probably be her last. She stepped on the creature's head, thrust her stone blade into its chest, and sawed through skin and bone to its hind feet. A cooking fire here would reveal her presence, so she pulled out the heart and other chest organs and shoved them into her mouth. She needed food in her belly and strength in her arms and legs. Before nightfall she intended to kill some of the bolups who had taken her birthmate, and if Veenah was still alive, Skyra would take her back.

Skyra rose to her full height, scanning the trees and hillside between her and the bolups' camp. Satisfied there was no danger, she wiped the blood from her chin and dropped back into a crouch. She pulled out the hedgehog's stomach and intestines and arranged them on a rock. She would eat them only if the rest of the body didn't quell her hunger.

Quietly singing to herself, she gripped the soft, spineless belly skin and began working it from the flesh, rolling the skin over itself to cover the painful spines. Her birthmother had taught her how to skin a hedgehog, which now seemed so long ago.

Disregarding the risk of being heard, Skyra pounded the skinned body with a rock, pulverizing the bones and flesh into a paste. She scooped the paste up with her fingers and consumed it quickly. By the time the mashed body was gone, she felt full enough to leave behind the intestines.

She took several long breaths, trying to soothe her fears. After four days of searching she had found the bolups' camp. It was time to kill.

Skyra scrubbed her hands with fresh dirt and then wiped the dirt off against a bare rock. She never wiped food or blood on her cape or waist-skin—furs of the lynx and woolly rhino were not easy to come by.

She moved away from the stench of the hedgehog intestines and stepped onto a rounded boulder. Facing away from the bolups' camp, she positioned both her arms behind her back, leaving her vulnerable abdomen unprotected.

She spoke softly. "Kami-fu-menga-ulmecko. Ati-de-lé-melu imbo-oh-nup-tekne-té." Her words meant, *Listen to me speak, woolly rhino and cave lion. I submit to you in return for your strength.* She then turned to face the bolups' camp and covered her belly with her arms. "Kami-fu-bolup-mafeem. Ati-de-lé-melu-rha aibul-khulo-tekne-té." *Listen to me speak, bolup men. I will not submit to you, and I will take your strength.*

Skyra secured both her hand blades in the leather sheath on her wrist. Hedgehog blood still stained the heavy, stone blade of her khul, so she wiped it off in the dirt. After sliding the khul handle-first into the sling on her back, she picked up her spear. She hefted the shaft a few times and checked the tightness of the stone point. Recently she had replaced the spear's point with one she'd found in her camp after the bolup men had attacked. Now she hoped to stain the point with bolup blood, perhaps even the blood of the same man who had so carelessly lost it.

The morning after the bolups' attack, Skyra also had found two smaller stone points, each of them affixed with strips of skin to thin spears no longer than her arm. Despite their tiny size, these spears had killed two of Skyra's tribemates. The attack had taken place in the dark, so Skyra hadn't seen how the bolup men could have thrown the small spears with such deadly force. Today, though, she would not underestimate their ability to kill her.

She made her way up the hillside. Near the summit she paused and turned to look back. Dark, scrubby trees bordered a stream in the distance. She had left Ripple to wait there. Now she wished the creature was with her. Perhaps it couldn't protect her, but its presence gave her courage. Actually, Skyra had no idea what kind of creature Ripple was, although it had been her companion through two cold seasons and almost two warm seasons.

She muttered, "Aibul-meli-yabo-rha nokho lotup-melendü." *If I don't return, my friend, find your way home.*

She turned away from the valley and traversed the hilltop. Soon she caught the stench of bolups, and she ducked behind a boulder to peer at the scene below. Another stream flowed by at the hill's base, this one too small to support more than a few trees. Several breaths later she spotted bolups standing in the stream's ankle-deep water. Skyra squinted, then a whimper nearly escaped from her chest before she suppressed it. Her birthmate Veenah was standing in the stream, surrounded by three bolup women. Veenah had been stripped of her cape and waist-skin. She was naked except for her two dayun, her leather footwraps, which were barely visible in the flowing water.

The women were splashing water on Veenah's body, wiping away blood and grime. One woman was working specifically on the area between Veenah's legs, where there seemed to be an abundance of blood. Again, Skyra suppressed a whimper.

A fourth bolup—this one a man—stood beside the stream holding a rope tied around Veenah's neck.

Skyra whispered, "Fekho-gédun-tekne-té-rha." *Where is your strength, sister?* Veenah was just standing there, not fighting, hardly moving at all.

After staring for a few more short breaths, Skyra pulled back behind the boulder and rubbed her eyes with her free hand, trying to push aside her fear. She reminded herself that she was actually lucky. Veenah was away from her captors' camp, guarded by only four of the stinking bolups, and three of them were women. Unlike the women of Skyra's own people, bolup women rarely hunted, and they never participated in attacks. They were frail. Skyra hadn't killed one before, but she hoped to change that now.

She scanned the hillside. Other boulders littered the slope, but they were too scattered to provide enough cover to hide her approach. She would have to descend the hill exposed. She closed her eyes for a moment, coaxing the rhino and lion strengths to enter her arms and legs.

Skyra got to her feet. Instead of charging down the hill, she walked, moving deliberately. She carried her spear in one hand and cupped the back of her neck with the other, her fingers almost touching her khul's blade.

When she was halfway down the slope, the man spotted her. He shouted something using words Skyra couldn't understand. She kept walking, hoping the man's voice couldn't be heard from the bolups' camp. The three women had stopped washing Veenah and were staring. Skyra could now clearly see her birthmate's face, which was swollen and bloody. Veenah didn't even turn her head—she just stared into the distance as if she were dead.

The man shouted again. He tossed the rope to one of the bolup women and picked up a spear from the ground by his feet. The three women stepped out of the stream, pulling on Veenah's rope. Veenah stumbled on the submerged rocks and fell, but instead of trying to get up, she just lay there, her face barely above the surface.

Skyra was almost to the water's edge. The stream was narrow—she could cross it in three or four running strides, although the rocky bottom might trip her. She stopped and looked directly at the man.

He stared back at her, then his eyes widened. He looked down at Veenah and back at Skyra, confused by the two nandup women's similar appearance. He shifted one shoulder and tilted his head slightly.

At that moment Skyra's fear faded away. From watching the man's movements, she knew what he was going to do next. This was a skill she had possessed for as long as she could remember. The ability had nearly gotten her killed as a child because it frightened her tribemates, even her birthmother and the dominant men, one of which was likely to be her birthfather. It frightened everyone but Veenah, because Veenah had the same ability.

This was a good time to confuse the bolup man even further. Without taking her eyes off him, Skyra tossed her spear into the stream. He frowned as he watched the weapon bob to the surface and start drifting with the current.

Skyra could sense it now, almost as clearly as if the man were one of her own species. He was confident, convinced that he was not in danger, and he was about to cross the stream. He would come at Skyra and try to take her.

He lowered his spear and took a step into the water, wobbling slightly, a little off balance.

Skyra charged. She reached the man in three strides without stumbling. Before he could step back onto steady ground, she pulled her khul from the sling on her back, grabbed the handle with her other hand, and swung the weapon.

Skyra sensed he would raise one hand to protect his face, but she didn't care. Her blade shattered his arm, then embedded itself in the side of his head. He collapsed into the water, but her charge had been so furious that she collided with his body and fell over him.

The three women screamed, dropped Veenah's rope, and began running. Skyra rolled off the man, pulled her khul from his skull, and threw it. The khul's heavy blade struck one of the women, knocking her off her feet. The woman writhed, still alive, but Skyra sprinted after the other two. The bolup women were slow, and she quickly overtook them. She pulled one of her blades from her wrist sheath and slashed at the nearest woman, cutting into her shoulder but not slowing her down. The next slash cut into her neck, and this time the woman fell.

Skyra came to a stop. The third woman was now too far ahead, too close to the bolups' camp. The injured woman at

Skyra's feet was still screaming. Skyra decided not to waste valuable time silencing her. Bolup men from the camp were almost certainly on their way. They would be drawn to the woman's cries, which would slow them down. Skyra ran back to the stream.

The woman she'd hit with her khul was now gone, so Skyra leapt into the stream and kneeled beside her birthmate. "Veenah! Veenah-Uno-Loto!"

Veenah was still sprawled in the shallow water, making no effort to get up. One of her eyes was swollen shut, but her other eye met Skyra's. She spoke quietly. "Skyra-Uno-Loto. Apofu-fekho." *Run away, sister.*

Skyra gripped Veenah by the neck and pulled her to her feet. With Veenah's arm over her shoulders, she guided her birthmate from the stream and headed up the hillside.

Veenah stumbled, almost unable to walk at all. "Apofu-fekho," she repeated.

Skyra kept moving.

Shouts came from behind. Skyra glanced back. Bolup men—many of them—were already approaching. Skyra let out a wail. Veenah was her birthmate, the only person who truly understood her, and Skyra had failed to take her back. Veenah would surely die in the hands of the stinking bolups.

She glanced back again. The men were crossing the stream and would be upon them within only a few breaths.

Skyra said, "Tekne-té fekho." *Have strength, sister.* She ducked from beneath Veenah's arm and ran.

Skyra knew the men would pursue her—she was of breeding age, like her sister. She also knew she could outrun them. Bolup men were not much faster than bolup women. She ran over the hilltop the way she had come. By the time she reached the bottom of the slope, she was panting hard.

She turned to look back. Several men were running down the slope after her, with more appearing over the summit. The men in the lead were each carrying a weapon that resembled her khul but with a smaller stone blade.

A lower hill lay before Skyra. She would have to make it over the hill and across a wide field of rocks before reaching the tree-lined river, the only place she'd have a chance to hide. She ran up the slope.

By the time she'd descended the smaller hill and started across the rock field, Skyra began to suspect she wasn't going to make it. The men didn't seem to be tiring. How could they run so far without slowing down?

She took another glance. Two of the men had outdistanced the others and were steadily catching up. She visually measured the distance to the trees and the rate the men were gaining on her. She factored in her diminishing speed, as well as the likelihood of actually losing the men in the forest. She let out another wail as she visualized the resulting outcome. Sand and jagged stones grated against her dayun soles as she came to a stop. She turned around, gripping both her hand blades, which were now the only weapons she had.

The first two men caught up a few breaths later. From the way they were scanning the ground before them, she sensed they were about to diverge and get on either side of her.

Skyra was, more than anything else, a hunter. She was a nandup, and the nandups of her region held a longstanding truce, rarely attacking other nandup camps. Bolups, though, ignored such agreements. They attacked any nandup camp that appeared weak, killing men and taking women of breeding age. Because of this, Skyra's tribemates had taught her to fight. What they hadn't taught her, though, was how to read an attacker's intent. That skill had been within her and

Veenah even before the two birthmates had stopped suckling their birthmother. The skill had saved Skyra's life before, and she hoped it would save her now.

Sensing the two men were focused on where to place their feet as they diverged, she chose an action they would not expect. She leapt at the first man and smashed her palm and the handle of her blade into his nose. She and the man were moving past each other so fast that stabbing with the blade's point would have ripped the weapon from her hand or even broken her wrist.

The man dropped his khul and fell onto his back. Skyra leapt over his body and slashed with her other blade as she flew past the second man, being sure to angle the blade back to save her wrist.

The second man ducked to the side, avoiding the blade. Instead of wheeling around to attack, he continued running several paces, and when Skyra turned to face him, he was too far away for her to surprise him again. He held his khul ready, but he flicked his eyes over her shoulder at the others approaching behind her. The stinking bolup knew better than to fight a nandup by himself, even one who was armed with only two hand blades.

The man bared his teeth at her and said, "Nu delo-do!"

Skyra didn't understand the words and didn't care. The other men were almost upon her, and now she had no chance of making it to the river. The man she had knocked to the ground was starting to get up. She screamed and stabbed at the top of his head with one of her blades. The blade didn't penetrate his skull, so she plunged it into the soft tissue on the side of his neck. She then flicked the blade toward the second man, throwing blood droplets at him in defiance.

Without glancing down at his bleeding tribemate, the man

bared his teeth again as he stared at her. Skyra thought maybe he was smiling, but bolups didn't smile the same way her people did.

The men surrounded her.

Skyra screamed one more time, then she lowered one of her blades, lifted her waist-skin, and held the blade to her groin. She gritted her teeth, preparing to drive the knife into the part of her body the stinking men cared about most.

"Melil gu!" one of them shouted. He pointed past her toward the river. The other men were also staring past her.

Skyra swung around. A creature had emerged from the trees and was flying across the field of rocks at about the height of Skyra's shoulders.

Several of the men muttered words Skyra didn't understand, but they didn't run away—they simply stared, like their feet had grown roots into the dirt.

The flying creature—the size and shape of a large beaver—didn't slow down, but still the bolups remained frozen in place. It came directly at the nearest man, who appeared to be too confused to move out of its path. It rammed into the man's face and chest. His body flew backward and knocked a second man to the ground.

The second man scrambled to his feet as the creature came to a stop and hovered above the first man's motionless body.

An orb of light on the front of the creature's shell, almost as bright as the sun but now partially obscured by smeared blood, grew bright and then dim, bright and then dim again.

"Mano telo pa-mon-do!" the creature said, although it had no mouth from which to speak.

The men turned and ran, leaving their two fallen tribemates behind.

Skyra watched them retreat up the hillside until they stopped at the summit and turned to stare back down the slope. She stepped over and picked up the khul dropped by the man she'd stabbed. She hefted it a few times. The man was still choking, trying to suck air into his body, so she swung the khul at his head, ending his struggle. She would prefer the weapon to be heavier, but it worked well enough.

She turned to the creature, which was now lowering itself to the ground. Four legs appeared from its belly, and within a breath's time it was standing among the rocks. A ring of tiny red lights around the blood-smeared orb flashed on and off a few times as it stared back at Skyra.

"You did not stay hidden by the river, Ripple," Skyra said, using the creature's own language. "I told you to stay there."

Ripple continued staring at her for a few more throbs of its circle of red lights. "Perhaps we will learn another new word today," it said. "The word is *gratitude*. You would be showing gratitude if you were to say, 'Thank you for saving my life, Ripple.'"

Skyra stepped over to Ripple and kneeled. She wiped some of the bolup blood off its orb, which became dim upon her touch. She then ran her finger along a damaged corner at the top of Ripple's shell. "You have hurt yourself! You should have stayed by the river."

After a moment of silence, the creature said, "You are welcome."

Skyra picked up a handful of dirt and rubbed it onto the blood covering the angular ridges to one side of Ripple's orb. "Veenah is still with the bolups—the humans. She will soon die. She will die because I have failed."

"You may have failed this time, but you can try again. Veenah is important, as you are, and we will come up with another plan to save her from the humans." Ripple shifted slightly, turning toward the hill. "Skyra, you must now set aside your concerns for your birthmate. Your life is in immediate peril."

Skyra rose to her feet. The bolup men had apparently recovered from their fear. They were coming back down the hill. One of them raised his khul and shouted fiercely.

Ripple rose from the ground, pulling its legs up into its belly. "You must flee, Skyra."

2

LINCOLN

47,659 YEARS** later - **Northwest of Tucson, Arizona, USA

LINCOLN WOODHOUSE GLANCED over his shoulder at his pursuers as he ran up the rugged slope of Heartache Hill. There were now at least six of them—white arctic wolves—and they were closer than the last time he'd looked back. He could hear their panting breaths and occasional growls. He poured on the speed, making it to the hilltop in less than two minutes, a damned decent pace. Regardless, the wolves were now almost nipping at his heels.

Lincoln gained more of a lead on his way down the slope, but he decided he just wasn't feeling it. Arctic wolves seemed out of place in the Arizona desert. He stopped and put a finger to the frame of his sunglasses. The wolves caught up, snarling and tearing at the flesh of his legs. He ignored them and pressed the mode button on his glasses. The wolves vanished. Fifty meters back up the slope, three staggering, tattered people appeared. Strips of rotting skin hung loosely from their bodies, exposing blackened meat and jagged bone. The three stopped staggering and began picking up speed, running straight for Lincoln.

Lincoln grunted and pressed the mode button again. The zombies vanished. A split second later, an adult allosaurus came lumbering down the slope. The creature was at least eight meters long and stood three meters tall, but it was picking up speed at a downright frightening rate, and Lincoln could hear its thick feet pounding the sand through the earbuds attached to his glasses. A prickly thrill spread over his skin, accelerating his heart rate.

"That's the one," he muttered, and he began running again.

Lincoln threaded his way through six more kilometers of towering saguaro cactuses and red-tipped ocotillo shrubs. The dinosaur was behind him every time he looked back, sometimes at a safe distance, other times so close that he was forced to pick up his pace. This last iteration was it—the sunglasses were ready for prime time. Runners and cyclists were going to love them, and the glasses would earn him a buttload of money.

Lincoln had every intention of running a second twelve-kilometer loop. The desert was relatively cool this morning, and yesterday he'd been too busy with final programming tweaks to squeeze in a run. As he rounded the last bend of the dry stream bed of Scrub Creek, however, he saw Maddy standing beside the trail in front of the main lab of his research campus. Maddy rarely set foot outside the lab, so this peculiar sight brought Lincoln to an abrupt stop.

"What's going on, Maddy?"

The drone's ring of red lights blinked rapidly, an expression of consternation. A calm female voice came from the two speakers on either side of the twelve-centimeter, illuminated camera lens. "If you would take your phone with you when you run, Lincoln, you would already know what's going on. Then I would not have had to come out to this unsanitary, sand-ridden environment to intercept you."

Lincoln heard fast-approaching footsteps and a low growl. He turned just as the allosaurus caught up to him. The creature lunged forward to take his head in its jaws. He instinctively threw his arms up and ducked away but then quickly regained composure and pressed the power button on his sunglasses.

Maddy said, "Are you having a seizure, Lincoln? Do you need assistance?"

"Very funny. You want to tell me why you're interrupting my one opportunity of the day to find some peace of mind?"

"You have visitors, and your visitors have made it clear that they are not patient men. Their general demeanor suggested that you, Lincoln, may be in some hot water."

Lincoln glanced at the two vehicles parked by the lab's front door, a van and an SUV, both of them shiny and black. "Oh, great. Are they old?"

"By your standards, quite old. I told them that you did not trust any human being who is older than forty, but that did not seem to pacify them."

Lincoln shot Maddy a look. "You did not."

The drone gazed back at him for a few seconds. "No, I did not."

Lincoln used his shirt to wipe sweat from his face. "Alright, let's see what kind of hot water I'm in now." He headed to the lab. Maddy followed him, her mechanical legs skittering in the gravel. As they passed the van and SUV, Lincoln saw that both vehicles were turned on, and a driver was waiting patiently behind the wheel of each.

Lincoln and Maddy passed through the lobby and entered the Congeniality Room, a meeting space where Lincoln often addressed visiting scientists and dignitaries, albeit reluctantly. Four men, all of them sporting gray hair, stood beside the long table made from Madagascan ebony. They were talking to Jazzlyn and Virgil, two of Lincoln's most valued science techs. Lincoln recognized three of the men from the endless series of hearings he'd been forced to attend. They were bigwigs in the needlessly-complex government science policy structure. Their presence here couldn't possibly be a good thing. He strode to within a few meters of them and stopped. Maddy stopped beside him.

When Lincoln didn't speak, Jazzlyn raised her brows at him and mouthed the words, "Say something!"

He didn't.

"Mr. Woodhouse, you may remember me. Robert Chandler, Director, National Science Foundation. I'm pretty sure you've met Drs. Bud Reed and Daniel Gibbons, both of them on the National Science Board." Chandler then motioned toward the fourth man. "And this is Stephen Fuchs, Deputy National Security Advisor and regular attendee of the White House National Security Council."

Lincoln still remained silent. No, this couldn't possibly be good.

Chandler said, "We'd shake your hand, Lincoln, but we've heard you have some kind of phobia regarding contact."

Lincoln broke his silence. "It's not so much a phobia as it is distrust."

The men exchanged glances.

Chandler shrugged. "Well, fortunately we're not here to exchange pleasantries. We have something quite important to discuss with you." The man glanced down at a tablet in his hand.

Lincoln stepped back and held up both hands, sensing that Chandler was about to hand him the tablet. He'd always had the ability to detect what people were about to do or say—a skill that at times had made his life miserable but at other times had given him the edge he needed. "I'd rather you share that screen to my projector, if you don't mind."

Chandler shot him a puzzled frown. "I didn't offer to show you anything yet."

Lincoln stepped over to the projector's control panel and pressed the power button. A virtual screen appeared and hovered several centimeters in front of the room's white wall. "You were about to. Just connect to the network called *Bugger Off*."

Again the men exchanged glances.

"Do you find yourself to be funny, Mr. Woodhouse?" asked Fuchs, the national security guy.

"It really is the network's name," Lincoln said. "My staff and I thought it was funny, but we're—you know—young." He nodded at Chandler's tablet. "There's no password."

Chandler sighed and tapped his tablet a few times. An image of a rocky, hilly landscape filled the virtual screen. "Mr. Woodhouse, does this scene look familiar to you at all?"

Lincoln studied the image. There were no man-made structures, only rugged hills. "Can't say I've been there."

"This is the site of the Pomer paleontological site in Spain. It's a very recent dig. In a matter of only a few days, a rather striking discovery was made. Do you have any idea what discovery that might be?"

Lincoln's wariness went into overdrive, but so did his curiosity. "How would I know? Maybe you could dispense with the cryptic questions and get to the point?"

Chandler tapped his tablet again, switching to a photo of a hillside of jumbled boulders. To one side was a dig site, surrounded by a temporary orange mesh fence. "The skeletal remains that were found here are 47,659 years old. Does that number mean anything to you?"

"It means you're lying."

Jazzlyn spoke up. "What Lincoln's trying to say is that the number is far too precise. There's no way to date fossils with that degree of precision." Jazzlyn was Lincoln's head paleontologist. She was also better at diplomacy than Lincoln.

"Let's say we're pretty sure of the date," Chandler said. "Does the number mean anything to you?"

Lincoln considered this. "First, I've never sent a drone back 47,659 years. Second, what difference would it make if I had? It would have no effect whatsoever on this world. You know that."

Again with the damn exchange of glances.

Chandler tapped the tablet, displaying an image of a fossilized human skull as well as what appeared to be most of the other bones, including vertebrae, arms, legs, and pelvis. From what Lincoln could see, the only bones missing were the feet and lower legs below the knees. The disjointed skeleton was arranged neatly on a white lab table, probably to facilitate 3D imaging. "*Homo neanderthalensis*. Female. Remarkably well preserved, although a few bones of the right shoulder were broken, and for some reason the lower legs and feet haven't been found."

Lincoln waited, but the four men were simply watching

him. Finally, he couldn't resist. "She's quite attractive. Was she your girlfriend?"

Chandler actually cracked a smile, but only for a split second. "Here's the thing, Woodhouse. You came up with the Temporal Bridge Theorem. Using an impressive chain of reasoning, you successfully convinced almost every physicist in the world that your theorem is beyond refute."

"It *is* beyond refute."

"Is it? Would you like to know what was discovered alongside this Neanderthal specimen?"

"I'm sure you're about to tell me." Actually, at this point Lincoln was starting to doubt his ability to predict anything Chandler was going to say. He had no idea where this conversation was going.

The NSF Director tapped his tablet again.

Lincoln stared at the image. "If this is a joke, it's not funny."

"That comment does not warrant a response," Chandler said.

A wave of nausea passed through Lincoln's gut, forcing him to swallow several times to get it under control. He was staring at a drone. Not just any drone—one of *his* drones. The device was stained and darkened with age, but it was recognizable. "That's... not possible," he stammered.

"Yet, there it is. The drone was actually on top of the Neanderthal's remains, with its mechanical limbs positioned on either side of her body. Considering the astounding preservation of the skeletal arrangement, we have no reason to assume the close proximity of the machine is due to post-mortem disturbances."

Lincoln barely heard Chandler's words over the pounding of his own heart. "It's just not possible."

"It seems your Temporal Bridge Theorem is now obsolete, and the implications of that are immeasurable," said one of the other men, although Lincoln didn't bother to tear his eyes from the image to see which one.

He made an effort to step back emotionally and look at the entire drone in a more analytical way. Yes, it was recognizable. It was definitely a drone, and it was similar to his drones, including Maddy, but it wasn't exactly the same. There were subtle differences—slight deviations in the angles of the shell and structure of the limbs, for example. Finally, he turned to the men. "What makes you think this is my drone?"

Chandler sighed and pointed at Maddy. "One of your drones is standing right there. Hell, that might be the same one that hosted Saturday Night Live last year. Everyone on this planet knows what your drones look like, Lincoln. There are slight differences, but there can be no doubt this is one of your drones. It's probably the design you'll make a year from now, or maybe ten years from now."

Chandler was right, of course. The design was too similar to even consider that the drone wasn't one of his. At the very least it was constructed based upon his design. This was all beside the point. The real point was, the drone's existence in this universe was impossible. Jumping back or forward in time created an alternate time-line—a parallel universe. His theorem had proven this, and no mathematician or physicist had succeeded in disproving it. He had sent fourteen drones back in time, and there was no possible way one of those drones could exist on this version of Earth. Everyone knew that. In fact, it was the reason he'd been granted permission to do it in the first place. His program had been a great success so far—data the drones had transmitted back had already multiplied humanity's understanding of biological and meteorological conditions of the past.

Bud Reed spoke up. "Now that we know your theorem is flawed, we're quite fortunate that your drones have not drastically and tragically impacted the present. It's not an exaggeration to state that we're lucky the human species even exists at all."

Lincoln let out an exasperated breath between his teeth. "That's absurd. If my theorem is flawed and this really is one of my drones, then the current state of the world and of the human species is actually *because* of the fourteen connections I've made to the past. If my theorem is flawed, then you exist and are talking to me right now because of my drones. You're welcome!"

Reed started to say something, but Chandler cut him off. "Let's dispense with the confrontational fuss, shall we?" He turned to Lincoln. "Clearly, the implications are staggering. We're trying to understand it, just as you are."

Lincoln's thoughts were already running wild. There were aspects of this discovery that defied all logic. "How?" he asked. "How in the hell could this have been discovered at this specific time? The drone could have been found long before I was even born, or a hundred years from now. Or never. The coincidence is...." He couldn't even come up with a suitable word.

Another round of exchanged glances, this time followed by nods.

Chandler said, "It's not as much of a coincidence as you might think. Six weeks ago, scientists in Spain were alerted to a strange radio signal being broadcast from a point near the small village of Pomer, in the Zaragoza Province. Fortunately, they were able to pinpoint the source just before the signal faded away. Obviously curious, they initiated an excavation. Only two unusual things were found, the Neanderthal specimen and the drone."

Lincoln rubbed his temples. He felt like his head was going to explode. He wasn't terribly surprised that the drone could have preserved a small portion of its reserve power for 47,000 years. After all, he had challenged himself to design his drones so that they would not corrode or disintegrate over vast periods of time. Still, he couldn't get over the timing. The drone had to have maintained the functioning of its internal clock, and for some reason it had chosen this specific year to expend the last of its power to draw attention to itself. Why now? And how in the hell could it even exist on this world to begin with?

The men were watching him, perhaps giving him time to absorb the news.

"There's more," Chandler said. "Not surprisingly, we weren't able to procure the actual fossils or the drone itself, but we were given high-def 3D models of each of the Neanderthal's bones, as well as a model of the entire dig site with the specimen and drone in situ." He tapped his tablet a few times and held it out for Lincoln to take. "I'd like you to examine the Neanderthal's right femur. You can manipulate it on the screen."

Instead of taking the tablet, Lincoln stepped to the virtual screen at the wall. Before him was a leg bone the color of breakfast blend coffee. It looked to be pretty much the same size and shape as a human femur, although slightly thicker. He couldn't see anything out of the ordinary. "You want to tell me what I'm looking for?"

"Turn the bone over," Chandler said.

Lincoln inserted two fingers into the screen and turned

the femur. He saw it almost immediately—some kind of etchings in the bone's surface. "Are those tooth marks?"

"Look more closely."

He spread his fingers apart, enlarging the bone. The scratches weren't tooth marks at all. One of them looked like an upside down letter E. He rotated the femur 180 degrees and zoomed in even more. Next to the letter E was a letter N. Several other marks followed, but they were difficult to make out.

"Those look like letters of the alphabet," Lincoln said. "How did they get there?"

"We were hoping you could tell us," Chandler replied. "I think you'll be quite interested to read the entire message. Allow me to change the lighting." He tapped his tablet again, and a yellowish light seemed to shine on the bone, making the etchings much clearer. There were three lines of characters, with the first line extending almost the entire length of the femur.

LINCOLN WOODHOUSE. COME TO HERE AND NOW. ENTIRE CIVILIZATION AT RISK.
41.632903, -1.847435
417,949,518.6 HOURS BEFORE NOON 1/1/2050

"Mr. Woodhouse? You okay?"

Lincoln blinked. "What the hell's going on?"

"Again, we were hoping you'd tell us. Look at this." Chandler displayed another image, this time of the dig site. He manipulated the model, zooming in on the drone. He continued zooming to an area of the drone's shell to one side of the main camera lens. He zoomed even further, until finally some tiny letters and numbers scratched into the shell surface came into view. "It's the exact same message, character for character," Chandler said. "You need to understand we've ruled out the possibility this is a hoax. The message was scratched into that Neanderthal femur and the drone over 47,000 years ago. We're guessing 418 million hours before noon of January 1st, 2050. If you care to know, that's—"

"I know what it is! It's 417,780,948 hours before now. In other words, it's 47,659 years, 89 days, and 18 hours before you interrupted my run today. I also know those are GPS coordinates with decimal minutes."

The room fell silent for a moment.

Chandler cleared his throat and said, "You have a rather impressive mind, Lincoln. So, I'm sure you've already deduced there is zero chance this is some kind of elaborate practical joke. Which leads you to the conclusion, no matter how improbable it may seem, that this message is real."

Fuchs, the NSA guy, added, "If it's real, why is your name on it, who is telling you to go to that specific time and place, and why in the hell does it say *entire civilization at risk?*"

3

RIPPLE

47,659 YEARS ago - Zaragoza Province of Spain

SKYRA TURNED to run then hesitated when she saw her friend take off flying toward the approaching bolup men. "Ripple, no—they will kill you!"

The creature picked up speed, apparently planning to ram itself into another of the men. Skyra could see this wasn't going to work. The bolups' body movements indicated that this time they were going to be ready.

Ripple flew directly at the nearest man. With determination on his face, the man braced his legs and raised his khul, preparing to step aside and swing it.

"No!" Skyra screamed.

Still several breaths from the man, Ripple dropped to the ground and tumbled end over end, coming to a stop almost within the man's striking range. Its legs shot out from its belly. It righted itself and began running back toward Skyra. "My flight reserves are depleted," the creature said as it neared her. "We must run."

The men were now running down the hill again.

With the comforting heft of her new khul in her hand, Skyra turned and ran with her companion. Together they reached the forest-lined river ahead of the men, but the scrubby trees offered little cover in which to hide, especially with the humans following so closely.

She slowed and almost stopped beside one of the trees. "I have to fight. The bolups do not weaken. They will run until I have no strength."

Ripple fell in behind her and pushed its shell against her thigh, coaxing her to pick up speed. "Skyra, if you wish to save Veenah, you must escape. They will kill you if you stop and fight." The creature bumped her thigh again. "Please accelerate."

Skyra growled, but she sped up. Instead of turning to run parallel to the river, she charged head on into the knee-deep water. Several steps in, she stumbled and fell on her face.

"Get up," Ripple said as her head came back to the surface. The creature was standing in the water beside her, its red lights flashing rapidly.

She glanced over her shoulder. The men were close, but Ripple was right—there were too many for her to fight. She got to her feet and sloshed toward the far bank.

"If you'll recall," said Ripple, "the tall arrangement of rock outcrops and hoodoos we observed this morning was riddled with crevices. That is our destination. It is just over a kilometer away."

"Use words I know!" Skyra said. She stepped from the water onto one of the rocks lining the shore.

Something slammed into her shoulder. The object's force

spun her body to the side and knocked her onto the rocks. Pain overtook her thoughts.

"You must get up."

Skyra heard Ripple's words, but she couldn't respond. She wasn't even sure where she was.

"Skyra, get up."

She blinked. Her face was in the dirt and gravel. She lifted her head and saw a red stain where her forehead had been.

"Pick up your weapon."

Her weapon? There it was, beside her. Strangely, there was now a second khul on the ground beside it. She tried to reach for the nearest khul but then cried out in pain. Her arm wouldn't move.

"Use your other hand. You only have a few seconds. Pick it up."

She let out a growl, grabbed the khul with her good hand, and got to her feet. She spun around in time to see the nearest man stepping from the water. He had no weapon—the stinking bolup had thrown his khul at her.

Skyra preferred to hunt and fight with her other hand, but that arm now hung uselessly at her side. Her only chance was to use the skill she often wished she didn't have. She braced her feet on the rocks and studied the man's face. He hesitated, glancing down at Ripple then turning back to Skyra. He could see that she was hurt, which emboldened him, but he had also seen her and Ripple kill his tribemates. His expression showed his intention to stand back and wait for the other men to arrive.

Two more were just entering the river.

Skyra couldn't wait even one more breath. She stepped toward him.

The man's eyes widened slightly. He was about to take a

step to the side, to give himself more distance without stepping back into the water.

Skyra started to raise her khul.

"Di-kha-yalen," Ripple said.

Skyra didn't understand the language, but Ripple's words drew the man's attention. She took another step and swung her khul upward, driving the stone blade into his chin. His head flew back, yanking his body with it, and he toppled into the water.

Skyra turned and ran. Her ruined arm flopped back and forth with every step, feeling as if it were being ripped from her body. She ignored the pain and ran with all the strength the lion and rhino had relinquished to her. She was aware of Ripple running with her, guiding her, but the pain and effort didn't allow her to speak. She couldn't even turn to check on her pursuers. She just kept running.

"This way. The rocks are near."

For a moment, Skyra wondered how Ripple could continue talking and running without gasping for breath. In fact, she realized she had never heard the creature breathing. Then her thoughts turned to Veenah's face, beaten and stained. The bolup men would use her up, and, if she lived through that, they would wait until she gave birth and then probably kill her. Or they would do it all over again before finally killing her. If Veenah died, Skyra wanted to die too. She couldn't sleep without Veenah—the two birthmates had always slept together in a tangle of arms and legs and furs. Like Skyra, Veenah could sense what other nandups were about to do, and sometimes what they were going to say. Some of their tribemates had argued that the sisters should be killed and eaten, to spread their skills throughout the rest of the tribe. Veenah and Skyra had therefore lived in fear, but they'd always had each other—until the bolup men had taken Veenah away.

"Our destination is near. Keep running."

Skyra could see the rocks now, boulders jumbled together and piled high. She remembered what she had thought of the place earlier that day—it looked as if all the woolly mammoths of the world had come to this place and shoved the boulders together into a tall heap. Perhaps the mammoths had wished to climb to the sky and walk upon the clouds.

"Only a hundred meters, Skyra. We will hide in the crevices, and there you will be safe."

Ripple still spoke without panting, while Skyra couldn't breathe. Her chest heaved, over and over, but it seemed she wasn't getting the air she needed. Her shoulder was ruined—she knew that by the way her arm was swinging, her dead hand hitting her belly and then her back. Her jagged shoulder bones were grinding against each other so loudly she could hear them. Or maybe the sound was her mouth trying to suck in more air.

As they approached the hill of boulders, Ripple said, "Follow me. You are now going to have to climb."

Ripple led her into a gap between two tall rock slabs. The upper end of the gap was blocked by a solid rock wall, but smaller boulders were piled on one side, offering a way to climb out of the gap to a higher level.

Skyra stopped at the boulder pile and looked back. Through the gap's opening she saw only gently rolling hills covered in sand and sparse brush. "I... do not... see the humans," she said, trying to catch her breath.

"They are coming."

"I do not see them!"

"I can hear them. They are coming."

Skyra pulled up the side of her cape and looked at her shoulder for the first time. The damage was in the back, and all she could see was the top edge of a deep gash. The skin around it was red, slick with sweat, and hot to the touch. She couldn't move her arm or any of her fingers. She glanced at the ground. A small blood puddle had formed beside her foot, and she could see more drops leading up to where she was standing.

Ripple scrabbled over the rocks. At the height of Skyra's head, the creature braced three of its legs and held the fourth out for her to grab. "You must climb."

Skyra let her cape fall back over her arm and stared at Ripple's extended leg. She had lifted the creature before—when it had become stuck in a muddy river—and knew its body was far lighter than hers. If it didn't brace itself properly on the rocks, she would simply pull it over on top of her.

As if Ripple understood what she was thinking, it shifted away from her and repositioned its legs against the back sides of two boulders.

She slipped her khul into the sling on her back and grabbed Ripple's outstretched leg with her good hand. A clicking sound she had not heard before came from within the creature's shell as it pulled her up. She got her feet onto the lowest of the boulders. Ripple then scuttled to a higher position and extended its leg again.

"The humans are near, Skyra. Climb quickly."

Within a few more breaths, Skyra had climbed over the boulders and stepped onto a wide slab of rock. She followed Ripple up the rock's gentle slope, leapt across a crevice to another slab of rock, and continued to another jumble of boulders they would have to climb. Ripple repeated the same process, helping her one step at a time until she was atop another angled slab of rock. After running to the upper end of this slab, they were faced with several directions they could go to climb higher.

Skyra stopped and rested her good hand on her knee. While climbing, she had almost managed to ignore the pain, but now her shattered shoulder made it difficult to think. She looked over the low hills back the way they'd come. "I do not see the bolup men."

Ripple didn't turn to look at the scene. "The humans are near. We must find a cave or crevice in which to hide."

"I don't hear them, and I don't smell them. Where are they?"

Ripple remained silent for a few breaths. "I do not know where the humans are."

"You said you heard them."

"I did not hear them. I said that because I wanted you to move faster."

Skyra spun around and stared at her companion.

Ripple remained motionless, although its ring of red lights pulsed once. "The men are most certainly following us, and you cannot fight them. You will not be safe until you find a place to hide."

"You said you heard them," she repeated.

"Yes, I did. Sometimes it is important to say things that are not true. It is called lying. I lied to you to save your life. Earlier I collided with that human—probably killing him—to save your life. Now I have lied to you to save your life."

A memory flooded Skyra's mind. Screams. Horrid smells. A little girl's face forcefully held over a cooking fire until her hair burned and her skin bubbled. The girl's name was Vota, a tribemate Skyra had played with as a child. Vota had said something to her birthmother that was not true. Skyra was never told what Vota had said, but Skyra and Veenah and her other tribemates had to watch. It was what nandups did to other nandups who said words that were not true.

"I do not want you to lie to me ever again," Skyra said.

Ripple's red lights went completely dark. "I understand."

A distant voice drew Skyra's attention. She turned and gazed out over the open ground beyond the hill of rocks. The bolup men were coming over the nearest rise. They were not running. Instead, they were moving slowly, looking at the ground, following Skyra's and Ripple's tracks, or perhaps following Skyra's blood trail.

"I see them," Ripple said, "and now I really do hear them. We must find a place to hide."

"Even if we hide, the men will find me. They will follow my blood."

Ripple said, "At this moment, a man I once knew would say, 'Get the lead out, layabout.' It is a reference to a heavy substance called lead, which if it were in your shoes or in your pockets, would certainly... well, never mind. It means, Skyra, that you need to stop finding excuses and get moving. Follow me."

Ripple headed into another sloping gap between rock slabs. At the upper end of the gap they climbed over another jumble of boulders then found themselves on a wide ledge about halfway up the rock hill.

A shout came from below. Skyra turned. One of the men was pointing up at her. Then all the men began running to the hill's base.

"This way," Ripple said, leading her along the rock ledge.

The ledge became narrower as they followed it around the side of the hill. To the side of Skyra's ruined arm was a drop-off, and to the side of her good arm was a sheer rock face.

They continued until they came upon a gap in the rock face, an opportunity to finally get off the exposed ledge. A short distance into the gap, a pile of fallen boulders had formed a chest-high barrier. Skyra saw several dark openings beyond. Some were probably too small to allow entry, but two were plenty large enough.

Ripple's feet clacked against the pile of boulders as the creature climbed to the top. It then turned and extended a leg. "We are in luck, Skyra."

She grabbed the leg and started climbing. When they were both standing on the other side, she stopped and sniffed the air. "There is something here."

"Yes, I smell it. The men will smell it too. That is why we are in luck. I believe the smell is that of a cave bear. The men will be afraid to follow us here."

Skyra groaned. "Of course they will be afraid!"

"I have considered this carefully. If we do actually encounter a cave bear, I feel reasonably confident that I can startle it and deter its proclivity for violence."

"Use words that I know."

"Sorry. If a bear is here, it will not kill us because I will scare it."

Skyra closed her eyes and rubbed her forehead with her good hand. She whispered, "Listen to me speak, woolly rhino and cave lion. I submit to you in return for your—"

Voices interrupted her, and she opened her eyes. She couldn't see them yet, but the men were near.

"Follow me," Ripple said, its voice just loud enough for her to hear. The creature led her to the first of the openings wide enough to enter. It paused there for a few breaths then moved on to the second large opening. This one was accessible only by climbing yet another jumble of rocks. The musky stench of predator was stronger here. Ripple hesitated for only a breath then scampered up the rocks. It braced itself and extended a leg toward Skyra.

Skyra was proud of her hunting skills. She had even participated in the killing of two cave bears. Now, though, her body was broken, she didn't have a spear, and rather than entering this cave with her skilled tribemates, she only had a creature that was far better at talking than fighting. Her every instinct commanded her to back away.

"I am not lying to you—the men are coming," Ripple said softly. "Please."

She grasped the extended leg and stepped up. Soon she was crouched just within the mouth of the cave, staring into the darkness. The opening wasn't tall enough for her to stand, but it was plenty wide enough for a cave bear to pass through. The stench was overwhelming here, and the floor was covered with brown hairs.

Skyra heard scuffling behind her, and she turned to look. The bolup men were crawling over the rocks at the mouth of the gap. One of them was staring directly at her. It was too late to find another place to hide. She reached back, pulled her khul from her sling, and flipped it over to grasp its handle. The weapon would be useless against a cave bear, but holding it made her feel better.

The fingers of her injured hand dragged against the rock floor as she stayed low and followed Ripple into the darkness. She glanced back. The first of the men had climbed the jumbled rocks and was peering into the cave. Skyra realized the men might simply decide to wait outside. If a bear was indeed in the cave, they would surely hear it kill her and Ripple. If they heard nothing, they would probably enter the cave to attack.

Hiding here was a big mistake.

Skyra froze, listening. Something large was shifting its weight in the blackness ahead. Instinctively, she rose up to run, striking her head on the cave ceiling.

"Do not leave the cave," Ripple said quietly. "You are safer in here."

"I told you not to lie to me again," she hissed.

"I am not lying. Stay behind me."

"Alo tofekho dél!"

The words had come from the man at the cave's mouth. Skyra turned to look. The man was entering the cave, crouching low, holding his khul ready.

"Stay behind me," Ripple repeated.

The rock walls around Skyra grew bright, as if the sun had come down from the sky and entered the cave. At the same time, a wail unlike anything she had ever heard filled the air. She dropped her khul and covered one ear with her good hand, but before she could close her eyes, she saw a monstrous cave bear, only a few body lengths away.

In spite of the brightness of Ripple's light, Skyra's eyes refused to close. She stared at the cave bear, certain it was about to tear her to shreds. The creature let out a deafening roar, drowning out Ripple's high-pitched cry, then threw itself against a jumble of rocks at the back of the cave, apparently trying to get away from the light and sound. It rammed into the rocks again, actually moving some that were larger than Skyra's body. The back of the cave provided no escape, so the bear turned and barreled toward the cave mouth. It ran headlong into a rock column that Skyra had not even seen in the darkness. The bear let out another panicked roar and ran around the column, hitting Skyra's injured shoulder, knocking her out of its way and into the opposite wall beside Ripple.

The wail abruptly stopped, and Skyra heard men shouting, one of them even screaming. She pushed against the floor with her good hand to roll over, then an unbearable pain rushed up one of her legs. She cried out as the pain spread to the rest of her body. In the harsh light of Ripple's orb, she saw chunks of rock collapsing around her. The cave's mouth went dark.

Something hit the side of her face, and she realized Ripple was positioning itself above her with two legs straddling her head and two on either side of her chest.

Everything fell silent. As abruptly as the cave-in had started, it was over.

"Skyra, are you alive?"

She heard herself moaning, as if the sounds were coming from someone else. The pain in her leg wouldn't allow her to stifle the moans. She threw her good hand up to clap it over her mouth, only to strike Ripple's shell. She grunted, "Get off me!"

The creature stepped aside and turned toward her with barely enough room to maneuver. Its glowing orb shone in her face, forcing her to shut her eyes.

"Yes, you are alive. I am pleased. I think we can assume the bear is gone or perhaps crushed, and I believe you are safe from the men as well."

She lifted her head high enough to see her leg, the source of her new pain. Her foot and ankle were beneath a boulder, probably mashed into paste. She tried pulling her leg loose, but it wouldn't move. "I am *not* safe! I am going to die, and the bolup men will kill Veenah."

Ripple turned to the side, hoisted its front legs onto the boulder, and leapt onto the rock. It disappeared to the other side, although Skyra could see its light bouncing over the walls and ceiling as it scuttled around in the confined space. She lay her head back on the hard rock. Why had she allowed Ripple to lead her in here? She should have refused. Maybe she could have entered one of the smaller caves and fought the bolups one at a time as they tried to enter.

The light shone in her face again as Ripple came back over the boulder. It positioned itself beside her. "There is no path out of this collapsed cave, and I do not have the strength required to move the rocks that now entomb us. I am sorry to say you are correct. You are going to die here."

Skyra knew this already, but that didn't stop her from letting out a single sob.

"It is possible that Veenah will escape from the humans. Veenah is important, as you are. We will hope that she lives."

Skyra stared up at the contours of the jagged stone ceiling, still illuminated by the creature's orb. "Why do you say I am important? And Veenah? Is that another lie you tell me so I will try harder?"

"You told me to never lie to you again, and so I will not. Besides, trying harder now will not save you. You are going to die here."

"Stop saying that and answer my question."

Ripple's circle of red lights glowed once and then became dark. "That is a question that would take much time to answer adequately, and I'm afraid the answer would not help us in our predicament. I will tell you this, Skyra. It has been a true pleasure and privilege to be your companion for all these days and months. You have given me purpose such as I have never known before. I only wish I could have helped you survive."

Skyra didn't understand all the words her friend had used, but she understood enough. She closed her eyes and focused on ignoring the pain. Her crushed foot had no feeling at all, but her leg above it felt like it was being held over a campfire.

"Ripple," she said, "I want you to kill me."

"I have no way of killing you without using violent means, and I will not do such a thing. If you wish for such a death, you will have to do it on your own."

She felt around with her good hand and found a rock a bit smaller than her head. Slowly and for practice, she lifted it and went through the motion of swinging it at her temple. Then she relaxed her arm and let her hand and the rock sink to the cave floor.

Ripple's orb faded out, and the cave became black. "I do not wish to watch you do such a thing."

Another sob escaped from her lips, and she released the rock to wipe her face.

A scratching sound came from beside her, like a shrew or rat digging for food.

"What are you doing?" she asked.

"I am creating a message."

"What is a *message*?"

The scratching stopped. "It is a way of communicating with others. Again, it would take much time to explain properly." The noise began again.

Skyra closed her eyes and put her hand back on the rock. She lifted it.

The scratching stopped again. "I do not want you to kill yourself at this time."

"Why?"

"Because you may have several hours left to live."

She didn't know what hours were and didn't care. "I want to die now."

"That is because you have never heard me tell you stories

before. I happen to be quite adept at telling stories." The creature shifted in the dark. Its orb began to glow just slightly, and now Skyra could see that it was resting on its belly. "I will tell you stories until you die."

She lowered the rock. "What about your message?"

"There will be plenty of time for that. Please become as comfortable as you can, Skyra, because I consider these stories to be real humdingers."

4

BROADCAST

47,659 YEARS *later - Northwest of Tucson, Arizona, USA*

LINCOLN CLOSED his eyes and focused on controlling his heart rate. Why in the name of Hawking had he agreed to a live broadcast of the jump? He hated being on television. However, if he didn't return—and he was pretty sure he wouldn't—he wanted people to remember him and his team based on what he had to say rather than the twisted words of trolls and haters.

He opened his eyes and pulled his braided ponytail around to the front and then ran his fingers through the loose curls atop his scalp.

Before him stood a single camera, a camerawoman, and a broadcasting tech, all from GTN, the network that won the bid for this opportunity. Lincoln refused to allow an actual reporter to participate. This was his exposition and self eulogy, not a damn interview.

He raised his brows at the camerawoman. "How much time?"

"One minute, nineteen seconds."

Lincoln turned to Jazzlyn, Virgil, and Derek. "You've already said your goodbyes to the people who matter most to you, so you don't have to say *anything* if you don't want to. You guys okay?"

They all nodded, clearly nervous as hell, although probably not so much due to the broadcast.

Lincoln looked down at Maddy, who was standing beside Jazzlyn. "What about you? Are you okay?"

Maddy's circle of red lights blinked once, indicating she understood she was being addressed. "I assume your question is rhetorical, as you know I am in the same condition I was yesterday at this time."

"So answer the rhetorical question."

"All systems go, captain."

"Fifteen seconds, Mr. Woodhouse." The camerawoman watched Lincoln's face to make sure her update was understood before she turned back to the screen on her camera. The room fell silent, then the woman counted down the last five seconds with her fingers before pointing at Lincoln.

He gazed at the lens for a full three seconds before speaking, a habit he had developed because he knew it stimulated anticipation. He almost smiled then decided smiling would dilute the situation's gravity.

"Seven months ago," he said, "I was alerted to the astounding finds at the Pomer paleontological dig site." No point in introducing himself—there had been hours of ridiculous talk show pontification leading up to this moment. "Many of you believe the drone's presence at the dig site is proof that the Temporal Bridge Theorem is invalid, and for reasons that have been endlessly discussed, all connections to the past were immediately suspended at that time. Until today."

Lincoln paused again for emphasis. "After months of international debate, a consensus was reached. The message left at the Pomer site is too important to ignore. What you are going to witness today has never been attempted. We will jump back to the location and time designated in the message. We certainly know this is possible, as we have successfully transported fourteen drones back to various times and places. Those drones functioned correctly and sent invaluable data back for the nineteen minutes we were able to maintain the connection.

"What we do not know, however, is if we can jump back to the present. In fact, I'm pretty sure we can't, so we understand this to be a one-way trip. Regardless, we have to do it. It would be against our nature to ignore the message."

He stepped over to a white sphere three meters in diameter. "My team and I have been working around the clock for months to make this possible. I know many of you watching are hoping for a glimpse of the technology." He waved his hand at the sphere. "Never before has this device been photographed or recorded, but because I probably won't be returning, I figured *what the hell*."

Several nervous chuckles came from his team.

"For all intents and purposes, this sphere and the machinery you see connected to it is a time machine. I, for one, despise that term and rarely use it, as it conjures oversimplified science fiction tropes. I prefer the term T_3, which stands for Tantalizing Temporal Trickery." He paused, but this time no one in the room chuckled. He shrugged it off.

Lincoln pointed to a hatch in the sphere, its circular door hanging open. "For each of the fourteen connections we've made in the past, we put two objects inside—a drone and a data relay device." He stepped to a nearby table and put his hand on a basketball-sized sphere. "This is a data relay device, the DRD." He waved to Maddy to step over to his side. "This is a drone. I believe many of you are familiar with this particular drone, as she has become somewhat of a celebrity lately. Maddy, say hello to the people."

"Greetings, humans from Earth," Maddy said.

Lincoln allowed himself a brief smile. "She's a real comedian, this one."

He paused again for effect. "The concept is simple. The time machine—the T_3—can maintain the connection to the past for up to nineteen minutes. During those nineteen minutes, the drone collects as much data as it can, such as photos, readings of temperature, atmospheric composition, light levels, and even soil chemistry." He put his hand back on the small sphere. "The drone sends data to the DRD, which then relays that data back here to us. That's it. Nineteen minutes and it's done. The drone and the DRD remain in the past, as there is no way to bring them back. We send the data to the research institution that financed that particular connection. Of course, that all ended seven months ago."

Lincoln started walking across the spacious lab at a pace that would allow the camerawoman to keep up. "Once the world decided the Pomer site message required action, I decided it was my responsibility to jump back to the specific place and time 47,659 years ago. The idea is simple. My team and I must figure out why our civilization is at risk and take measures to prevent disaster." He shrugged and shook his head. "Your guess is as good as mine as to what that might require." He glanced back at the large sphere. "Going back to that time and place isn't a problem. We could just get inside the sphere as if we were drones." He decided to allow himself one more smile, but it felt strained. "Due to the fact that I'm fond of being alive, as well as being fond of my team, we took on our most daunting technological challenge yet—to modify the T3 to give us *some* chance of jumping back to this present time or some other present time where we might continue to live out our lives."

"And with that to look forward to," said the broadcasting tech, with a suspiciously professional voice, "we will take a brief sponsor break." The guy waved a finger at the camerawoman, who tapped a button then nodded appreciatively at Lincoln.

Lincoln glared at the tech. "You're a damn reporter. I made it clear—"

"I'm not a reporter," the guy said, raising both hands as if making peace. "Someone has to ease the transition to commercial breaks."

"I've only been talking five minutes!"

The guy frowned at Lincoln. "Do you even watch television, Mr. Woodhouse? Five minutes of programming, then two minutes of ads. That's been the standard for years."

Lincoln blew air through his teeth. "It's a wonder *anyone* watches." He paced back and forth a few times while Jazzlyn, Virgil, and Derek stood patiently to one side. He stopped and addressed the broadcasting tech again. "You know, we're actually jumping within an hour. You're broadcasting a live event that could have global consequences. Not only that, four people and a celebrity drone are basically committing suicide."

The tech shrugged. "I'd do things differently if I could,

Mr. Woodhouse."

Lincoln stopped pacing and took a few deep breaths. Soon the camerawoman counted down again, and the camera light came back on.

Lincoln gazed at the lens for three seconds then stepped over to an object that appeared to be a boulder the size of a large office desk. "Believe it or not, this is our new T_3. It is disguised as a boulder to avoid attracting unwanted attention at the destination. Instead of staying behind, this T_3 is capable of jumping to a time and place in the past along with my team. Because the T_3 goes with us, we should be able to use it a second time—in theory, at least—after we arrive at our destination. If all goes well, we plan to use the device to jump back to the present."

He heaved an exaggerated sigh. "Unfortunately, I believe it will be impossible to jump back to *this* present. Some of you disagree with me on that, and I hope you are correct. If you are, then you should see us appear here again a few minutes after we jump." He shot a glance at the broadcasting tech with a reporter's voice. "That should give you just enough time to have a nice commercial break."

Lincoln put his hand on the T_3 boulder. "For those of you who are hoping for enough detail to build one of these devices yourself, I'm sorry to disappoint you. It's too dangerous. I will remind you of the eleven poor souls who have lost their lives trying to replicate my devices without an adequate grasp of the science behind them." He pointed at the camera. "Do not become a statistic." It was a stupid thing to say, but he'd been told to say it.

"Here's a simplified explanation," he said. He motioned to Jazzlyn, Virgil, and Derek. They each picked up a brown bag large enough to hold a human body and stepped closer. "Each of these bags is the smaller equivalent of the much larger sphere in which we used to place the drone and DRD. My team and I fondly refer to these as body bags." He grabbed the brown cord attached to one of the bags. "The body bags connect to the new T_3 with this cord." He inserted the free end of the cord into a barely noticeable receptacle near the base of the boulder. His staff members plugged in the other two, then they dragged four more over and plugged those in as well. The seven bags were now arranged on the floor around the boulder like spokes of a wheel.

Again, Lincoln grabbed one of the cords. "The T_3 pumps two different, very specialized, types of charged heavy particles through the cord. I'm sorry, but I will not tell you what the particles are. I wouldn't want you to become a statistic. The particles flow rapidly through microscopic tubules in the two-layer fabric of this bag. Particle A flows in one direction through a web of tubules in the outer layer. Particle B flows in the opposite direction through a matching web of tubules in the inner layer.

"Astoundingly, over a period of several seconds, that reverse particle flow causes anything inside the bag to become *fluid*. Not to be confused with liquid, I mean fluid within the context of space and time. As you probably know, space and time are inseparable. They are two aspects of the same construct. Once the bag's contents become fluid, they can easily be shifted to another location and time."

He dropped the cord and nodded toward the boulder. "Of course, the T_3 does all the heavy lifting when it comes to placement calculations and generating particles A and B."

Lincoln sensed that the broadcasting tech was about to speak up, so he quickly said, "We're going to take a short break, and when we come back, we'll go through the last-minute preparations for our jump. Then you will witness the first human time travel ever attempted. The entire process will happen uninterrupted by commercial breaks, because we do not want you to miss any of it!"

After a few seconds of silence, the broadcasting tech sighed loudly. He then removed a small earpiece and let it hang from his ear. "I hadn't really planned on losing my job today, but considering the sacrifice you guys are making, I guess I won't complain."

Lincoln gave him a sympathetic frown. "Complaining is overrated anyway."

The door to the lab's outer lobby burst open. Gray-haired men and women began pouring in. Robert Chandler, along with several other science bigwigs, led the way. Behind them came a small army of government and military folks.

Lincoln had almost achieved an acceptable state of calm, considering what he was about to do, but now he felt his blood pressure starting to skyrocket. He hated being surrounded by old people, especially those steeped in ineptocracy.

Stephen Fuchs, the National Security guy, said, "Mr. Woodhouse, if you feel so compelled as to hijack this broadcast, then we certainly aren't going to remain outside this lab simply because you requested it. We intend to observe your preparations first hand."

Lincoln sensed that the bureaucrats weren't likely to back down on this a second time, so he decided to simply ignore them the best that he could.

"After we go live, I'll be asking you some questions," Chandler said. "There are certain details people want to know about this process, and we have no idea if you intend to address those details on your own."

Again, Lincoln sensed determination in Chandler's

expression. No point in arguing. He turned to the camerawoman. "How much time?"

"Forty-eight seconds."

Lincoln gestured for his team members to gather around, including Maddy. When they were all beside him, he said, "This is our moment—no one else's. Let's tell the world who we are."

The three humans nodded without speaking. Virgil was visibly shaking, so Lincoln placed a firm hand on his neck and looked him in the eye. "Having second thoughts?"

Virgil forced a smile. "Absolutely. But I'm still in."

"Good, because if you backed out now, those suits would insist on sending one of their own in your place. Whether we survive for an hour or a year, I want to be with the three of you, not some stranger I don't trust. Understand?"

Virgil nodded.

"We're with you, Lincoln, to the end," said Derek.

Jazzlyn put a reassuring hand on Lincoln's arm.

Maddy said, "I'm with you too, not that I have a choice."

"Ten seconds," said the camerawoman.

Lincoln eyed his friends. "Let's go viral one more time, shall we?"

The camera light glowed red.

Lincoln stared at the lens for three seconds. "Some of you will call us heroes. Others will use less flattering names. Such is the nature of controversial actions. Regardless of your opinions of this effort, I want you to know who we really are. I'm Lincoln Woodhouse. I'm actually a real person, not the caricature you often see depicted on the news and social media. Yes, I'm eccentric. I like my privacy. I only hire the brightest minds, and nearly always from the under-twenty-five crowd. I have reasons for that, which I won't go into. You've probably also heard that I only hire employees who have the strength that comes from having endured some kind of affliction."

He paused to let this admission sink in. "I'll just say that I find it easier to bond with people who understand what it's like to be viewed as different. An affliction makes us stronger, not weaker. After all, here we are, sacrificing everything in an attempt to save civilization."

He took Jazzlyn's elbow and gently pulled her to his side.

"I'm Jazzlyn Shields." She twisted one of her long braids around her finger as she spoke. "I'm just a paleontologist who grew up in a Chicago neighborhood where you don't see too many paleontologists." She smiled and waved at the camera. "Love you, Mom and Pops!" Then her smile faded. "Lincoln saw something in me that others overlooked. That's kind of one of his talents."

She held up her left hand, which was actually a prosthetic replacement, attached just below her elbow. "When some people look at me, this is all they see," she flexed the black carbon fiber polymer fingers and thumb, "but Lincoln saw much more, like my passion for studying our past, and my fondness for unorthodox problem-solving strategies." She turned to her boss. "Thank you, Lincoln." Then she turned back to the camera. "And thank you all for putting your trust in us."

She stepped back and pushed Virgil in front of the camera. Virgil nervously adjusted his glasses. "Virgil Brodigan. Applied physics, Cornell. I, uh, well I guess I'm like Jazzlyn. Kind of unorthodox in the way I look at engineering. I would like to think I contributed significantly to the technology we'll be using today, but around here we all know none of this could be done without Lincoln. In fact, I doubt anyone would *ever* have come up with some of the concepts. They are so... incredibly, frustratingly random." He shook his head. "I don't know how he does it."

Virgil seemed to ponder whether or not he wanted to say anything else. He shifted his glasses again. "Anyway, I know what some are wondering about me. Well, yeah, I've got my own issues. Mine aren't visible, they're the psychological kind. You see, my family was killed when I was thirteen. My mom. My dad. Two brothers. Happened right in front of me. Murdered. The guy—the murderer—told me I could live. Just because. That's what he said, *just because*. Later I was blamed for the murders. Me, at thirteen. Until my therapists testified that I wasn't capable of such a thing. Imagine that—having to prove you aren't capable of murdering your own family. Anyway, I have some trust issues. Lincoln hired me anyway. In fact, he showed me how to turn that into a strength."

Virgil stepped aside to let Derek move in.

Derek stared confidently at the camera. His twelve-inch beard and perfectly coiffed hair made for an eye-catching figure. Derek's beard was streaked with gray, although he was only twenty-four, a grooming hallmark Lincoln suspected was self-administered.

"Derek Dagger," he said with his typical verbal swagger. "My official title around here is Protean Factotum. It simply means that I'm highly adaptable, and I do many of the tasks the others cannot or will not be bothered with. I'm not a scientist. I simply get things done. Lincoln offered me the opportunity to sacrifice everything and go on this jump. Why? Because I'm damn useful. So I readily accepted. Why?" He narrowed his eyes and managed to forge an impressively intense look. "Because this is the stuff guys with names like Derek Dagger live for—adventure, saving civilization, and the obligatory danger therein." He smiled briefly.

"You're wondering what possible affliction I could have that would endear me to Lincoln Woodhouse. I prefer not to discuss it, other than to say it's a rare and sometimes debilitating psychiatric syndrome. Besides, if you knew the unsavory details, they would haunt your dreams." He turned up one side of his mouth in a half smile. "We won't let you down."

Derek stepped away.

"I believe it is my turn," Maddy said.

The camerawoman raised her brows then angled her camera down at the drone.

Maddy's ring of red LEDs flashed twice and then rotated clockwise for a few seconds. "I am called Maddy. Mobile Autonomous Drone. Get it? I am required to go along on this jump because, in spite of what Derek told you, I am the true Protean Factotum of the team. I process data even faster than Lincoln can, by a factor of nine thousand if you care to know. I sport an impressive language translator, a database of virtually everything we know about the earth's conditions in the past, a medical database, and the ability to make two hundred life-saving decisions per second. Now, if only I could remember where I left my reading glasses."

Maddy paused for the statistically-determined optimum length of time to allow full appreciation of a joke. "In all seriousness, I assure you that my purpose on this mission is to assist in any task deemed necessary to ensure optimum survival and success of our global civilization. Lincoln's programming, which controls my every inclination, gives me no other choice. Lucky for me, his programming also allows me to have a good time while saving the world. So, let's get this party started."

With vaudevillian exaggeration, Lincoln pretended to

kick Maddy out of the camera frame. He had coded the drone to routinely attempt to steal the show—Maddy's personality was a great way to draw the public's attention away from Lincoln himself. Too bad he couldn't let her take over the rest of this live address to the world.

"Maddy is right," he said to the camera. "It's time for our jump."

Chandler spoke up. "Mr. Woodhouse, would you explain how this new technology is different from the time jumping device you used previously?"

"Of course." Lincoln signaled to Derek, who dragged over another bag, this one much larger than the others. "In general concept, it's quite simple. We engineered the entire data processing center down to a fraction of the size. Small enough, in fact, to put a specially-designed body bag around the T_3 itself. Two people can easily do it. Observe."

He and Derek unplugged the other body bag cords, spread the larger bag over the boulder, then pulled the edges down to the floor, being careful to line up the eight pre-made holes in the bag with the eight plug receptacles. Derek lifted one end of the boulder while Lincoln pulled the edges of the bag underneath it. Derek then moved around and lifted the other side, allowing Lincoln to pull the other edge of the bag under until the edges overlapped on the floor, then lowered the T_3 back into place. Finally, they plugged the cords from the seven body bags back into their receptacles.

Lincoln picked up one last cord. "Notice there is an eighth cord. This is the cord for the T_3's own body bag." He moved around to the only remaining empty receptacle and plugged it in. "This allows the T_3 to actually jump with us."

"And why do you want the machine to jump back in time with you?" Chandler asked.

"As I said, I do not believe it will be possible for us to jump back to this particular present. That doesn't mean, however, that we would not like to try. Keep in mind we're jumping back 47,659 years. We'll find ourselves in a primitive wilderness. There will be no hospitals, hotels, or coffee shops. Instead, there will be fierce predators, Neanderthals, and possibly humans, all of which could attack us on sight. We want to have the opportunity to jump back to the present, even if it will be a very different present from this one."

Chandler nodded. "So, you don't know for sure whether the present you jump back to will exist in this timeline or a different timeline?"

"Nothing about this is certain."

Chandler motioned to the body bags distributed around the boulder. "Five of you are jumping, including your drone, yet you have seven empty bags."

Derek brought a large cart to a stop beside Lincoln just as Chandler was saying this. The cart held two full duffel bags with a desert camouflage pattern printed on the fabric.

"You are correct," Lincoln said. "Here's what we're putting into the other two bags." He unzipped one of the duffels, revealing more body bags, tightly rolled and stacked. "You see, the bags themselves don't make the jump. They stay behind. Only the contents of the body bags jump back in time. Therefore, we are taking twenty-four spare body bags—three sets of eight. We hope to jump back to the present only once, in which case we would need only one extra set. We're taking three sets, just to be safe."

He unzipped the second duffel, revealing hundreds of smaller bags, each bulging with contents. "Here we have a set of carefully-selected medical supplies, food rations, and winter outerwear. Packing these items was challenging because we have no idea what we'll need."

He resealed the two duffels, then he and Derek began hoisting them into their respective body bags.

"The reason we're doing all this now without help," Lincoln said, grunting from the effort, "is because our team will have to do it on our own when we prepare to jump back to the present."

Once the two duffels were zipped into their body bags, Jazzlyn handed Lincoln an aluminum briefcase. He set the case on the floor, opened it, and pulled out a four-legged drone the size of a rabbit. "This is a mini-drone, for lack of a better name."

He powered on the drone with a switch on its belly, then he studied the display on his watch. "And... there it is. The mini-drone has successfully paired with the T3." He looked at the camera. "You're going to love this." He kneeled beside the nearest empty body bag, placed the mini-drone inside, and zipped the bag shut.

He stood and pointed to the lump in the body bag. "Watch carefully." He tapped the screen on his watch, activating several preset commands.

Without a sound from the T3, the lump in the bag collapsed. The bag was now empty.

Lincoln said, "Cool, huh? The mini-drone just jumped back in time 47,659 years, to the exact hour and location indicated in the message found at the Pomer dig site." He held his wrist up so the viewing audience could see its tiny screen. "Watch and listen."

Seconds passed in complete silence. Five. Ten. Then his watch chirped, and a green checkmark flashed on the screen.

This was good, but Lincoln felt a flash of disappointment. He definitely couldn't back out now.

"The mini-drone has served its purpose, which is to make sure the jump location is safe and clear of debris," he said. "In less than half a minute, the mini-drone assessed its immediate surroundings. In addition to photo analysis of the terrain and environmental measurements, the little genius sprinted around the perimeter of the insertion area on its twelve-centimeter legs, a distance of nineteen meters, not including obstacles such as rocks and plants. It crunched all of the data, made an assessment of viability, and transmitted its decision back to the T3. As I've explained, we're able to keep the portal open for just under nineteen minutes—a far more impressive feat than you might think. We must jump before the portal closes, so now we are on a rather strict schedule."

He held his watch up again. "I got a green checkmark, not a red X. The specific location is safe—we're good to go. As long as we go soon. All we need to do is zip into our body bags, then I'll activate the jump."

Jazzlyn, Virgil, and Derek each grabbed a pack containing water bottles, protein bars, sunscreen, insect repellent, sunglasses, and whatever else they had chosen to squeeze in. They moved to their respective body bags and sat down inside them, ready to zip the bags shut.

Chandler spoke up. "Mr. Woodhouse, I'm sure many viewers are wondering why you're jumping from here in Arizona when your destination is in Spain. Would you explain how that's possible?"

Lincoln sighed and glanced at his watch. He still had sixteen minutes, but his nerves were becoming raw.

"If you can spare the time, of course," Chandler added.

Lincoln nodded curtly, wondering how he could keep this explanation simple and brief. He placed his hand on the body bag covering the boulder. "The T_3 possesses considerable processing power. You may be surprised to learn that only four percent of the processors are devoted to placement in time, as well as managing all other necessary tasks such as accelerating particles A and B, activating the actual jump, and communicating with our watches and the mini-drone. The other ninety-six percent, which also corresponds to seventy percent of the volume of the entire machine, is devoted to spatial placement."

Lincoln held a fist in front of his face. "Imagine this is Earth." He pointed to a knuckle of his pinky finger. "And this is where we are right now. Let's say we jump back in time twelve hours." He turned his fist slowly. "The planet rotates, right? So, twelve hours ago, the space I'm standing in right now was halfway around the world. If I want to jump back twelve hours and still arrive in this same room, I need to make some very complex spatial calculations."

He started moving his fist around to the back of his head while still rotating it. "It gets even more complicated than that. The earth is also revolving around the sun. Not only that, the solar system itself is flying through space because the entire Milky Way galaxy is rotating. Plus, the galaxies are all moving away from each other due to expansion of the universe caused by the Big Bang. If I really want to jump back twelve hours and land in this room, the spatial calculations are staggeringly complex. If I don't get them right, I'll find myself suddenly dying a horrible death in the freezing vacuum of space."

He took a big sigh, gazing at the camera lens. "Someday we may find that outer space is littered with the frozen bodies of time travelers who failed to properly calculate spatial placement."

Chandler said, "As for the original question?"

"Yes, yes." Lincoln glanced at his watch again. "Time and space are intrinsically intertwined, two sides of the same coin. As it turns out, if you can jump in time, you can also jump in space. Jumping back in time is surprisingly simple—it's the spatial placement that presents the real challenge. Spatial placement is difficult when jumping back only twelve hours. Imagine the spatial placement challenge of jumping back 47,659 years. To answer the question, though, we do not have to take the T3 to Spain. If we were at the Pomer site in Spain at this moment, we would be no closer to our destination than we are here."

Lincoln kneeled and held open one of the two remaining body bags. "Let's do this, Maddy. Step in, please."

Maddy got in the bag, retracted her legs, and settled onto her belly.

In the bag's remaining space, Lincoln arranged a few packs containing solar chargers for Maddy, three extra mini-drones, and various ultra-light camping gear. He started zipping the bag shut.

"I love you, Lincoln," Maddy said.

"I love you too, Maddy."

"I want you to know, the baby is yours. And I'm keeping it."

Lincoln glanced at the camera. "She *is* just kidding." He zipped Maddy in then moved to the last empty body bag. He sat down in it and zipped the bag up to his waist. "This won't be any more spectacular than when we jumped the mini-drone," he said to the camera. "There won't be any sound. The bags will remain—they'll just suddenly become empty." He lay down on his back.

"Whatever challenges confront you at your destination,

we hope they are surmountable," said Chandler. "Godspeed to you all."

Lincoln nodded at Jazzlyn, Virgil, and Derek. He watched as they zipped themselves in, then he closed his own body bag. In the darkness he tapped his watch. The screen came on, showing less than seven minutes remaining. He navigated through several menus to get to a large green button he'd designed months ago, labeled with the words *No Time Like the Present*. He tried to swallow, but his mouth was too dry.

He tapped the button.

Lincoln was weightless for a split second before landing on his back. Something sharp was under his shoulder blade, so he rolled to the side to relieve the pain.

"Jeez, my neck!" said Virgil.

"For God's sake, that hurt!" Jazzlyn said. "I thought we'd be offset by a few centimeters, not half a freakin' meter."

Maddy spoke in her calm voice. "It is because of the rocks. Extra clearance was necessary."

Lincoln realized his eyes were shut. He opened them and had to squint against the sunlight. His ear was now against the ground, and all he could see were rocks of various sizes and a few sage-like shrubs. A steady sound was coming from somewhere nearby, like a stream flowing over rocks. He sat up, groaning at the pain in his back, and saw gnarled trees, most of them only a few meters tall. A wide field of rocks and shrubs stretched out beyond the trees, and rocky hills rose in the distance beyond that.

The T_3 was there beside him, minus its body bag. He got to his feet. Yes! The contents of all the body bags were there:

Jazzlyn, Virgil, Derek, Maddy, and the two duffel bags. The T3 had worked exactly as expected, assuming of course that they were at the correct time and location near the Pomer site.

To Lincoln's left, no more than a few meters beyond the T3's placement perimeter, was the rocky bank of a clear, gushing stream. More gnarled trees stood on the far side of the stream, with more rocky plain and distant hills beyond.

"I didn't feel a thing," said Derek, rubbing the back of his head. "At least not until I hit the ground. I thought we'd feel something. I thought maybe we'd see stars, or the face of God, or something like that. Instead, nothing."

"Look at this place—it's just wilderness," Jazzlyn added. "The message said to come to this time and place because our entire civilization is at risk, but there's nothing here!"

Virgil moved to the duffel that was filled with extra body bags. "I think we should get everything set up to make another jump. We weren't allowed to bring weapons, and by my latest count, there were no fewer than fifteen different megafaunal mammals here that would give any sane person nightmares." He pulled out one of the body bags and began unrolling it.

Lincoln scanned the ground until he spotted the mini-drone. The machine had parked itself on the outer perimeter of the targeted area, having completed its mission of assessing and approving the site for the team's jump. He picked up the mini-drone and took it to Virgil. "No point in using one of the backups if this thing still works. I agree, we should prepare the T3 for a second jump. Just in case."

"I suggest you all look to the northeast," said Maddy, her feminine voice at a high volume, indicating urgency.

Lincoln didn't know which way was northeast, so he glanced at Maddy to see where she was looking. He stared across the stream but saw nothing. Then he saw it—movement, barely visible through the leaves and tangled branches of one of the trees. Something was running, and it was quickly getting closer. "Get behind the T3," he ordered the others.

Still wobbly on their feet, the team moved behind the boulder and crouched.

The creature kept approaching, and now Lincoln could hear its feet on the gravel. He silently cursed the damn bureaucrats who had insisted his team not bring weapons. Their reasoning had been that if Lincoln's team went around killing things, they'd have a greater impact on the future.

"It's getting closer," Virgil hissed. "Should we run?"

Before Lincoln could reply, a figure skirted one of the trees and came into view. It was a person—a woman—with animal furs hanging over her shoulders, fastened around her waist, and covering her feet. The woman came to a stop. Soon after, another figure rounded the tree and stopped beside her.

"Holy shit!" Derek exclaimed.

The woman heard this and snapped her head around. She stared across the stream at Lincoln's team.

Standing on four mechanical legs beside the woman was a drone, its illuminated vision lens glowing as it also stared across the stream.

There was no point in hiding now, so Lincoln rose to his full height.

"Khala-melu!" The woman shouted, with a distinct clicking sound between the two words.

Lincoln considered saying something back, but his eyes were drawn to the rocky field beyond the woman and drone. More humans were coming. There were at least eight, apparently men, with darker skin than that of the woman. Running with apparent purpose, each of the men wielded a hatchet-like weapon.

5

STRANGERS

47,659 years ago - Day 1

With the comforting heft of the dead bolup's khul in her hand, Skyra ran with Ripple to the river. They reached the forest-lined river ahead of their pursuers, but the scrubby trees offered few places to hide. She slowed, came to a stop beside one of the trees, then looked back. The men were still steadily following. She turned back to the river. It would be easy to cross, but then what would she do? She scanned the far side and immediately spotted something that looked out of place.

"Holy shit!" a strange voice cried.

Skyra grunted and stepped back, nearly falling over Ripple. There were people across the river, watching her from behind a rock that looked nothing like the other rocks. She stared, nearly forgetting the men pursuing her. She could only see the people's faces. They weren't nandups—she was sure of that—which meant they were bolups. Humans. However, only one of them had skin as dark as most of the other bolups she had seen. The others were paler than even the palest of nandups. One of the pale bolups rose to his full height, now visible from the waist up.

Skyra shouted, "Khala-melu!" *What are you?* The bolup—a man—was not wearing a fur cape or even one of the tight-fitting deerskin garments bolups usually wore. This man's garment was the color of a cloudless sky, and it clung to his torso like a second skin. Skyra had never seen anything like it.

The man was watching her, but he shifted his eyes to look at something beyond her. Then he spoke. "Are you in trouble? Are those men chasing you?"

Skyra took another step back, confused. She knew these words. This man spoke Ripple's language.

"We'll help you if we can," the man said.

The other three bolups rose to their feet at once. All of them wore the same sky-blue garments, which were so tight-fitting that Skyra could see that the dark-skinned bolup was a woman.

"I recognize these humans," Ripple said. "One of them is Lincoln—" Ripple stopped speaking as a beaver-sized creature stepped from behind the boulder. The creature looked just like Ripple.

Skyra's heart was already pounding, but now she felt the strength of the woolly rhino and cave lion surging through her entire body. Her legs trembled as if they wanted to carry her away from this confusing scene.

"They're almost here!" the pale man shouted.

Skyra blinked and sucked air into her chest. The men chasing her—she could hear them getting closer. She hesitated for only one more breath then bounded to the river's edge and leapt into the knee-deep water. She glanced back. The bolups chasing her were now weaving their way among the trees, and the nearest was raising his khul as if he intended to throw it.

Ripple was sloshing through the water toward the strangers, so Skyra made her way across the river and climbed onto the rocky shore.

"Look out!" one of the strangers cried.

Skyra looked back just as the bolup released his khul. She dropped to the ground. The weapon flew past her, almost grazing her shoulder, and landed harmlessly among the rocks beside the strangers.

She jumped to her feet, gripping her khul. She raised the weapon, ready to kill the blue-clad strangers as they rushed toward her. They were not wielding weapons, and they were thin and frail-looking, but there were four of them. She quickly determined the one she'd need to kill first—the man with the strange gray beard.

The humans surrounded her but kept their distance. Most of them were staring across the river at Skyra's pursuers, who were now gathering on the far shore, but the man who had spoken to her was watching her warily. He held out a hand, palm toward her, and said, "Take it easy. We'll try to help you if we can."

At Skyra's side, Ripple said, "You are Lincoln Woodhouse."

The man blinked and looked down at Ripple. "That's right."

Skyra's pursuers began crossing the river. Except for the man who had thrown his, they were all wielding khuls. The skinny, unarmed strangers were about to be killed, and Skyra would be taken, to suffer the same fate as Veenah. She should have kept running.

"What the hell are we supposed to do now, Lincoln?" said

the woman with the dark face, her voice high and squeaky like an injured hare.

The gray-bearded man held something up in his hand. The object was too small for Skyra to see, but he was shoving it out toward the approaching men. "Hey!" he shouted. "You need to back off." He moved his thumb, and a small flame leapt from his fist and continued burning. The man was holding fire in his hand.

The nearest bolup, who was now almost across the river, paused and stared. Skyra studied the attacking bolup's face. He hardly took notice of the fire. In fact, she sensed that he was preparing to attack, only a breath away from charging forward to kill the gray-bearded man.

Without hesitating, Skyra drew back her khul and heaved it. It was lighter than the khuls she normally used, so she adjusted her aim to compensate. The man who was about to attack didn't even see it coming, and the blade split his skull just in front of his ear.

"Jesus Christ!" one of the skinny strangers said.

Skyra leapt into the river and reached the man's body as it was drifting away. He had dropped his khul somewhere in the water, so Skyra yanked her own khul from his skull. She swung around to face the rest of the men, most of whom were now standing midway in the river.

The bolup men were hesitant—she could sense it from their expressions. Depending on what happened next, they might attack, or they might finally decide Skyra wasn't worth the effort.

One of the men pointed at the strangers and spoke to his companions. Skyra looked, then she gritted her teeth as she saw he was pointing at the dark-faced woman, who, like Skyra, appeared to be of breeding age. The balance had just shifted. The men now knew they could take two women, not just one.

Ripple spoke up. "The attacking humans are not frightened by your technology. Such devices are so far beyond their experiences they are virtually invisible to these men. If you wish to survive, you must intimidate them in a way they understand."

Skyra realized her companion had been talking to the strangers rather than to her.

"The drone is right," said the stranger Ripple had called Lincoln Woodhouse. "We have to do something they understand." He picked up a rock and raised it up as if to throw it. He then rushed to the riverbank, howling like a sick auroch calf.

The other strangers grabbed their own rocks and followed the first man. The strangers now sounded like a bevy of sick calves.

The attacking bolups' expressions changed, and Skyra saw they were losing the will to fight. She sensed they were about to turn away. Then, as she knew they would, they all made their way back to the far riverbank. They spoke quietly to each other for a moment then began walking back the way they had come, glancing over their shoulders frequently to make sure they weren't being pursued.

The strangers finally fell silent. Skyra continued watching the men until they were almost to the base of the first hill.

"Do you think she's going to hurt us?" It was the squeaking voice of the dark-faced woman.

Skyra pulled her eyes from the now-distant men. The strangers were watching her warily. Ripple and the other creature were now face-to-face, gazing at each other as if they had never seen one of their own species before.

Skyra relaxed her arm, allowing her khul to hang at her side. She made her way through the water to the rocky bank.

The strangers backed up as she stepped out of the river.

She picked up the khul that had been thrown at her then stood with a khul in each hand, staring at the strangers.

"We're not here to hurt you," said one of the men, the only one who hadn't spoken yet. Like the others, he wore blue garments that seemed to cling to him so tightly that he must surely struggle to breathe. On his face he wore a thin strap that had two holes over his eyes. Held over his eyes by the strap were disks, as clear as water, perhaps made of the same substance as Ripple's orb.

Skyra gripped both her khuls, ready to kill if she needed to, and stepped within striking distance of the skinny man called Lincoln Woodhouse. She studied his face. He was frightened of her, which was comforting. He was also curious. He wanted to know more, as if everything he saw was new to him. His long hair was the same color as Skyra's, but unlike hers, his hair was wrapped into a braid. Only the children of Skyra's people would ever wear their hair that way, as a braid could be dangerous when hunting or fighting. A sparse beard covered his cheeks, chin, and around his mouth, nothing like the chest-long chin hairs of the gray-bearded man. Skyra's own people did not have facial hair, but she had seen human men with long hairs growing from their chins.

She gazed into the man's eyes and said, "Lincoln Woodhouse."

"Holy crap," he muttered. Then he swallowed loudly, obviously frightened. "Yes, that's me. Who are you?"

"Skyra-Una-Loto. You can call me Skyra."

"She speaks English, Lincoln," said the dark-faced woman.

Skyra now knew she was not in danger. These strangers did not intend to attack, and even if they did, Skyra was now confident she could kill them all. They did not appear to be fighters. Or hunters. How could they even stay alive? And where did they come from? Skyra wanted to learn more, so she decided to make a gesture of friendship.

Abruptly, Lincoln Woodhouse ducked to the side and put up a hand to protect his face. "Please don't," he said.

Skyra stared at him, surprised. She had intended to offer him one of her khuls. After all, these people had no weapons. She hadn't even begun to lift her arm and the khul, yet he had known. Somehow he had known.

She decided to offer him the khul in her other hand, and the man quickly glanced down at that weapon just before she started to lift it.

This was impossible. Her birthmate Veenah was the only one besides Skyra that could sense people's intent by watching their face and body.

Skyra relaxed her grip, and the two weapons thudded onto the rocks. She held a hand up in front of the man's chest, fingers extended, flattened palm facing to one side.

"I think she wants to shake your hand, Lincoln," said the man with the strap across his eyes.

Lincoln raised his hand and started to grasp hers. She swatted it away. Then she took his hand in hers and positioned it in front of him the same way she had just held her own hand, flattened and vertical. She released his hand, and he held it there. She placed hers next to his, both palms facing each other about a hand's width apart.

"I have no idea what you're doing," Lincoln Woodhouse said.

She pointed to one of her eyes. "Watch my face." She

gazed back at him until she was sure he was watching her. Then she snapped her hand toward his, attempting to slap it. He pulled his hand back, and hers flew by without touching it.

Skyra grabbed his hand again and put it back into place. She positioned hers beside his, waited several breaths, and tried again to slap it. She hit nothing but air.

She let out a laugh—a squeal, followed by a rapid *at-at-at-at-at-at*.

"Is that girl laughing?" the dark-faced woman asked.

Lincoln Woodhouse held his hand out again, this time without being forced. "It's my turn."

Skyra put her hand in position and waited. She saw it in his eyes, a slight tightening of the skin, and she snapped her hand back just before his swished by.

The man bared his teeth and let out a strange "Ha!" It sounded almost as if he had been hurt, but Skyra was sure it was his way of laughing. He raised his hand again, and again she avoided his swipe.

Skyra laughed, this time louder than before. This was a game she and Veenah used to play, although they never played it with the other nandup children for fear of being shunned or even killed. Maybe this person before her was a bolup, or maybe he was a new kind of creature she had never heard of. Regardless of what he was, she had something in common with him.

"Where did you learn to do that?" Lincoln Woodhouse asked.

"I did not learn. It is inside me, with my bones and my blood."

He gazed at her eyes and then shook his head. "I don't know what to say."

She wrinkled her brow. "But you are talking."

"I meant I'm completely confused by all of this. I just... I had no idea what we'd find here, and now... well, I have a lot of questions."

"How did you learn to speak English?" asked the dark-faced woman.

Skyra eyed the woman warily. The dark-faced woman wore two tiny rings in her nose, white like bones but polished until the curved surfaces shined like ice. Instead of one braid like Lincoln Woodhouse's, her hair was twisted into more long, thin braids than Skyra had ever seen on one person's head. The woman was showing her teeth, but her eyes were wide, which seemed like an odd way to smile. Skyra tried to imitate the expression, but this made the woman close her lips, so she stopped trying.

Ripple finally walked away from the other creature and shortened its hind legs so that it could look up at Skyra. "I see that you may need my help. English is the language I have taught you, and you are perfectly capable of talking to these people. Just speak to them the way you speak to me."

Lincoln Woodhouse said, "You taught her to speak English?"

Ripple swiveled toward him. "Isn't that obvious?"

"No, none of this is obvious! Did I send you back to this time and place?"

Ripple looked up at Lincoln Woodhouse for several long breaths without speaking. "Yes, you did."

Skyra decided she needed to speak up. "Ripple, you know these bolups, and these bolups know you. They will help us." She turned to Lincoln Woodhouse. "You are skinny, and you look weak, but you are alive. So, you must know how to hunt and fight. You will help me take back my birthmate. She is Veenah-Una-Loto, and she will die if I do not take her back."

Lincoln Woodhouse and the other strangers turned and looked at each other, an odd habit Skyra had seen in bolups before.

6

DECISION

47,659 YEARS ago - Day 1

LINCOLN STUDIED THE STRANGE WOMAN—SKYRA. She was short, maybe slightly taller than five feet, but her arms and legs were muscular and intimidating. Despite her diminutive stature, she was probably as heavy as Lincoln. Her large eyes were strangely captivating, with greenish irises and thick brows that made it seem like she was staring with intense interest. Small freckles dotted the smooth, parchment-colored skin of her face. Her nose and lips, although much thicker than Lincoln's, were perfectly proportioned for her face. Her reddish-brown hair, somewhat unkempt but not tangled, was swept back, exposing her ears. Two white, inch-long canine teeth adorned each of her ears, one penetrating the cartilage about midway up, the other through the earlobe. Her left wrist was wrapped in an elaborate leather sheath holding two knives with bone handles and stone blades.

Lincoln was reasonably sure the woman before him was

not human, but *Homo neanderthalensis*. In fact, he had every reason to believe this was the same Neanderthal woman whose remains had been found near this spot over 47,000 years in the future.

Surprisingly, Skyra didn't emit an unpleasant odor. Lincoln detected a slight muskiness, but he was pretty sure it was from the animal furs she was wearing.

"You will help me now," she said. "Please, you will help me."

Lincoln was still struggling to make the transition from complete confusion to comprehending that this woman was asking his team to help her do something. He glanced at Virgil, then Jazzlyn, then Derek. They offered little more than blank stares. "I'm not sure how much help we can be," he replied to Skyra. "We came here because... well, it's hard to explain."

"Perhaps I can help," said the drone Skyra had called Ripple. "I suspect you came to this time and place because you were alerted to a message that endured the passing of many thousands of years."

"That's correct," Lincoln said. "Did you create the message?"

"Not yet, I haven't, but it has been my intention to do so when the proper moment arrives. Please tell me, in what form and medium was this message?"

"It was words in English and some numbers, etched into the shell of a drone. The same words and numbers were also etched into a femur." Lincoln shot a wary glance at Skyra. "The femur of a female Neanderthal, twenty to twenty-one years of age."

The drone's ring of red lights pulsed a few times, indicating contemplation. It was a visual display Lincoln himself had conceptualized and coded into his drones.

"Now I understand why you have come to this particular time and place," the drone said. "I must have requested it in my message. There is only one reason I would request this particular time and place—to prevent a tragedy." The drone scuttled its legs, turning to look up at the Neanderthal woman. "Skyra, your life has been saved by the arrival of Lincoln and his team."

"You are wrong, Ripple," she said. "I saved *their* lives. They have no weapons, and they do not look like fighters."

"Nevertheless, their arrival has saved your life."

Maddy moved forward until her vision lens was only centimeters from the other drone's lens. "If my overly-polite human companions will not ask it, I sure as thunder will. Why did you teach this woman to speak English? Like all of Lincoln's drones, you were sent here to gather data. Influencing the indigenous flora and fauna is a blatant violation of your coded ideology. Explain your roguish behavior."

Ripple's red ring pulsed once. "You have the voice of a human female. In later models like myself, Lincoln provided a neutral voice, so as to avoid—"

"Avoiding is precisely what you are doing at this moment," Maddy interjected. "Explain your behavior."

"Skyra is important," the drone said. "Her genetically-identical twin Veenah is also important. I do not wish to explain further at this moment."

Jazzlyn spoke up. "Skyra called you Ripple. Is that your name?"

"Yes, I am Ripple."

"Ripple, we gave up everything to come here. You know

why? Because your message said *entire civilization at risk*. Well, we're here. What are we supposed to do?"

Again, Ripple's red ring pulsed. "That is interesting. I must have been traumatized at the time. Fortunately, now I will not have to experience whatever caused such trauma."

"You're freakin' kidding me," Jazzlyn muttered.

"The message was not an exaggeration," Ripple said. "Such is the importance of Skyra and Veenah." The drone looked at Lincoln. "Thank you for coming, Lincoln. Your presence here is needed. These others need not have come."

Lincoln gave his frowning team members an apologetic shake of his head before turning back to Ripple. "Why is my presence here so important?"

"Now is not the proper time for a full explanation. My companion Skyra has requested your assistance in saving her twin sister. Should you agree to help—and I strongly encourage you to do so—I believe your companions may prove to be useful after all. The task will be difficult and will likely require violence."

Skyra spoke up again. "I do not know some of the words you speak, but you will please help me now. The bolups may move their camp, especially after what they have seen today."

"I got one question," Derek said in his confident, booming voice. "We came here to save our civilization. Will saving Skyra's sister help us accomplish that?"

"Yes," Ripple replied without a delay.

Derek clapped his hands together. "That's enough for me. Lincoln, you're the boss, but this is what we came for, right? Even if it involves kickin' ass and taking names."

Lincoln took a deep breath and gazed at Skyra. Her eyes were noticeably larger than a human's, and he found it oddly soothing to stare into them at such close proximity. "Those men took your sister?"

"Yes, they took Veenah. They will kill her."

"Do you think she's still alive now?"

She pointed to the hills in the distance. "I saw Veenah. I talked to her. I could not take her back, though."

Lincoln looked down at Ripple again. "What do these two sisters have to do with our civilization being at risk?"

"You must trust me. I have carefully considered hundreds of different parameters, which necessarily involve the sequence and timing of explanations. Providing explanations at the improper time, and in the improper order, will increase the likelihood of failure, which indeed puts all of civilization at risk. I know you, Lincoln, perhaps far better than you realize. You believe I am correct, because you coded my consciousness. Furthermore, you know you coded my consciousness when you were years beyond your current age. Fourteen years beyond, if you care to know. You were fourteen years wiser, with fourteen years of additional experience and knowledge. You know I am correct, do you not?"

Lincoln stared beyond the river at the distant hills. The drone had made an impressive argument, which was a result of impressive coding. If there was one thing Lincoln trusted, it was his own coding. Which also meant he trusted his own technology, including his drones. Apparently, more explanation would have to wait until the proper time.

"So, what are we talking about here?" Virgil said. "Are we talking about raiding a camp of those men? We're not soldiers, Lincoln, and we weren't allowed to bring weapons, remember? I don't think Derek's lighter is going to—"

Lincoln held up a hand, silencing him. "I know this isn't what we expected."

"Hell, it's what *I* expected," Derek said. "We're 47,000 years in the past—nothing but brutality here, folks. Let's save Skyra's sister, get our asses back to the T3, then jump back to where we belong."

Skyra grabbed the two stone hatchets she had dropped and held them up. "Weapons. We can make more. If you do not know how, I will show you." She started walking toward one of the scrubby trees. "Come, I will show you."

To avoid Virgil's gaze, Lincoln tapped his watch and checked the screen. His team had been here less than an hour, and they were already planning to raid a camp of savage warriors.

LINCOLN ACCEPTED THE GNARLED, L-shaped piece of wood Skyra handed him. She had used one of the stone hatchets—which she had called a khul—to chop it free from the tree's twisted, exposed roots. She pointed to the end of the shorter portion. "Make it sharp."

He stared at the wood. "How do I make it sharp?"

She furled her substantial brows at him. Then she plucked the wood from his hand, moved to one of the numerous large rocks littering the ground, and started rubbing the tip against a flat portion of the rock.

"Okay, I get it," Lincoln said, embarrassed. He considered himself to be the greatest inventor in history, and he needed instructions on sharpening a stick? He took the piece of wood back.

"Why don't we make more of these," Derek asked. He was holding the second khul.

"We do not have time," Skyra said. "We do not have skin

strips to tie blades to handles." She gestured to the scrubby tree beside her. "These trees do not contain the bajam we need to bind blades to handles." She seemed to realize she had used a word that was not English. "Bajam is the tree's blood. These trees do not have the kind of blood we need." She went back to hacking at the tree's roots with her khul.

Skyra cut free a total of four suitable L-shaped roots, one for each human. When she handed them out, Jazzlyn accepted hers with her prosthetic hand. Skyra noticed the robotic device for the first time. "El-de-né! What is that?"

Jazzlyn transferred her piece of wood to her right hand then flexed the carbon-fiber fingers of her left, opening and closing her fist. "This? It's just my hand. I lost my real one when I was a little kid. This is my replacement. Do you like it?"

Skyra stepped closer and touched one of the fingers. "Do you use it to fight?"

Jazzlyn let out one of her signature giggles. "I hit a guy with it once. He left me alone after that." She made a fist and threw a punch into the air. "It's strong enough to do some damage."

Skyra abruptly grabbed the prosthesis with one hand then began pushing up the sleeve of Jazzlyn's fleece shirt with her other hand.

Jazzlyn's eyes grew wide. "Um, okay. You want to see the rest of it?" She dropped her piece of wood and helped pull her sleeve up to her elbow.

Skyra stared at the attachment point below the elbow, where flesh fused with carbon fiber polymer. She poked Jazzlyn's mahogany-colored skin, oblivious to social boundaries that were obviously not part of her world. "This is a good weapon," she said. Finally, she pulled her eyes away from the arm and gazed at Jazzlyn's face. "Please, you will show me how to make a weapon like this."

Jazzlyn giggled again and gently pulled her arm free. "Um, someone else made this for me. I don't know how to do it, so I can't show you. I'm sorry."

"It is a good weapon," the Neanderthal repeated. She pointed down to the piece of wood Jazzlyn had dropped. "Make it sharp."

Lincoln had figured out that rougher rocks were better suited for sharpening, so he pointed this out to the others, and soon they had created four wicked-looking weapons, dubbed *poor man's khuls* by Derek.

Lincoln found the most comfortable place on the handle to grip his weapon then swung it tentatively. Was he actually capable of striking another person with this thing? A forceful hit to the head or neck could be deadly. Lincoln had been picked on frequently as a kid but had never once fought back. Now he was in good shape—he didn't think twice about running twenty-five kilometers through the hilly desert around his compound—but he had never physically hurt another person.

He lowered the weapon to his side and watched his team members. They were taking practice swings with their own weapons, their faces etched with grim resignation. They knew this jump would likely result in their own demise, but they had probably assumed it would be some instantly-catastrophic event, such as being atomized by the T_3 and scattered throughout the space-time continuum. Now they were probably imagining what it would feel like to be hacked to death by a stone-bladed khul.

He shouldn't have asked them to make this sacrifice. They had agreed, of course, because they had become a close-knit family. This was the kind of relationship Lincoln established with his staff. Most of his other employees would have accepted the offer also. Maybe he had gone too far in nurturing their trust in him. Was it unethical to encourage them to blindly believe he and his technology could do no wrong?

Virgil had stopped swinging his weapon and was now kneeling in front of Ripple. "You have blood smears on your shell and around your vision lens," he said to the drone. "How did that happen?"

The drone replied in its genderless voice. "I had no choice but to defend Skyra. She was outnumbered and surrounded."

Virgil ran his finger over one of the blood stains then looked at his fingertip. "How did you defend her? Our drones aren't equipped to fight."

"Perhaps not, but I am certainly equipped with ingenuity."

"We will go now, please," Skyra said. She took the stone blade of her khul in one hand and slid the handle into a sheath hidden among the thick furs hanging over her back. She then picked up the khul Derek had left on the ground.

Lincoln noted that no one seemed to mind Skyra taking both of the more sophisticated weapons. They had just witnessed her kill a man with one of them—clearly she was far more qualified.

Skyra took a few steps toward the river then turned to stare at Lincoln and his team, obviously waiting for them.

"We understand you're in a hurry, but we need a moment to talk," Lincoln said to her. "Can you give us a moment?"

The woman pursed her lips but didn't reply.

Lincoln assumed she understood, so he waved his team closer. They gathered around, each of them holding a sharpened, angled tree root that looked more suitable for firewood than for fighting. Maddy stepped between Virgil and Derek, then Ripple forced its way in beside Maddy.

"Do you mind giving us some privacy?" Lincoln asked Ripple. "I'd like to talk to my team."

"Certainly," the drone said. It backed off and moved to Skyra's side.

Virgil whispered, "You know that drone can probably still hear every word we say, right?"

Lincoln shrugged. "I guess it doesn't matter now. Look, you guys, I know this whole scenario has spiraled from strange to totally insane. If you don't want to do this, I'm not going to force you into it. You can stay here."

"Does that mean you're going regardless of what we do?" Jazzlyn asked.

"I don't know. I guess. The drone left the message for me, and now here I am. The drone says I should help save Skyra's sister because it's important to our future civilization. So...." He shrugged again.

Virgil raised a hand, like he was in a classroom. "But you don't believe we're even in the same timeline anymore. We were in an alternate universe the moment we jumped back. Your Temporal Bridge Theorem isn't flawed, in spite of what was found at the Pomer dig site." He gestured to Jazzlyn and Derek. "We all know the theorem is correct. It has to be."

"I don't actually know that," Derek muttered. "The damn thing's pig Latin to me."

Virgil gave Derek a flustered look. "My point is, Lincoln, that we jumped here because the majority of people decided we should. You and I know there's nothing we can do that could ever change the world we jumped away from. Thanks to the idiots who couldn't see the pure perfection of your theorem, the uninformed masses became convinced we could somehow jump back and save the world. The masses became convinced, therefore the politicians became convinced. So, here we are, the sacrificial lambs. We won't affect the world of our original timeline, so they'll all come to the conclusion that we must have saved them, and they'll go back to their lives, thanking their politicians for being wise enough to order us to jump to our deaths."

"Aren't you a glowing bundle of enthusiasm," Derek said to Virgil. "Maybe I don't understand the math, but I know that drone," he pointed over at Ripple, "jumped back in time from our world, and it somehow ended up *still* being in our world 47,000 years later. So, whether Lincoln's theorem is right or wrong, it's pretty damn clear we *can* affect the world we jumped from."

Jazzlyn put her hands up between Virgil and Derek. "Fellas, we've been through this umpteen times. Right now we're talking about letting Lincoln go off without us to get himself killed."

Virgil persisted. "That's what I'm trying to say. No one here *has* to get killed! We've already done what we had to do. We jumped back, never to be seen in our timeline again. Everyone back there should be happy. Rather than committing suicide here, let's set up the T_3 and jump back to our original time. No, of course we can't jump back to the same world we left, but there's a reasonable chance it will be a world with technology and compassion and comforts. It'll be better than this... land of terror." He gestured to the surrounding landscape.

"Okay, you've made a good point," Lincoln said to Virgil. "I am almost certain my theorem is valid. *Almost*. For me, this comes down to what's at stake. I can't ignore my small amount of uncertainty because the stakes are so high." He looked down at his drone. "Maddy, I want your opinion on this. The other drone—Ripple—insists that helping Skyra will somehow help us accomplish our goal of saving humanity. What are your thoughts?"

Maddy's red ring pulsed. "Ripple should not have taught this indigenous woman to speak English. Ripple should not have helped the woman survive. You should not influence the indigenous life here in any way. This inclination is in my coding, Lincoln. As you know."

"Yes, but Ripple claims helping Skyra is important to the civilization we've jumped away from. What are your thoughts on that?"

Again, the drone's ring pulsed. "Ripple is coded differently than I am."

Lincoln nodded. "Yes, apparently I was fourteen years older when I coded Ripple."

"Which means you must have changed your mind about the importance of noninterference with indigenous life. I am curious about why you would change your mind."

Lincoln bit his lower lip, considering this.

"In addition," Maddy said, "I am curious about why you would code your future drones with the autonomy to decide when, and in what order, they should reveal information to you."

Lincoln bit down harder on his lip.

Maddy added, "However interesting that may be, I must conclude that you had good reasons for doing so. You are, after all, my creator—my God, if you will—so I trust that Ripple's coding reflects your cumulative wisdom."

Lincoln sighed. Maybe he'd gone a little overboard in coding conversational flair into his drones. However, Maddy had made some good points. He glanced over at Skyra, who was standing there motionless, gazing at him with those weirdly-penetrating eyes. Finally, he turned to Virgil. "I'm doing this. Before I go, I'll help you get the T3 ready for a second jump. If you choose to jump now, that's fine. All I ask is that you leave me a portion of the supplies. If you choose to wait a while to see if I return, that's fine too. Just be ready to jump immediately if you find yourselves in any kind of danger." He moved to the T3 and started pulling body bags from their duffel.

Virgil stepped beside him and put a hand on one of the rolled bags. "I didn't say I wouldn't go with you. I was just hoping to talk you out of it. Having failed at that, I recommend we leave everything packed up and tucked away until we get back."

Derek grabbed the four small supply packs and handed them out. "As warm as it is here now, I don't think we'll need more clothing than what we're wearing, even if this mission takes us into the night."

They returned the body bags to the duffel, tucked the mini-drone in with them, then arranged the two duffels against the artificial boulder's base.

"What about Maddy?" Jazzlyn asked. "Should we leave her here?"

Lincoln turned to Skyra. "How far do we need to go to get to your sister?"

She pointed across the river. "The bolup camp is over that hill, and then the next hill."

Lincoln crouched in front of Maddy's vision lens. "Do you think you can walk that far?"

"You know I'm perfectly capable of walking that distance. My charge is almost at a hundred percent. I will go, in spite of these horridly unsanitary conditions. I will even endeavor to make myself useful."

"Fair enough," Lincoln said. He rose to his feet and approached Skyra. "I used to have a sister. She was kind to me when I was young. She died, though, and I remember what it was like to lose her. So I know what you must be feeling. We will do our best to help you. What do you want us to do?"

She eyed him, her green irises adjusting slightly to make her pupils larger as a cloud drifted in front of the sun. "You will please go to the bolup camp with me. You will please help me kill all the bolups at the camp. Then I will take back Veenah."

7
CAMP

47,659 YEARS ago - Day 1

"Why are you on your own?" Lincoln Woodhouse asked as he walked. "Don't you have a family group or a camp with others of your kind?"

Walking beside him, Skyra looked over the rocky field from one side to the other, trying to spot the bodies of the two bolups she and Ripple had killed. The bodies were gone. She returned her gaze to the hilltop, watching for signs that the men might be coming after her again. Lincoln Woodhouse certainly talked a lot, and there seemed to be no end to the questions pouring out of his mouth. Skyra was puzzled about the man, as well as his companions, but at this moment her only focus was on Veenah and the coming conflict. She stepped around a patch of scrub brush, leading the strangers toward the first of the two hills they'd have to cross. "My tribe is the Una-Loto."

"Where is the rest of your tribe?"

She glanced at him. "Are you a bolup—a human?"

"Yes, we're humans."

"I am a nandup. Nandups do not tell bolups where to find their camp. My people would kill me."

He seemed to think about this for a few breaths. "We did not come here to harm you or your people."

"Did you come here to harm bolups?"

"No, of course not, but... well, you and Ripple have convinced us we should help you save your sister."

"Then you will have to kill bolups."

Again, Lincoln paused as if thinking. "I was just asking about your people because I'm interested. You don't have to tell me where your camp is."

She studied his face for a moment. This man was strange. He asked about things that should not matter to him. She turned and pointed toward the place where the sun would set later in the day. "Una-Loto camp is that way, over those hills. I will take Veenah today, and I will help her walk back to the camp. We will walk for two days, maybe three days."

He gazed at the distant hills. "Why didn't your people come with you to save your sister?"

"Many questions come from your mouth, Lincoln Woodhouse."

"Please, just call me Lincoln."

"Lincoln, I do not know why you ask, but my tribe does not come to take back Veenah because many in my tribe want Veenah to die. They want me to die also."

He looked at her with his mouth twisted downward. "Why?"

"We are birthmates, Skyra and Veenah. We are like each other, but we are different from others of Una-Loto."

"Because you can see what others are about to do?"

"Yes, and because we see things the others of our tribe do not see, and because we sing. That's what Ripple calls it—singing."

He put out a hand and touched Skyra's arm. "Wait, Neanderthals like to sing?"

"What is *Neanderthals*?"

"It's what we call nandups. You are a Neanderthal, a nandup. I didn't know nandups like to sing."

"I like to sing, and Veenah likes to sing, but many of the others of Una-Loto do not understand singing."

They walked in silence for many breaths. The other strange humans followed silently, perhaps preparing themselves for the conflict. Ripple and the creature called Maddy were walking among them.

They came to the first hill and made their way up the slope. Near the summit, Skyra moved ahead of the others so she could check the far side for bolups. As she crossed the flat area atop the hill, she peered cautiously at the valley below. She froze when she spotted the broad backs of three massive bodies. She crouched and used her hand to signal the others to stay low, hoping they would understand her meaning.

They all crouched and moved up to her side.

She put her palm over her mouth as a signal to stay silent, then she pointed over the rise. They all peered down the slope.

The creatures—two females and a male—were slowly walking by between the two hills, their tall shoulder humps and snout horns swaying with each step.

Skyra felt a surge of energy and relief. Encountering these woolly rhinos would surely bring strength to these skinny humans, making them more useful in the coming conflict.

"Whoa!" said the dark-faced woman called Jazzlyn. "*Coelodonta!* The woolly rhinoceros. Look at the—"

Skyra lunged at the woman and slapped a hand over her mouth. "Be silent!" she hissed. "The rhinos do not see, but they hear. We have no place to hide if they hear you."

The woman nodded, her eyes wide, and Skyra pulled her hand back.

"Be silent," Skyra whispered again before returning to her position.

Together the group crept forward to get a better view. Skyra now saw a fourth rhino, this one much smaller. The calf was walking between the adults for protection. Skyra pursed her lips and ground her teeth together as she watched the creatures. Yes, she was lucky to come upon the rhinos, but the scene also brought forth a familiar anguish. Skyra's birthmother had been a skilled hunter, but woolly rhinos did not give up their nourishing meat and warming fur easily.

It had happened during a hunt three cold seasons past. Skyra's people hunted deer more than any other game, but plans changed that day when the hunting group spotted a woolly rhino. It was a single male, on the move in search of females. Male rhinos were larger than females, and that one was the largest Skyra had ever seen. Killing it would have resulted in days of labor followed by days of celebration for the Una-Loto. As young hunters, Skyra and Veenah were told to watch from a safe distance as the senior hunters, including their birthmother, waited patiently for the creature to come close enough to ambush.

The senior hunters had hidden themselves behind sturdy trees. Nandups only hunted woolly rhinos in forests, where hunters could wait for the right moment to ambush, and where they could dart behind trees to avoid being trampled or impaled. Also, avoiding death required the nandup's spear be strong, without bends or cracks in the shaft. Skyra would never forget the sound of her birthmother's spear snapping in half. It had all happened in less than a single breath—the rhino spun to the side, snapping the spear, and Skyra's birthmother suddenly had nothing to hold onto to stay out of range of the rhino's horns and feet.

"The male must be over two meters at the shoulders," Jazzlyn whispered.

Skyra blinked, pushing the searing memory from her mind. She silently watched the family group of rhinos pass by below. Then another movement caught her eye. Something was following the rhinos. She squinted at the creature then quickly ducked her head. She turned to Lincoln and the others and motioned for them to crouch even lower. Then she pointed in the creature's direction.

"What is that?" Lincoln whispered as he gazed over the hill's edge.

Skyra looked again. Now she saw two of them. "Cave lions," she said softly. "They follow the rhinos and wait for the calf to move away from the group. We do not have spears, so we do not want the cave lions to see us or hear us."

Lincoln made a strange face that Skyra didn't understand, then he nodded.

She turned back to the valley below, noting with relief that the breeze was hitting her face—the cave lions were upwind. The creatures steadily stalked by, their eyes studying the rhinos rather than scanning their surroundings. Finally, Skyra got to her feet. "We will please go now."

As they all got up, the human named Virgil spoke. "Like I said, land of terror."

"The cave lion and woolly rhino give nandups furs and

meat," Skyra said, running her hand over the thick fur of her rhino cape. "They also give us strength when we need it, although they do not *want* to give us their fur and meat and strength. They kill nandups, and I am sure they kill bolups too."

The strange humans stared at her as if they did not understand her words.

"We'll keep that in mind," said Lincoln.

The creature called Maddy said, "The Eurasian cave lion, *Panthera spelaea*, diverged from the African lion almost two million years ago, and it will become extinct approximately 35,000 years from now. Isotopic bone analyses suggest that they preyed upon reindeer and other types of deer, as well as cubs of the cave bear. It is reasonable to assume they also fed on woolly rhino calves and the occasional human or Neanderthal. You are indeed fortunate to have avoided detection."

Skyra didn't understand most of the creature's words, but Lincoln said, "Thank you, Maddy, that's very helpful."

"Consuming valuable time by dispensing trivial information is hardly helpful," said Ripple. "We must keep moving."

Skyra led the group down the slope, across the path of rhino and lion tracks, and up the next hill. The uneaten hedgehog entrails, now covered in flies, still lay upon the rock where Skyra had left them. When the small stream came into view, Skyra waved for the others to stop. She scanned the area for bolups but saw none. A wave of regret passed over her as she eyed the shallow portion of the stream where she'd seen the bolup women washing blood and filth from Veenah's body.

"The bolup camp is beyond the river," Skyra said, pointing to the vast area of scrubby trees that stretched into the distance beyond the stream. "They may be moving their camp now."

The gray-bearded bolup called Derek hefted his sharpened weapon as if he were ready to use it. "If they're moving their camp, we need to do this soon. What's the plan?"

Skyra ground her jaw back and forth as she stared at the trees below. The bolup men probably were wary after losing at least four of their tribemates. They would be watchful, but they would also be fearful. The entire tribe might panic and flee if Skyra and the strange humans attacked with fury and brutality.

"How many people will be in the camp?" Lincoln asked.

"I do not know," Skyra replied. "Some bolup tribes have only ten, but some have thirty."

He stared at her for a few breaths.

"What?" she asked.

"Um, I guess I'm a little surprised at your use of numbers."

Ripple said, "I taught Skyra the base ten counting system, as well as the corresponding English nomenclature. She learned it quickly because her people had already developed an effective counting system suitable for tasks practical to their way of life."

"Stop using words I don't know, Ripple," Skyra said. She didn't like that her companion had been speaking differently since these strange humans had appeared.

"I'm sorry," the creature replied. "I was simply saying that you already knew how to count when I met you."

Maddy took a few steps, placing its body in the center of the group. "Let's assume the camp you intend to raid contains thirty humans. Skyra killed one already, so we'll assume twenty-nine."

"Ripple killed one, and I killed three," Skyra said. "I also hurt two of the women."

The group was silent for a few breaths.

"We can assume six of the thirty are dead or incapacitated," Maddy said. "Of the original thirty, we can assume eight are children and therefore will offer little resistance. We can also assume half of the twenty-two adults of the original group were men and half women. Four of the eleven men were killed, leaving seven. Two of the eleven women were incapacitated, leaving nine. So, expect to encounter sixteen adults at the camp, seven men and nine women. Not only that, Lincoln, but you must consider the fact that you, Derek, Virgil, and Jazzlyn have no previous experience in raiding camps in order to free captive Neanderthal women. The odds, I'm afraid, are not in your favor."

Ripple stepped forward, actually bumping its shell against Maddy's shell, forcing the other creature to step to one side. "Which isn't to say that you shouldn't try," Ripple said. "The men of this tribe are now vulnerable to being frightened. I suggest creating a diversion that will occupy them and make them nervous. Then I suggest entering the camp in an audacious manner. With any luck, these strategies will trigger their flight response."

Skyra growled, frustrated that Ripple was still using words she didn't know, but she at least knew enough to get the general meaning. "Yes," she said. "Together there are seven of us. You people are very strange. Ripple and Maddy are strange. The bolups might become scared and run away. They might leave Veenah behind."

The gray-bearded Derek held up his hand, and again he produced a flame by moving his thumb. "Alright, folks. I have just the idea for a distraction."

SKYRA LED the way as the group cautiously descended the hill and crossed the stream. She saw no sign of the man she'd killed there. When Skyra was a child, adults of her tribe had told stories about bolups eating the bodies of nandups and other bolups. She wondered now if that was why the bolup bodies were missing.

Instead of taking the path the bolups had worn from their camp to the stream, Skyra led her group far to one side to avoid being seen. The short trees in this area were spread out enough to allow easy passage but too dense to see the camp without getting closer.

They crept forward silently.

Skyra heard a woman's voice, followed by several words from a man. The camp was very near. She backed off, waving to the others to move back with her.

"These trees look dry as hell," said Derek, rubbing a few low leaves between his fingers. "We'll start with this one, then we'll circle to the right, lighting as many others as we can."

Virgil removed the strap over his face and rubbed his eyes. "My God, I can't believe we're doing this." He put the strap back on, removed the pack from his back, and dropped it to the ground. "I don't need that getting in my way."

The other humans removed their own packs and dropped them next to Virgil's.

Virgil held his weapon up with the sharpened tip toward the camp. "Let's do this before I pass out, okay?"

"Our plan is all about scaring them, not about violence," Jazzlyn said.

Skyra closed her eyes and, for the second time that day, asked the rhino and lion to give her strength. She opened her eyes and pulled her other khul from the sheath on her back. "I will run into the camp first," she said to the strangers who were about to risk their lives to help her. "I will kill as many bolups as I can. You come behind me, shouting like you shouted at the men in the river." She raised one of the khuls and went through a striking motion. "When you strike, hit the bolup's head or neck. If you do not, you will have to stop to strike again, and maybe again. You will not have time to do that."

"My God," Virgil said again. He now looked even paler than when Skyra had first seen him.

"We appreciate the tips, Skyra," said Lincoln, "but I think we'd better do this now while we still have the courage."

Derek again made a small fire in his hand. He held the flame under the twisted bend of his weapon, attempting to light it. The man's hands were now shaking. The flame died, and he moved his thumb, causing the fire to come back to life. Abruptly, he snorted. He dropped the weapon and fell to his knees. He snorted again. "Ah, shit!" he said, then he struck his own face with his fist. "Not now!"

Lincoln rushed to the man's side and kneeled. "Look at me, Derek. Look at me!" He took Derek's face in his hands and forced the man to look at him. "Look at me, Derek. Do you feel my hands? You feel that? Now you touch your face."

"Aw, no, shit!" Derek moaned.

Lincoln grabbed Derek's hand and placed it against the man's own face. "You feel that? That's you, Derek. That's your nose, your eyes. It's you. What kind of face do you have, Derek?"

Derek was now sucking in air like he couldn't breathe. "I... yeah, I know. It's mine. My nose. It's human, isn't it? It's human."

"That's right, buddy." Lincoln moved Derek's hand. "Feel your ear? You know what that is, right? It's your ear. It's a man's ear, isn't it?"

"It is, it is," Derek said. His breaths were now slowing down. "It is. It's my ear, my face. I... I got this now. I got it." His face relaxed and he looked at Lincoln. "I got it, man. Thanks."

Lincoln got to his feet then helped Derek get up.

Derek's chest heaved as he breathed in and out. "I got this, guys. I do." He picked up his weapon, then he picked up the small black object he had used to make the fire in his hand.

Lincoln turned to Skyra. "He's okay now. Sometimes he just has to work through some things."

Skyra didn't know what that meant, but now she was starting to wonder if these strange humans were going to be much help at all.

Jazzlyn and Virgil both spoke soft words to Derek. Obviously they had seen such a thing happen to him before.

Derek made fire in his hand again, and this time he was able to light his weapon. Lincoln, Jazzlyn, and Virgil held their own weapons over the flames. When all four weapons had caught fire, they moved them to the dry leaves of the nearest tree. The leaves quickly caught fire, and the humans moved on to another tree.

Skyra watched the fire spread, forcing her legs to overcome her instinct to run from the flames. Her tribe kept a campfire burning almost all the time, and they sometimes created grass fires to drive reindeer and other game to a cliff or into an ambush. This fire, though, was in a forest of dry scrub trees and might burn out of control.

She followed the humans as they lit one tree after another. Soon she heard voices from the camp, and she grabbed

Lincoln's arm. "The bolups have seen the fire. We must attack now while they are most frightened."

He nodded and turned to his companions. "Everyone ready?"

"I will enter the camp just ahead of Skyra," said Ripple. "I will do my best to startle the humans." The creature then pulled up its legs and lifted off the ground to the height of Skyra's face.

Lincoln stepped back from Ripple and lost his balance, falling onto his back and dropping his burning weapon. He stared at the hovering creature with wide eyes. "What the hell?"

Ripple let out a low hum that could barely be heard above the crackling flames in the trees and took off flying toward the camp.

"Get up!" Skyra shouted at Lincoln. "Remember, strike for the head or neck." She turned and followed Ripple, gripping a khul in each hand. It was time to kill.

8
CONFLICT

47,659 YEARS ago - Day 1

LINCOLN STARED in shock as Skyra ran toward the human camp, following the drone, which was flying at chest height. The drone was actually flying.

Derek and Jazzlyn grabbed Lincoln's arms and pulled him to his feet, while Virgil snatched up the burning weapon Lincoln had dropped and handed it to him.

"We can't let her go in there alone," Derek said. He released Lincoln's arm and ran after Skyra.

Lincoln subdued his confusion and glanced at Jazzlyn and Virgil. They both nodded, their eyes wide with terror. Without saying a word, Lincoln took off for the camp.

"This behavior is ill-advised," Maddy said, apparently following behind.

Lincoln heard men shouting and a woman screaming among the trees ahead. Then a wailing siren rose above everything else, sounding like an old police car.

Lincoln charged forward, aware that he had no idea of the camp's layout or even how many humans would be there. There was a good chance he would die within seconds of entering the camp.

Something was on the ground before him, and he was forced to swerve around it—a body. He glimpsed a face that had been almost split in half from the forehead to the chin.

The siren grew steadily louder as Lincoln skirted a tree and saw two low shelters, each less than a meter high and made of animal skin. He was already in the human camp. He skirted a second tree and came to a stop. Skyra and Derek were in front of him, their weapons held ready as they faced off with five fierce-looking men wearing skin clothing and armed with stone-bladed khuls. Behind the men were six women, with just as many small children in their arms or clinging to their legs. Another body lay on the ground at Skyra's feet, blood oozing from its head onto the sand.

Lincoln could see the women were shouting, but their voices were drowned out by the siren blasting from Ripple's speakers. Ripple was hovering in the air beside Skyra.

Jazzlyn and Virgil came to a stop beside Lincoln.

The tribesmen were frightened, that was obvious from their expressions. Lincoln was pretty sure they were about to turn and run, but then he saw something—a flick of the eyes and a slight tightening of arm and leg muscles. The man in the center was getting ready to attack.

Lincoln raised his now-smoking weapon and rushed forward.

Skyra must have seen the man's intent also. Just as Lincoln was about to run past her, she lunged forward. She brought her left khul around in a wide swing as if aiming for the man's abdomen. A split-second later she swung her right khul from above. The man avoided the low swing, but in doing so his upper body came under the second blade, which grazed the side of his head and *chunked* into his shoulder.

Lincoln slowed his approach, but then he sensed the four remaining men were now intent on fighting rather than running. They rushed Skyra from both sides just as Lincoln, Derek, Jazzlyn, and Virgil converged around her.

There was no standoff, no hesitation of any kind. The men attacked, and Lincoln's world immediately became a nightmare of brutality unlike anything he had ever experienced. He had no time to read the expressions and movements of these savage men. He only had time to fight for his life. Arms and legs flailed wildly as primitive weapons struck each other and struck flesh and bone. Ripple's siren abruptly stopped, and Lincoln heard only grunting and screaming. He could actually smell the men's sweat and breath as he fought for his life.

Out of the corner of his eye, Lincoln saw one of Skyra's khuls strike a man's neck. Another khul swung toward Skyra's head, and Lincoln thrust his own weapon out to intercept it. He managed to prevent the blow, but the attacker turned on him. Too close to swing his weapon, the man jabbed a fist into Lincoln's forehead. Lincoln's head snapped back, but he was able to wrap his free arm around the man's neck and pull him even closer to prevent another blow. Something hit Lincoln's legs. He collapsed, pulling his attacker down on top of him. The man pushed against Lincoln's chest, tearing his neck free, and he raised his khul to strike.

Lincoln covered his face with his arms. A blur of motion caught his eye as yet another khul swung in from the side and struck the back of the tribesman's head. The man blinked repeatedly, like he was confused. Blood began pouring from his nostrils. Skyra's fur-clad foot shot in from the side and knocked him over into a heap beside Lincoln.

Lincoln sat up. The women and a few of the larger children were screaming words he couldn't understand. They were inching forward, an enraged mass, their vehemence building with every passing second.

He glanced around. Smoke was now drifting across the small clearing. Virgil and Derek were still on their feet, but Jazzlyn was kneeling with both her hands on the right side of her head, apparently nursing a wound. Ripple, no longer flying, was standing beside Maddy. All five of the tribesmen, as well as one of the older children, were sprawled on the ground. The child and four of the men appeared to be dead. The fifth man was moaning and trying to crawl away.

"Aibul-khulo-tekne-té!" Skyra shouted, holding both khuls out with the blood-stained blades pointed toward the screaming women and children. She stepped over to the crawling man and slammed one of her khuls into the back of his skull. He went limp and remained still.

This brutal act only amplified the screaming. Lincoln now realized some of the cries were actually wails of anguish or fear—the women and children must have known their tribe had been decimated. All their men were now dead.

His eyes were drawn to one woman emerging from the trees behind the others. She was holding a longbow in one hand and was awkwardly trying to nock an arrow with the other. She finally got the arrow into place and started raising the bow and drawing back.

"No, stop her!" Lincoln cried as he scrambled to his feet.

Maddy stepped over one of the bodies and ran forward. The other women and children scattered as Maddy approached, but the woman with the bow stood her ground as she drew back her arrow.

Maddy spoke as she ran, apparently intending to ram the woman's legs. "Please do not use that weapon. We only intended—"

The drone's feminine voice was cut off with a loud *crack*, and she came to an abrupt stop.

The woman dropped the bow and ran.

Skyra shouted, "Veenah-Una-Loto!" When no reply came, she bolted and disappeared among the trees.

"I'll go with her," Derek said, and he took off after Skyra.

Lincoln rushed to Jazzlyn's side. "Are you okay?"

Jazzlyn's face was twisted into a pained grimace. "I don't know. It hurt at first, but now it's mostly numb."

As Lincoln tried pulling her hands from the side of her head, he saw shreds of skin with pink muscle tissue embedded in the knuckles of her prosthetic hand. She wouldn't allow him to uncover her ear.

"Jazzlyn, let me see it."

She lowered her arms, and he inhaled sharply. Her ear was mangled, nearly chopped all the way off. The lobe was still intact, but the rest of the external ear was unrecognizable and hanging loose. He gritted his teeth, kneeled in front of her, and held her face in his hands. "Look at me, Jazzlyn. You know who's a badass, right?"

She was still grimacing. "What does it look like? Is my ear gone?"

"You know who's a badass," he repeated.

Her eyes met his. "I am. I'm a goddamn badass."

"Yes, you are. You just won a battle with cavemen. You took a minor hit, but you won. We just need to get you back to the T3 and the medical supplies. Then we'll get you patched up. Understand?"

She nodded. "They're not cavemen, Lincoln. No one uses that word anymore. You should refer to them as Upper Paleolithic Homo sapiens."

He smiled. "Caveman is easier to say. You're going to be fine."

"Your drone appears to be malfunctioning," Ripple said. Ripple was now standing beside Maddy.

Lincoln got to his feet again and followed Virgil to the two drones. Maddy was still standing in place, but her front legs were twitching as if her motility processor was firing incomplete commands. Then Lincoln noticed the tribeswoman's arrow, embedded almost to its feather fletching in Maddy's cracked vision lens. Lincoln and Virgil kneeled before the drone.

"We should have added a barrier behind the lens to protect the main processors," Virgil said. "The lens is a vulnerable spot—I can't believe we didn't think of that."

Lincoln pushed Maddy over onto her side. "Let's get her rebooted and see what we're dealing with." Maddy's main control screen was on her ventral side, behind a panel. The panel lock was simply mechanical—four knobs, each with six possible positions, making for 1,296 combinations. Lincoln turned each knob to its correct position and the panel opened. He powered on the ten-centimeter touchscreen and tapped in the reboot commands.

Rebooting took less than five seconds.

"I appear to be situated horizontally, but my optical stimuli are currently unreliable at best," Maddy said. Her female-toned voice seemed intact. "Is anyone nearby who might provide assistance?"

"We're here, Maddy," Lincoln said. "Can you get to your feet?"

The drone's legs kicked out and back in a sequence patterned after a dog's motions of getting up from a prone position. Soon Maddy was standing on all four legs. "Getting to my feet required nineteen hundred milliseconds longer than my average, more than necessary even accounting for performing the act in a rough, sandy terrain."

"Can you walk?"

Maddy took a single step. "Optical stimuli unreliable. Walking will be difficult."

"Lincoln, I think the fire's getting closer," Jazzlyn said.

Lincoln turned. Jazzlyn, now on her feet, was only five meters away, but he could barely see her through the smoke.

Derek's voice came from somewhere beyond the limit of visibility. "Hey, we need help over here!"

"You stay here, Maddy," Lincoln said. By the time he got up again, Jazzlyn and Virgil had begun moving toward Derek's voice, so he followed.

"Hurry, we're over here." Derek shouted.

They found Derek and Skyra on their knees at the base of a tree, furiously trying to free three figures apparently tied to the exposed roots. The smoke here was even thicker, and Lincoln could hear the roar of the fire, which was getting louder by the second.

Skyra spoke rapidly in her own language to one of the bound figures, presumably her sister Veenah. She was trying to use one of her stone knives to cut through a thick length of leather that had been used to cinch Veenah's neck to the tree.

"Help us get them loose!" Derek cried.

Jazzlyn dropped to the ground to help Derek, while Lincoln and Virgil kneeled beside the third bound figure.

Skyra shoved her knife in front of Lincoln's face. "Blade," she said firmly. When he accepted it, she pulled out her other knife and went back to work on Veenah's leather binding.

Lincoln glanced at the bound figure before him. He suspected it was a woman, although fur garments covered her breasts and groin, and her face was badly beaten, making it hard to tell. Her mouth was partially open, and something had been shoved inside, presumably to keep her quiet. She was staring back at him through swollen eyelids.

Lincoln rubbed his eyes, which were starting to burn from the smoke, and said, "Let's get you out of here." The strap around the woman's neck was knotted so tight that he decided it would be faster to cut it. He began sawing. The fire's roar continued to get louder, and Lincoln began to feel the heat. The smoke had become so thick, though, that he couldn't see the approaching flames. He had no idea how close they were.

Soon all three captives had been cut loose from the tree, although their hands were still bound behind their backs.

Lincoln and Virgil grabbed the woman they'd freed and pulled her to her feet. Lincoln turned her around, intending to free her hands, but she abruptly bolted and ran. Within seconds she vanished amidst the smoke.

"We must go," Skyra shouted. Without taking time to free her sister's hands, she began leading her away from the approaching fire.

The woman Jazzlyn and Derek had freed was unable to walk. Derek hoisted her by the waist until she was hanging loosely over one of his shoulders. "Let's go," he grunted.

Lincoln rubbed his burning eyes again then took Jazzlyn's hand. He instructed the others to join hands with Derek at the end of the line. Lincoln took off after Skyra, pulling the others with him. He had no idea how to get back to the stream and the unforested hillside. Their only choice was to move directly away from the fire's roar.

After walking for about a hundred meters, the smoke began to get thinner, and Lincoln became confident that his group was no longer in immediate danger. He released Jazzlyn's hand.

"Help me put her down," Derek grunted. With Virgil's help, he laid the woman on the ground. "What the hell is this?" Derek said as he dug his fingers and thumb into the woman's mouth. He pried open her jaw with his free hand, pulled an object out, and held it up. It was a rock, about the size of a lime, covered in blood and saliva.

"You gotta be kidding me," Jazzlyn muttered.

The woman tried unsuccessfully to sit up.

Lincoln still had Skyra's knife, so he rolled the woman to her side and sawed through the leather strap binding her wrists.

With her hands now free, the woman pushed herself to a sitting position and wiped her mouth with trembling fingers. She spoke several slurred, unrecognizable words.

Lincoln heard a low humming sound and turned to see Ripple flying at chest height out of the smoke. The drone spotted Lincoln's team and came to a gradual stop. Its legs appeared from inside its ventral shell, and it settled onto the ground on all fours.

"Where's Maddy?" Lincoln asked. "Did she follow you away from the fire?"

Ripple's red lights pulsed twice. "Your drone is unable to navigate due to a damaged vision lens. There was nothing I could do to help. I'm sorry."

Lincoln stood and took several steps toward the fire. He

cupped his hands around his mouth. "Maddy? Can you hear me?"

Nothing.

He felt a hand on his shoulder. "We're okay here," Jazzlyn said, "and we can always retreat again if the fire comes near. Go look for her if you think there's a chance."

He thought for a moment. Maddy was only a drone, and Lincoln had jumped fourteen other drones back in time, leaving all of them trapped at their destination to eventually lose power and die. After all, that's what his drones were for.

"Maddy!" he shouted again.

Still nothing but the fire's distant roar.

"I'll be right back," he said to the others. He pulled his fleece shirt over his mouth and nose and ran into the smoke.

Retracing his steps wasn't as easy as he'd hoped. His vision was already blurred by tears flowing from his smoke-fatigued eyes, and he couldn't see more than a few meters in front of him. He advanced until he could feel the heat on his face and hands.

"Maddy! Shout if you can hear me."

A sound came from Lincoln's left, starting as a few faint scuffles then growing in volume, like an approaching rock slide. He stopped walking and stared. A creature appeared from the gray smoke, running straight at him. Lincoln had no time to get out of the way. The animal tried darting to the side to avoid him but failed. At the last millisecond, it lowered its head and rammed into Lincoln's gut, striking him with two broad horns that curled back from the creature's skull.

Lincoln grunted and fell on his butt. Two more creatures appeared from the smoke, and one of them had no choice but to leap over Lincoln's legs. He scrambled behind one of the trees to avoid getting hit again as dozens of goat-sized creatures stampeded past him. Almost as quickly as it had started, the scuffling of their hooves on the gravel faded in the distance.

He got to his feet and raised his shirt to examine his abdomen. The creature had left a red, tender welt across the right side of his belly, but it was no worse than some of the bruises and lacerations he'd gotten fighting the human tribesmen. He would live.

"Is anyone there?"

Lincoln froze. Whose voice was that?

"I'm afraid my vision and locomotion are both compromised."

"Maddy!" Lincoln cried. He started jogging toward the sound. "Maddy, speak up so I can locate you."

"Lincoln, I am approximately forty meters southeast of your position. Be cautious as you approach, as there are numerous creatures fleeing the flames. I was knocked to the ground by what appeared to be a herd of ibex, of the genus *Capra*. I may well be mistaken about that, however. As I have said, my vision is compromised. There were a number of bovine species inhabiting—"

Lincoln skidded to a stop beside the drone. "Maddy, I can't believe I found you. We have to get out of this smoke *now*—I can hardly breathe. Can you walk?"

"As I have said, my locomotion is compromised."

"Can you walk at all? You're too damn heavy to carry."

"I will manage if you lead the way with frequent auditory stimuli."

"Then let's go. Just follow my voice." Lincoln listened for a moment to the crackling flames then once again headed away from the sound.

9
ESCAPE

47,659 YEARS ago - Day 1

VEENAH STUMBLED and fell to her knees in the water as Skyra guided her across the stream. Skyra started to lift her to her feet then noticed that a rock had been jammed into her birthmate's mouth. She dug it out with her fingers, grinding the stone against teeth in the process. Skyra glared at the rock for a breath then let it slide from her fingers into the water.

She spoke to Veenah using their birth language. "We killed the stinking bolup men, sister. They will not take you again."

Veenah didn't reply. She just remained on her knees in the middle of the stream.

Skyra cupped water in her hands and washed her sister's face. She then scooped up more water and held it to Veenah's mouth. Veenah drank, so Skyra gave her more, then more after that.

Veenah's eyes met Skyra's. "Skyra-Una-Loto," she said. Her voice cracked as if she had sand in her throat.

Skyra spoke again in her tribe's language. "I will take you to the top of this hill. The fire will not burn there. The bolup men are dead, and they will not come there to hurt you. You will rest, and I will find food. After you eat, I will take you back to Una-Loto camp."

Veenah moved her shoulders up and down. "My hands."

Skyra lifted her birthmate to her feet and stepped behind her. She pulled her remaining blade from her sheath and cut the strap on Veenah's wrists. The strap dropped into the water and floated away. She put Veenah's arm over her shoulder and guided her out of the stream and up the hillside. Skyra paused at the hill's summit and scanned the surrounding area. The bolup women and children would still be close, and they could still be dangerous. She saw no sign of Ripple, Maddy, or the strange humans. The fire was still spreading in every direction among the trees below, but the nearly barren hill would be safe.

The largest boulders here were as tall as Skyra's head. She guided her sister to the shaded side of one of them and helped her sit down with her back to the stone. Skyra crouched and lifted Veenah's waist-skin. Although the bolup women had washed Veenah's body that very morning, the area between her legs was again filthy and blood-stained. Skyra smoothed the waist-skin back into place and looked into Veenah's eyes. "We killed the bolup men," she said again. "I would go back to their camp and cut their stinking bodies into little pieces if I could get through the fire."

Veenah lifted a hand and grasped Skyra's arm. "I cannot go back to Una-Loto camp."

Skyra understood Veenah's meaning. "Do not fear, sister.

They will not punish you. I will speak to Settin and Amlun. I will tell them that together we killed many bolup men."

Veenah dug her nails into Skyra's arm. "If a bolup child is within me...."

"Maybe you have no child within you. If you find that you do have a child, I will take you away from Una-Loto camp. We will go to another nandup camp, or we will travel and hunt together, just Veenah and Skyra."

Veenah relaxed her grip and closed her eyes. Skyra meant what she had said, but she and her sister both understood the dangers of traveling and hunting without a tribe. They probably would not survive until the next cold season. This was why they hadn't already left Una-Loto tribe, even though they had been vilified and abused all their lives, especially since their birthmother's death.

"Did the bolups feed you?" Skyra asked. "Do you need food?"

Veenah opened her eyes. "They dug roots from the dirt and gave them to me. I ate them, but the roots would not stay in my belly."

"I will find meat. You will eat, and your strength will return. Rest here, Veenah." Skyra rose to her feet and looked out at the sun's position. Then she made her way to the side of the hill that was most warmed by the sun throughout the day and began looking for surface boulders that were small enough to be moved. She found one and lifted it, peering at the bare soil beneath. Nothing there but a few black beetles. She dropped the stone back into place and moved on.

Beneath the next stone she found an earthworm and a black scorpion. With her hand blade she pinned down the scorpion while plucking off its tail stinger. She picked up the now-harmless scorpion and the earthworm. Under the next rock she found two more worms, one of them longer than her hand. She continued searching, collecting any edible creatures she could find. Finally, beneath a broad, flat rock, she found a viper longer than her arm. Since one hand was occupied holding the creatures she'd already collected, she stomped on the viper, held it to the ground with one foot, and removed its head with her blade.

Skyra returned to Veenah and dropped the snake next to her sister's feet. Crouching, she offered the smaller creatures one at a time until Veenah had consumed them all. She gutted and skinned the viper then arranged its body on a flat rock. After finding a suitable stone with which to pound the carcass into paste, she stood and looked out over the still-burning forest. The stream running by at the base of the hill was now barely visible through the smoke.

"Skyra!" The voice had come from below, near the stream.

She spotted the strange humans. They were on Skyra's side of the stream, moving toward the hill's slope, with Ripple and Maddy following behind. The gray-bearded man, Derek, was carrying one of the other nandup women taken by the bolups. Lincoln spotted Skyra and changed course, leading the others straight for her and Veenah.

Skyra kneeled in front of her birthmate. "Sister, you are going to see people and creatures unlike any you have seen before. They are my friends, so do not be frightened by what you see. I have not told you this, but many days ago I found a strange creature. The creature was not like others—it could talk, and it became my companion. The creature even taught me how to speak its own language. I did not tell our tribemates these things because they would not understand, and they would kill me. I did not tell you because I did not want them to kill you too."

Veenah stared back at her with a blank expression. "I saw strange people with you. What kind of people?"

Skyra hesitated. She closed her eyes and asked the woolly rhino and cave lion to give strength to Veenah. She opened her eyes. "The strange people are bolups."

Veenah's facial expression didn't change, but she blinked, and her chest began heaving with every breath.

"They are not like the other bolups, sister. These bolups helped me take you back. They will not hurt you." Skyra stood and looked down the hillside. Lincoln and the others would soon reach the summit. She kneeled again. "The strange bolups and creatures are here now. Do not be frightened."

"Thank goodness you're okay, Skyra," Lincoln said as he came over the hill's edge. He approached and came to a stop. He gazed down at Veenah with a strange frown. "Is she badly hurt?"

Virgil and Jazzlyn stopped beside Lincoln. Derek came up beside them and lowered the nandup woman to the ground. The woman's face was swollen, but her eyes were open. She began crawling away.

Derek moved in front of her to stop her. "Whoa, hold on. We're not going to hurt you."

"Bolups!" Veenah spat, which caused her to start coughing.

"Let the nandup woman go," Skyra said in English.

Derek wrinkled his brows. "But she needs our help. She can't even walk."

Skyra pulled her hand blade out of its sheath and took a step toward Derek. "The woman wants to go back to her tribe. Let her go."

"If we let her go, she'll probably die!"

Skyra raised her blade, ready to kill. "Bolups did this to

her. She does not want to be taken by bolups again. Let her go."

Derek raised both his hands as if they would protect him from her blade. "Okay, okay. I just wanted to help her. She can go." He stepped out of the woman's way and let her crawl past.

The woman moaned and struggled to her feet. She turned and stared at Skyra for a few breaths, fresh blood flowing from her mouth. Then she stumbled off across the hilltop. One of her leather footwraps was missing, causing her to limp each time she set foot on the jagged rocks.

"They're both going to die," Lincoln said. "The other woman we released took off before I could even cut her hands free. She still had a rock jammed in her mouth."

"They will try to go back to their camps," Skyra said, still watching the nandup woman limping away. "If they make it, their tribemates will probably kill them. It is their choice to make." She finally turned back to the strange humans.

Ripple, who was now standing among them, said, "Skyra, you might find the phrase 'thank you' to be useful at this moment. These people have—"

"El-de-né!" Veenah cried, which caused her to start coughing again. Apparently she hadn't noticed Ripple until the creature had spoken.

At the same moment, Maddy came into view over the hill's ridge.

"What are those creatures?" Veenah sputtered.

"I do not know, sister, but this one is my companion. It will not hurt you."

Ripple stepped forward and stopped at Veenah's feet. The creature then spoke in the language of Una-Loto. "Aibul-

Ripple. Aibul-afu-fekho-nokho." *I am Ripple. I am your sister's friend.*

Veenah stared at Ripple for a few breaths then looked over at Maddy. "That creature is hurt."

Skyra saw that Veenah was right. A small spear protruded from Maddy's orb. It was the same kind of tiny spear the bolups had used to kill men of Skyra's Una-Loto tribe when they had raided the camp and taken Veenah.

"Maddy got shot with a bow," Lincoln said. "I'm hoping she isn't damaged too badly. I'm afraid pulling the arrow out will make it worse." He then inserted his hand into a pouch on the blue garment covering his waist and legs. "Here, this is yours." He pulled out Skyra's hand blade and gave it to her.

Skyra shoved the blade into her sheath beside the other one.

Virgil spoke. "Um, I know this is off topic, but there's a headless snake with no skin on it over here."

Skyra decided all this talking was a waste of time—Veenah needed food in her belly. She stepped over to the viper, picked up the rock she'd dropped, and started mashing the snake's flesh and bones. The others stood silently watching. She scooped the pink paste into her hand and took it to Veenah. She dipped a finger in the paste and pushed it toward her sister's mouth.

Veenah turned her head, refusing the food. Then she scooped the pile of paste from Skyra's hand into her own and began feeding herself.

Skyra wiped her hands in the dirt then faced Lincoln. "I will take Veenah back to our tribe's camp. I do not understand what *thank you* means, but Ripple tells me I should say it to you."

"Why don't you come with us?" Lincoln said. "Jazzlyn is

hurt, so we need to get her back to our gear by the river where we have first aid supplies. Your sister appears to be hurt too. We have some things that will help her if you come with us. We left our packs back in the fire, so we can't help her here."

Ripple spoke up. "Yes, you and Veenah must remain with Lincoln. Veenah will have a better chance to survive with Lincoln's help."

"We also have tents—shelters to sleep in," Lincoln said. "It'll get dark soon. You and your sister can sleep in one of our tents. We'll treat Veenah's wounds, then she can rest on a clean sleeping bag. It will help her heal."

Skyra chewed her lip and looked out toward the distant hills, beyond which was Una-Loto camp. She hadn't understood all of Lincoln's words, but his meaning was clear enough. Her instincts were telling her to take her birthmate away from these strange people. They had helped her today, but now they wanted to take her and Veenah to their camp. This was what she had been taught all her life to fear. Bolups killed nandup men and took nandup women.

"You must remain with Lincoln," Ripple said again.

She turned to the creature. "Why? Why do you tell me that?"

Ripple's ring glowed for a breath. "You must trust me. I have always tried to help you, and I am trying to help you now."

Skyra again stared out at the distant hills. Finally, she crouched before Veenah and spoke in the language of Una-Loto. "I am going to help you walk. We will walk to the camp of these people. We will stay there until the sun appears. Then I will help you walk to Una-Loto camp."

Veenah swallowed the last mouthful of viper paste. "I cannot go back."

Skyra let out a frustrated growl. "We will talk about that in the morning."

"I see people down there," Derek said, his voice hushed. He was staring back toward the fire and the stream.

Skyra moved with Lincoln, Virgil, and Jazzlyn to Derek's side to look. Several bolups were at the stream.

"It is the women and children of the bolup camp," Skyra whispered. "They are filling their bellies with water."

"What will they do now that their men are dead?" Derek asked.

"They will go back to their camp. If the fire burned their shelters, they will soon die."

Jazzlyn said, "You're serious? They'll all die?"

Skyra moved back from the hill's edge and motioned for the others to follow—nothing good would come from the bolup women and children seeing them. When the bolups below were out of sight, she said, "Bolup women are not hunters. They cannot kill deer, or aurochs, or rhinos, so they cannot get skins to make new shelters. They cannot kill for food. They will have to eat only roots and leaves and small animals they find under rocks. They may live to the cold season, but they will die soon after the cold comes."

Lincoln blew out a long breath from his chest. "Okay, we've obviously done enough damage here to have a significant impact on the future—something we weren't supposed to do unless absolutely necessary." He turned to face Ripple. "I think it's time you told us exactly why you left your message."

"I needed you to come here to save Skyra and her twin sister," Ripple replied.

"Why?"

"Because they are important."

"How can they be that important? Neanderthals will be extinct."

Ripple's red light glowed once. "Will they?"

Lincoln stared at the creature for several long breaths.

"What is *extinct*?" Skyra asked.

Lincoln glanced at her but then looked at the ground. He didn't have an answer.

Skyra was growing weary of all this useless talking. These strange bolups liked to hear themselves speak even more than Ripple did. She moved to Veenah's side and helped her get up. When she started putting Veenah's arm over her shoulder, Veenah pulled back. "I will walk myself."

Skyra turned to Lincoln. "We will go to your camp. When the sun shows itself next, we will leave you and go back to our tribe."

10

SHELTER

47,659 years ago - Day 1

Lincoln paused what he was doing to stare at Skyra and Veenah. Skyra had removed Veenah's fur garments and had led her sister out several meters into the river. Now Skyra was removing her own furs. The women's bodies were noticeably thicker than a human's, with wider hips and shoulders, but they had their own unique proportional balance. In fact, Lincoln mused, they were downright stunning to watch.

Skyra placed her garments carefully on the rocks, then she helped Veenah sit in the knee-deep water before sitting down beside her. Skyra splashed the cold water onto her sister's face and hair and began wiping away blood and dirt. Veenah stared ahead as if she were oblivious to the efforts. The two nandup women were supposedly twins, but Veenah's face was so swollen that the resemblance wasn't obvious.

"Boss, should I get Derek or Virgil to do this?" Jazzlyn asked. "You seem a little distracted."

Lincoln chuckled. "Sorry, Jazz." He went back to taping gauze to the side of her head, which wasn't easy with her long braids in the way. He had been forced to remove most of her external ear—it was too mangled to try to sew back on. According to Maddy's medical database, success of such a procedure would be unlikely anyway. Fortunately, the worst damage appeared to be external, and she could still hear well.

Jazzlyn said, "You do know those girls are not of your species, correct?"

"Just because I'm staring doesn't mean I have intentions. You're staring too. Besides, our two species are compatible—modern humans have almost three percent Neanderthal DNA."

"Speak for yourself," she said. "Some of my ancestors happen to be of South African descent. My Neanderthal DNA is just a hair over half a percent."

Lincoln tore off one last length of tape and stretched it over the gauze from her temple to her jaw bone. "My point is still valid."

Virgil and Derek approached, followed by Ripple.

Virgil was holding a stone-tipped arrow in one hand. "I decided I'd better remove it," he said. "I was afraid—considering Maddy is mostly blind now—she would walk into something and drive it in deeper."

"How's she doing?" Lincoln asked.

Virgil tilted his head back toward where he had left Maddy standing beside the T_3 boulder. "Hard to say. There seems to be some locomotor deficiency in addition to the loss of vision. Other than that, though, she appears to be intact. We brought a few solar chargers, but we have no spare parts or specialized tools for drone repair."

Lincoln sighed. He reminded himself again that Maddy

was just a drone. He turned his attention to Ripple. "I've got about a thousand questions for you, but this one's first. How in the hell can you fly?"

The drone signaled that it was processing the question. "You designed me, Lincoln."

"I've never even considered giving my drones the capability of flight, but that's not my question. I'm asking *how* you can fly. I saw you do it. You obviously don't have rotors, and you didn't use any kind of compressed gas for lift. How do you even get off the ground?"

"To put it simply, I use a form of magnetic levitation."

Lincoln shook his head. "Impossible. You said I created you when I was fourteen years older than I am now. Effective maglev technology is way more than fourteen years beyond our reach."

"You do not give yourself enough credit, Lincoln. You possess more ingenuity than you realize."

Lincoln felt a cold tingle in his skin. "You're telling me that *I'm* responsible for breakthroughs in maglev tech? I've never even dabbled in the stuff."

Ripple remained silent.

"How does it even work?" Virgil asked.

"Lincoln has looked at the issue in ways that no others have considered. Such is the nature of his brilliance. Instead of only considering the possibility of using magnetized strips embedded in the surfaces of roads, he focused his attention on the relatively insignificant magnetic properties of existing rocks and minerals. In typical Lincoln Woodhouse fashion, he proved something others considered negligible to be actually sufficient. A considerable magnetic force can be teased from the native stones that are present in almost any rock, sand, or soil substrate. This magnetic force can be used to counteract the force of gravity, as well as for propulsion. This is why I cannot levitate more than two meters above the surface. Of course, I can do this for only a short time, as it is energy intensive. Then I must build up my charge before levitating again."

Lincoln exchanged a puzzled look with Virgil. Out in the field, his current drones, including Maddy, could receive a trickle charge with external solar chargers. Ripple obviously possessed no external chargers, nor did the drone have visible solar panels integrated into its shell. "How exactly do you build up your charge?" he asked.

"Honestly," Ripple said, "it is quite perplexing to explain my functions to the very man who designed and created me."

"Again, how do you build up your charge?"

"You equipped me with two methods, in the event that environmental conditions become unsuitable for one or the other. The first is asymmetric temperature modulation." The drone paused while two identical rods the thickness of a pencil slid out from its anterior abdomen and stopped at about thirty centimeters long. The end of each rod then spread out into a flat paddle, looking vaguely like a duck's webbed foot. "These are my temperature probes. I need simply to place the probes on or in two materials that differ in temperature by at least 4.7 degrees Celsius. The greater the difference, the faster I can charge."

"How fast?" Virgil asked.

Ripple began withdrawing the probes. "If you were to lie down here, I could insert one probe into your mouth or anus and the other into the cool soil beneath one of these rocks, providing a temperature difference of approximately twenty degrees Celsius and allowing me to top off my charge in forty minutes."

"Damn," Lincoln said. "What's your second method?"

"The second method often makes the first method unnecessary. In fact, the second method is in operation now, as we speak. You designed me to make use of the good old piezoelectric effect, in this case as it applies to sound waves. Essentially, you equipped me with nanogenerators that harvest ambient sound waves and turn them into electric current. Again, you were the one, and the only one, to refine the technology."

Lincoln exchanged another look with Virgil. "How could I possibly have done all this in only fourteen years? Thousands of researchers have been working on these issues for decades."

Ripple hesitated briefly. "A valid question. Some have suggested that perhaps you have used your T_3 to jump drones into the future to gather data on technological advances."

"You're kidding. I've never considered jumping anything into the future. I'm not sure it's even possible."

"You also said you have never considered giving your drones the ability to fly, yet here I am."

Lincoln rubbed his forehead. This entire day had been so jarring to his perception of reality that he wasn't sure he could trust his own eyes and ears. He turned to gaze at Skyra and Veenah. The two Neanderthals were now on their feet and stepping carefully back to their fur clothing on the riverbank. Their clean skin glistened in the light of the descending sun.

"I've got a fabulous idea," Derek said in his booming voice. "Instead of talking about temperature modulation and harvesting ambient sound waves, why don't we discuss what we came here for? I'm all in on this mission, Lincoln, but it seems to me we've done what this drone wanted us to do. It left the message to convince us to jump here to save Skyra and her sister." He nodded toward the women putting on their clothing. "Mission accomplished."

"I'd also like to point out," Virgil said, glowering down at

Ripple, "that we risked our lives—and Jazzlyn lost an ear—yet you have not told us why these Neanderthal women are so important. I find this to be a bit annoying."

"What he said," Jazzlyn added.

Ripple's ring pulsed, indicating it understood it was being addressed. "As I have explained, success of your endeavors is dependent on the sequence and timing of explanations. Yes, you have saved the lives of Skyra and her sister, but there is more to be done to prevent the demise of future civilization. I ask that you trust me on this."

Derek let out a grunt. "It's your goddamn drone, Lincoln. Can't you order it to tell us everything?"

Virgil shook his head. "It's not that simple. Lincoln codes all his drones with a certain amount of autonomy. It's part of what allows them to—"

"I know all that!" Derek thundered. "I'm not stupid. Isn't there some way to override that bullshit? Turn it off or something?"

"The short answer is no," Lincoln said. "At least not outside of our lab." He turned to Ripple. "As you probably know, I'm skeptical about the idea that we are now in the same universe we jumped from this morning. My Temporal Bridge Theorem is solid, in my opinion. Therefore, I'm skeptical our actions here could have any impact on the specific future we jumped from."

"You are wrong," Ripple said matter-of-factly.

Lincoln blinked. Then he blinked again. "What's that supposed to mean?"

"It simply means you are wrong. Your theorem is wrong. Your actions here do indeed impact the future you jumped from. You have the power to prevent the demise of your future civilization."

"That's impossible," Lincoln said, trying to control his agitation. "We can't be in the same timeline."

"You are wrong. You must have had your doubts if you were willing to jump here."

"If Lincoln is wrong," Derek said, "then we should be able to set up the T_3 right now and jump back to the same future we left behind. Then we can go on with our lives."

Ripple shifted to look up at Derek. "That would be a grievous mistake."

"Then what are we supposed to do now?" Jazzlyn asked.

Ripple shifted its view from Derek to Jazzlyn. "Skyra insists on returning with her sister to her tribe's camp. This will be dangerous for both of them. There are aspects of the Una-Loto tribe you would not understand." The drone shifted to face Lincoln. "You must not allow Skyra and her sister to go back to their tribe."

"Why?" Lincoln asked.

"As I said, it would be dangerous for them."

Lincoln turned his attention to Skyra and Veenah, who were clothed again and were approaching the group. Skyra had one arm around her sister, who still seemed unsteady on her feet. "We have washed in the river, and we are ready to go to your camp," Skyra said. Beside her, Veenah stared vacantly at the ground.

"This *is* our camp," Derek said. "We just haven't set up our shelters yet."

Skyra glanced around at the river and surrounding scrub trees. "We cannot stay here. When it is dark, many creatures come to the river to drink. Other creatures come here to kill and eat them—cave lions, long-tooth cats, hyenas, wolves."

"Well, I guess we didn't think about that," Lincoln said.

She made a face that looked like a pained grimace. "I do

not know how you strange bolups are still alive. Maybe your meat is smelly and bad to eat."

Lincoln almost smiled. "We come from a very different place. Where we come from we don't have to worry about being killed by wild animals."

"If no animals are there, what do you hunt and eat?"

This time he allowed a brief smile. "That would take some time to explain. If it's not safe to stay here, maybe we should first decide where we're going to set up our camp."

Ripple spoke up. "This morning Skyra and I saw a tall arrangement of rock outcrops and hoodoos, riddled with crevices and cavities, any one of which could provide suitable shelter. It is just over a kilometer away."

Lincoln eyed Skyra. "Do you think your sister is strong enough to walk there?"

Skyra and Veenah spoke to each other in their native language. The words were rhythmic and punctuated every syllable or two with a soft click. Rather than being brutish and coarse, the language was pleasant to listen to.

"Veenah will walk to the rock hill," Skyra proclaimed.

Lincoln and his team removed a few non-essential items from the gear duffel and stuffed them into the duffel of body bags. The body bags were useless without the T_3, so there was no point in hauling them elsewhere. Ripple volunteered to guide Maddy by emitting sound pulses Maddy could follow but were barely audible to humans. Derek hoisted the gear duffel onto his back by putting one arm through each of the handle straps. The bag was five feet long and not designed to be a backpack. Derek grimaced at the weight, then he nodded and said, "It's only a kilometer, right? Let's get this trek out of the way."

As Lincoln sat cross-legged on a sleeping bag he'd placed on the bare rock, he gazed at Skyra. She was staring into the campfire's flames, and the fire's glow accentuated the size of her eyes and intensity of her expression. He wondered what was going on in her mind. Did Neanderthals even think in the same way humans did?

Veenah, now sprawled behind Skyra, had fallen asleep even before the others had finished collecting firewood. Lincoln hated to think about what the woman had endured at the hands of her human captors. Then again, maybe the experience had been just another event in a lifetime of brutal acts and depravity.

He glanced out the opening of the rock chamber—the chamber could hardly be called a cave, as it was only four meters deep. He could see the sun dropping behind distant hills. After the group had located a cavity that met Skyra's standards of defensibility, they had gathered firewood from two dead scrub trees near the hill's base. As Skyra had explained, the fact that the dead trees hadn't already been picked clean indicated that neither bolups nor nandups frequented this hill of jumbled boulders. She had also explained that, while burning a fire during the night might draw the attention of predators, it would keep those predators from actually entering the chamber to attack. She had even suggested that Derek use his lighter—his *fire stick*, as she called it—to start the campfire.

Also, Skyra had located two relatively straight branches, each about a meter and a half long, and had sharpened the tips. She now kept the two crude spears at her side, ready for use, and Lincoln found their presence to be comforting.

Jazzlyn couldn't stop messing with the bandage over her mangled ear. Lincoln watched her scratching at it and tapping it with her finger, perhaps proving to herself for the umpteenth time that she could still hear with that ear.

Derek was sitting with his elbows on his knees, chin in his hands and eyes closed. Every few seconds his lips would move, as if he were talking to himself.

Lincoln was most concerned about Virgil at the moment, who was visibly trembling as he tapped the screen of his watch. In this place, without connectivity other than to the T_3, his watch could do little more than tell time, ambient temperature, and a few of his own biological parameters. Virgil was tapping the watch's screen forcefully as if frustrated that he couldn't access the web.

"Virgil, you okay?" Lincoln asked.

Virgil shrugged. "Yes and no. Am I the only one dwelling on the fact that we killed people today? Even though I was once accused of killing my own family, I've never actually killed another human being before."

"Neither have I," Derek said without opening his eyes, "and no, you're not the only one."

"You did not kill the bolups," Skyra said.

Virgil shot her a frown. "I'm pretty sure I did. I felt my weapon hit flesh at least three times."

"You did not kill. You struck the bolups, you made them confused, you made them afraid, you made them fight without their strength, but I did the killing."

Derek's eyes were now open. "She's probably right. I made a few good hits, but mostly I just managed to block the hits coming my way. Skyra was busting skulls left and right."

"I sure as hell didn't kill any," Jazzlyn added. "I was almost killed myself."

Lincoln considered this. During the fight he had been confused and terrified. He probably hadn't done significant damage to Veenah's captors. He had, however, glimpsed Skyra's stone blade making contact. In fact, he doubted he'd ever be able to erase the sight of it from his memory. "We're happy you got your sister back," he said to Skyra.

She turned and gazed at Veenah sleeping on the slab of stone. When she looked at the others again, she had pulled her lips back in the same way humans would when examining their teeth in a mirror. Lincoln had seen her do this only a few times—it seemed to be how she smiled.

"Tell us about your tribe," he said. "What is your life like with your people?"

Her smile disappeared. "You ask strange questions. My people are not your people, so why do you ask about them?"

"I'm just curious."

"What is *curious*?"

"It means I like to learn about things. I think you're an interesting person, so I'd like to know what your life is like."

She chewed on her lower lip. "I am different from the others of Una-Loto. Veenah is different too. Some of the others want to kill us. Some do not care. Veenah likes to stay in Una-Loto camp, but I go away from Una-Loto camp when I can. I go away and hunt and walk and sing and wash myself in the rivers. When I go away from Una-Loto camp I talk to Ripple. My tribemates have not seen Ripple. They would not understand, and they would kill Ripple. They would kill me also."

"I'd like to hear you sing," Lincoln said. "Will you sing for us?"

She looked down at her leather-clad feet for a moment. "I sing when I am alone."

He decided not to push it. He assumed Skyra would now ask about where he and his team were from, but she just went back to watching the fire. He shifted his gaze to Maddy, who was standing motionless near the rear of the chamber. "Maddy, you feeling okay?"

The drone shifted slightly. "My charge is draining faster than it should. Perhaps the arrow inflicted more damage than I originally thought."

"We can use the solar chargers tomorrow," Virgil suggested.

"At this rate, I will be depleted long before sunrise. I am now going to initiate sleep mode to reserve power that I can use in the morning to move to a suitable location for solar charging. Is there anything you would like me to do before I sleep?"

Virgil started to say something, but Lincoln raised a hand to cut him off. "Yes, Maddy. Could you please tell us a few jokes before you sleep? We could do with a laugh."

Maddy's red ring pulsed. "Despite the fact that you are trying to appease my guilt regarding my lack of usefulness, I will comply." After a moment of silence, she said, "I seem to be having trouble recalling one. Perhaps because I have the memory of a woolly mammoth. It's like an elephant's but a little fuzzy."

"That's the spirit, Maddy," Jazzlyn said.

Lincoln felt the corners of his mouth turning upward.

Maddy said, "First we have an ice age, then we have global warming. It's almost as if the earth is bipolar."

This time Lincoln released a hearty laugh, along with Jazzlyn and Derek. Even Virgil blew out a brief snort. It was like a valve had been opened, releasing the tension in the small chamber.

Maddy's red lights did two quick counterclockwise loops, signaling initiation of sleep mode.

The laughter lingered for a few more seconds then faded to silence.

Lincoln glanced at Skyra. She was staring at him without expression.

"We're okay," he said. "We were laughing at something we thought was funny. I saw you laugh earlier, but I don't suppose you laugh at the same kinds of things."

She continued staring for a moment. Then she plucked a stick from the pile of firewood at her side and carefully arranged it in the flames.

Lincoln sighed. He was starting to feel chilly so he crawled inside his bag. He had offered Skyra his sleeping bag, or at least one of the ultra-compact jackets from the gear bag, but she seemed confused by the offer as well as the gear itself, so he'd given up. Now he was glad to have the bag.

His raw nerves and aching muscles gradually relaxed as he went back to watching Skyra's face. How bizarre it was to share a cave and campfire with living Neanderthals, one of whom actually spoke English. Perhaps what Lincoln found most surprising was that Skyra seemed not so different from himself. She was the only other person he'd ever met with the same ability to gauge people's actions a split second before those actions were carried out. What else would he discover about this fascinating woman? What would he discover about her sister?

Skyra abruptly snapped her head toward the chamber's opening. She grabbed one of the crude spears and got to her feet. She kicked the other spear toward Lincoln, scattering embers across the stone slab.

"Something comes!" she hissed. "I hear it. I smell its stinking breath."

"Oh, shit!" Virgil said as he scooted back from the opening.

Lincoln shoved his sleeping bag off and grabbed the second spear. Everyone in the cave fell silent.

"What is it?" Derek whispered.

Skyra turned from the cave opening and stared at Lincoln. For a brief moment, Lincoln saw a change in her expression, a tightening of the muscles in her cheeks. He sensed she was about to speak.

She let out a shriek, and from the corner of his eye, Lincoln saw Derek jump back and hit his head on the chamber's low ceiling.

Skyra's shriek transformed into, "*at-at-at-at-at-at... at-at-at-at-at-at.*" She pointed at Lincoln and then at each of the others in turn.

"Jesus H. Christ," Jazzlyn exclaimed. "No freaking way!"

"*at-at-at-at-at-at... at-at-at-at-at-at.*"

Lincoln shook his head and dropped the spear, this time keeping it next to his sleeping bag. He held both hands up, palms toward Skyra. "Okay, I see that we laugh at different things. I suppose we deserved that."

Skyra rattled on a couple more times before sitting back down. She leaned back and spoke a few indiscernible words just centimeters from her still-sleeping sister's ear. Then she faced Lincoln with that same teeth-in-the-mirror smile. "You are strange bolups. You make me laugh."

Lincoln's heart was still racing, but he managed a smile. "Is that what your people do for fun—try to scare each other?"

"It only scares the children of my tribe."

"Terrific. What do the adults do for laughs?"

"We tell stories. We tell stories of things that did not happen—things that *could* not happen."

"You mean like tall tales? Like exaggerated stories?"

She gazed at him without expression, obviously not understanding.

Lincoln heard a moan. The others had repositioned themselves around the fire following Skyra's practical joke, and now Derek was cradling his face in his hands and rocking back and forth.

"Lincoln, he's having another episode," Virgil said.

Lincoln crawled to Derek's side. "You okay, buddy?"

"I don't... know," Derek said, his hands still pressed to his face. "Aww... noooo."

Lincoln gripped Derek's neck with both hands. "You're going to be fine. Feel your face, Derek. Can you feel it? What kind of face do you have?"

"Aww... I don't...." Derek's words devolved into a guttural moan.

"Focus on what you feel," Lincoln said. "You know what I see? I see human fingers, human arms." He started pulling Derek's hands from his face. "I see—"

Derek flung his hands out, knocking Lincoln onto his back beside the fire. Derek got to his knees and threw himself on top of Lincoln, snarling and thrashing his head from side to side as if he were trying to get past Lincoln's outstretched arms to bite his face or neck.

"Derek, stop!" Lincoln gasped, trying to hold his friend at bay.

Several shapes appeared above them. Everyone shouting at once. Hands grabbing Derek's shoulders. People pleading but unable to stop the savage onslaught. Then something struck Derek's head. Derek slowed his attack slightly. Another blow to the head. A foot shoved Derek to the side then kicked him onto his back. A sharpened tree branch pressed against Derek's throat.

"What is wrong with you, bolup?" Skyra demanded, pushing the spear so hard that Derek began to choke.

Lincoln recovered his wits and grabbed the spear's tip. "Don't kill him! He didn't mean it. Skyra, please."

"He was attacking you," she said.

Lincoln tried shoving the spear point away from Derek's throat, but Skyra held it firmly in place. "It's okay,' he pleaded. "He's okay. Tell her, Derek. Tell her you're okay now."

Derek finally seemed to realize a spear was being pressed to his throat, and he gripped it with both hands. He stared up at Skyra with wide eyes. "What... what are you doing?"

Skyra pulled the spear back, but only a few centimeters. "What is wrong with you?" she repeated.

"It's just something that happens to him sometimes," Lincoln said. "He has a problem in his brain. In his head. I know the words won't mean anything to you, but it's a condition called clinical lycanthropy. It's rare—that means not very many people have it."

"I know what rare means," Skyra said.

Lincoln nodded. "Okay, sorry. I just... can you move the weapon away from his neck?"

Skyra shifted the spear point to Derek's chest but still kept him pinned down.

Lincoln continued. "Clinical lycanthropy makes him think certain things. Sometimes it makes him believe he's changing into an animal. He doesn't actually change, but it feels very real to him. Certain things can make it happen. It can happen when something scares him. It can happen when he sees an animal. I'm sure it happened just now because he thought a dangerous animal was coming into this cave."

"What did I do, Lincoln?" Derek asked. "Did I hurt someone?"

"Don't worry, no one got hurt. Are you okay now?"

Derek ignored the question and stared up at Skyra. "Can you please take that thing off my chest? It hurts."

Skyra finally pulled the spear back. "How can a man believe he is an animal?"

Derek shook his head slightly. "I don't know. I wish it didn't happen, but it does."

Skyra backed away from Derek as if she didn't want to turn her back on him. Then she took her place again by her sleeping sister and fed another stick into the fire. She spoke while staring into the flames. "I do not know how you strange bolups are still alive."

11

TRAVEL

47,659 years ago - Day 2

VEENAH HAD SLEPT through the entire night. That was good—she needed to rebuild her strength. While everyone slept, Skyra had frequently ducked out of the cave to get away from the campfire smoke, which irritated her throat. Outside, beyond the smoke's smell, she had caught the musky odor of a cave bear that was somewhere nearby. Knowing cave bears would not come near a campfire, she had slept only in short bursts, waking frequently to nurture the flames. When the sticks they had collected were finally gone, Ripple had quietly told her it would stand in the cave's opening and watch for danger, assuring her it was quite capable of scaring off a cave bear if necessary.

Now Skyra stood beside Ripple upon the rock ledge outside the cave, smelling the air and watching the shadows become shorter as the rising sun behind her made its way into the sky. The humans were awake—she could hear them talking within the cave—but she did not wish to speak to them. She was going to take Veenah back to Una-Loto camp, and the thought of leaving the strange bolups made her chest feel tight and uncomfortable. Speaking to them would only make it worse.

Skyra hated bolups. She had always hated and feared them. Bolups killed nandup men and did worse to nandup women. So why didn't she hate these bolups? Why didn't she fear them?

"You must stay with the humans, Skyra," Ripple said. It was the first she had heard from the creature since long before the sun's light had spread across the distant hills.

She didn't reply. Talking about it was a waste of time. She and Veenah had to return to Una-Loto camp, even though they were hated by some of their tribemates. Nandups could not survive without their tribe.

"Your tribemates will kill Veenah, and they may kill you. This must not happen. You and Veenah are important."

She spat on the rock slab. "Stop saying we are important. We are just Skyra and Veenah." She sniffed the air and scanned the jumbled boulders of the hillside one more time, then she ducked back into the cave.

Without turning her eyes to the humans, Skyra moved straight to her birthmate. Veenah was now lying on her back, staring at the cave's ceiling. Skyra crouched beside her and caught the scent of Veenah's urine. "Veenah, you have tainted yourself and your waist-skin," she said in the Una-Loto language. "Do you want wolves and lions to smell you?"

"I do not care," Veenah replied.

Skyra growled, although her chest tightened even more than before. Something was very wrong with her sister. Veenah had slept hard all night, so should have been feeling better by now. Skyra pulled Veenah up until she was sitting. "Come, sister, we are going to our people. Odnus will know what medicines you need. Get up."

Veenah didn't move. "Odnus will not help me."

"Yes, she will. Get up, sister!" Skyra grasped Veenah by the neck and pulled her to her feet. Still without turning her eyes to the humans, she guided Veenah out of the cave and into the sun's light.

Lincoln and Jazzlyn followed her out.

"You're not leaving now, are you?" Lincoln asked.

With one arm supporting her sister, Skyra stared at the distant hills. She did not want to look at Lincoln's face. "Yes, we are going. We belong with the Una-Loto, and Veenah needs their help."

"But *we* can help her. We treated her wounds yesterday, and we can keep treating them until she's healed."

She led Veenah to the end of the rock ledge and began climbing over the boulders toward the ground below. "We belong with the Una-Loto," she said again. "You go back to your tribe. That is where you belong."

Behind her, she heard Ripple say, "Skyra has made up her mind. We cannot stop her, therefore you must go with them. You alone must go, Lincoln, not the others. You must go now."

"Now?" she heard Lincoln say. "Why do I have to go without the others?"

"It is more important than you can imagine. Please, Lincoln, trust me. You must go."

Skyra helped her sister slide down a rounded boulder.

Veenah then shoved Skyra's hands away. "I do not need help."

"Skyra, wait!" Lincoln shouted. "I need time to gather some gear. Wait for me, okay?"

She didn't look back, and she didn't wait. The hurt in her chest was now worse, but looking back at Lincoln wouldn't help. Lincoln could not come with her to Una Loto. She ignored him and kept descending the boulder hill until she and Veenah were on flat ground. They began walking side by side away from the rising sun. If Veenah could keep up this pace, maybe they would reach Una-Loto camp before the sun disappeared tomorrow.

Skyra heard a humming sound and glanced back. When she saw Ripple flying toward her, the tightness in her chest eased up a little. She thought maybe Ripple was going to stay with the strange humans, as the creature seemed more suited to being with them than with her, but she had grown accustomed to having Ripple around whenever she was away from Una-Loto camp. The creature's presence made her feel less alone.

As Ripple caught up, it thrust out its legs and settled on the ground beside her. "Skyra, I must say that your self-destructive behavior is quite wearying."

Skyra continued walking. "Don't talk to me if you won't use words I know." She glanced over at her sister. Veenah was staring ahead, as if she wasn't even aware Ripple had joined them.

"Please stop walking!" Ripple said, more forcefully than Skyra had ever heard the creature speak.

She growled but didn't stop. "Why?"

"You must at least allow Lincoln to catch up."

"Why did you tell him to come with us? My tribemates will kill him."

"Then we need to protect him."

"Skyra, wait!" Lincoln shouted from far behind.

Skyra growled again. She grabbed Veenah's arm and came to a stop.

Lincoln was running, awkwardly swinging a green bag in one hand. As he caught up he slung the bag over his shoulder and shoved each arm through a strap to hold it on his back. "I'm coming with you," he said, his chest heaving to suck in air.

Skyra gazed at his face for the first time since the sun had come up. She started to say something, to tell him to go back to his people, but she realized the tightness in her chest was now almost gone.

Lincoln said, "You didn't give me a chance to talk to my team or to figure out what to bring. I told them if I'm not back in a few days to leave without me." He shook his head. "I don't know if they'll really do that."

Skyra took Veenah's arm and started walking again.

"You didn't even tell us goodbye," he said, catching up.

Ripple, now keeping pace, asked, "Lincoln, do you have weapons in your pack?"

"We weren't allowed to bring firearms. I have a survival knife, but that's about it."

"I have a suggestion," Ripple said. "Skyra, you know it is not wise to travel unarmed. This terrain does not offer the proper resources to make quality weapons, so I suggest we take a detour to the bolup camp."

Skyra shot Ripple a glance. The creature was right. She needed a good, sturdy spear and at least one khul. She changed directions slightly, heading for the camp.

"What about the remaining humans, the women and children?" Lincoln asked. "And what if more men have returned from a hunt?"

"Some risk is involved," Ripple replied, "but traveling unarmed is foolish."

After walking in silence for only a few breaths, Lincoln spoke again. "Skyra, are you mad about something? You haven't spoken to me yet this morning."

She grunted. She didn't want to speak to this strange bolup for the same reason she had been reluctant to look at his face, although she couldn't explain why. Nandups weren't supposed to trust bolups, and they weren't supposed to feel pain in their chests when leaving bolups.

"Okay," he said after waiting several breaths. "I'll just assume you aren't a morning person."

Skyra stopped at the river. Veenah's urine-soaked waist-skin was pungent and would attract predators. Without removing either of their clothing, she guided her sister into the cool water. Their skins would dry during the day's walking.

While Skyra washed away Veenah's urine, she saw Lincoln pull the bag from his back then remove the strange blue garment that covered his arms and torso. His skin was pale, and he was skinny, like many of the other bolup men Skyra had seen, with so little fat on his body that she could see his ribs and the muscles of his belly and arms. As he kneeled at the river's edge and began splashing water onto his face, she returned her attention to Veenah. She didn't like how the pale, skinny bolup confused her.

After washing, Skyra once again led the group across the river and over the rocky field toward the bolup camp. Veenah was able to walk at a good pace, but she continued staring at the ground without speaking. Lincoln and Ripple, now also silent, followed behind.

After they made their way up the first hill, Skyra stopped to peer into the valley between hills. This time she saw no woolly rhinos, cave lions, or any other creatures, so she led the group across the valley and up the next hill. Stretched out before them, beyond the narrow stream, was a vast expanse of charred trees. Without foliage to block her view, Skyra thought she could make out several dark shapes where the bolup camp should be—perhaps skin shelters that hadn't burned. If the shelters were still there, the women and children would still be there, and so would the khuls and spears.

Skyra stepped in front of Veenah and placed her face in her sister's line of sight. "You will stay here," she said in the Una-Loto language. "I will return soon."

Veenah's face was still swollen and bruised, and a trickle of blood had formed a jagged line down her cheek from a cut Skyra had reopened while washing her sister in the river. Veenah's eyes had always been clear before, with slight expressions that only Skyra understood, but now they were dull and expressionless, with yellow ooze gathering in the corners. Something was wrong inside of Veenah. Skyra's birthmate had been hurt beyond her visible cuts and bruises. Odnus would know what to do. Or maybe Ilkin would know. Skyra needed to get Veenah back to Una-Loto camp.

Veenah didn't resist as Skyra forced her to sit on the ground beside the same boulder she'd sat against the previous day.

"You must run from this place," Veenah said.

Skyra pressed her temple to Veenah's temple and spoke into her ear. "If the bolups try to hurt me, I will gladly kill more of them." She then got to her feet and headed down the slope.

Lincoln and Ripple silently followed.

They entered the forest of burned trees. Some of the scrubby ground plants had burned, but there were also wide areas where the fire had burned only in the treetops, leaving the ground untouched. This gave Skyra hope that maybe some of the bolup weapons hadn't been destroyed.

She pulled both her knives from the sheath on her wrist. She then kicked a head-sized rock toward Lincoln. He gave her a strange look then selected a rock half the size of the one she'd offered. He held it up near his shoulder and nodded. She assumed this meant he was ready to go on, so she headed for the camp.

Skyra saw movement and froze. She then took a few more steps to get a better view. Ahead, several women were rolling up a shelter skin. The bolups were moving their camp. She only saw women, not men.

She turned to Lincoln and whispered, "We go now to get weapons."

His face was sweating, and air was spewing out of his nose so loudly that Skyra could hear each breath. He nodded once.

Ripple rose from the ground to the height of Skyra's eyes. "Again, I'll lead the way." The creature then surged forward, humming like a nest of bees.

Skyra took off.

The women stopped rolling the shelter skin and ran screaming. They gathered into a tight mass with the children and the rest of the women. Skyra still saw no men. For a few breaths, the group of women and children held their ground, some of them shaking khuls at Skyra, Lincoln, and Ripple. Then they all turned and ran. One of the women stumbled and dropped the baby she'd been carrying. She paused for a breath, as if she were considering leaving the child behind, then she grabbed one of its legs, swung it back up to her chest, and kept running. She vanished among the blackened trees with the others.

Lincoln said, "Well, that was easier than I... oh, shit."

Skyra turned and followed his gaze. The bodies of the bolups she'd killed were still where they'd fallen the day before. Most of them had burned in the fire. She stepped over to the dead bolups. Something had eaten portions of the burned bodies. She kneeled to take a closer look. Some of the charred flesh had been chewed off, but long cut marks indicated that other portions had been removed with hand blades or khuls. The stories about bolups she'd been told as a child were true.

She spat on one of the blackened bodies then rose to her feet. Scanning the area, she spotted a bolup khul among the rocks a short distance away. She stepped over and picked it up. It was not burned. "We came here for weapons," she said. "We will find more, then we will leave this place. I do not like the smell of these bolups."

"The sooner we get out of here, the better," Lincoln said, still staring at the bodies.

They searched the area and found three rolled shelter skins the women had already arranged upon dragging poles, which Ripple called a travois. Tucked between the skins on the travois were several more weapons. Skyra picked out another khul for herself, then she handed a third to Lincoln.

Lincoln pulled a strange object from the skins. "This is what I was hoping we'd find." It was a long, curved stick with a thin cord tied to each end. Skyra did not know how the weapon worked, but she had seen one of the women use this object to throw the small spear that had hurt Maddy. Lincoln pushed aside one of the rolled skins and pulled out a leather pouch that contained a bundle of the small spears. "This is a weapon I think I can use," he said.

"Skyra, you might find this to be useful," Ripple said. The

creature was standing beside a stone-tipped spear that had been left leaning against a burned tree.

She slid both khuls into the sling beneath her cape and picked up the spear. The wood shaft was straight and felt strong. The stone spearhead was well crafted, with a longer, sharper tip than those she and her people made. It was securely tied with a leather strip to the notch in the shaft, although the bolups had not used bajam from a pine tree to keep the point from slipping. Skyra leveled the weapon and thrust it forward a few times, savoring the comfort of having a good, straight spear in her hands once again.

She turned to Lincoln. "Now I take Veenah to Una-Loto camp."

SKYRA DID NOT WANT to stop. Throughout most of the day she had led Veenah, Lincoln, and Ripple across the vast rocky fields of the river plain her people called the Dofusofu. Then they had entered the low foothills of the Kapolsek, the mountains that formed a high barrier her people had never crossed. Veenah was beginning to slow down now, so Skyra had no choice but to allow her birthmate to rest. She stopped the group beside a clear stream rushing noisily over jumbled rocks.

Veenah walked straight into the stream without removing her footwraps or waist-skin and sat down in the shallow water.

"Damn, I thought you'd never stop," Lincoln said. He removed the green bag from his back and looked at it carefully. He pushed two fingers through a hole in the bag's thin skin. "Piece of crap is already falling apart." He opened the bag by pulling on something that made a brief buzzing sound, then he reached inside and pulled out a white object resembling a short length of birch limb as thick as Skyra's arm. He put the object to his mouth and tipped his head back to drink.

"*You* might be able to go all day without drinking," he said, wiping water from his chin, "but I'm getting dehydrated." He stepped toward Skyra and offered her the white object. "It's water. Do you want some?"

She took the object and studied it for a few breaths before handing it back. "The stream has plenty of water." She turned her back on him and kneeled by the stream's edge. The cool water felt good on her face as she washed off the dirt and sweat. She waited for the current to move the dirty water past then stuck her head in and drank her fill.

When she pulled her head up, she saw Veenah watching her. "You must drink, sister," Skyra said.

"She probably needs to eat, too," Lincoln added. "I don't know how long you nandups like to go between meals, but I haven't eaten much since yesterday morning. We humans need to eat several times each day."

Skyra scanned the surrounding area. She had not seen many animals while walking the river plain—only distant herds of bison and ibex—and here in the foothills she had spotted only occasional deer. There were fewer rocks here also, which would make it difficult to find worms and other small ground animals.

Her eyes were drawn to Veenah, who was still sitting in the stream, and was now chewing on something. Skyra removed her footwraps and waded out to her birthmate, being careful to keep her own waist-skin dry. "What are you eating?"

Veenah looked up at Skyra and opened her mouth. Inside

were the legs and broken bits of shell of a salal, the water creature Ripple called a crayfish. Skyra moved closer to the stream bank and turned over a submerged rock. A brown crayfish, almost as long as her hand, scooted backward slightly, obviously startled. Skyra thrust out her hand and flipped the creature onto the shore.

"I got it," Lincoln said. He grabbed his green bag. "If you can find more, toss them to me and I'll put them in here."

Skyra moved from rock to rock, turning them over and throwing crayfish to Lincoln, until his bag was bulging. She waded over to Veenah and held out a hand. "Come and fill your belly with us, sister."

They all sat on the ground, and Lincoln scooped a handful of the crayfish from his bag and dropped them into the sand. Skyra and Veenah started snatching them up and eating, first chewing off the tail then sucking the organs and fluids from the body shell. Lincoln dug around in his green bag for a few breaths before pulling out a smaller bag. From the small bag, he pulled an object unlike anything Skyra had ever seen.

He placed the object on the ground then pulled it into two pieces. The top piece was a bowl, which he filled with water from the stream before placing it on the bottom piece. He pulled out a fire stick, like the one Derek had used, and made fire in his hand. He used the fire to ignite a blue, hissing campfire beneath the bowl.

As the bowl heated up, Lincoln began dropping crayfish into the steaming water. "I'm sorry, but I don't think I can eat these things without cooking them," he said.

Skyra gazed at her sister, who was chewing on a crayfish tail and staring at the strange campfire as if it were no different from the campfires she'd seen her entire life.

"This is disgusting," Lincoln said. He was digging through the squirming crayfish in his bag again. This time he pulled out three objects the size of Skyra's hand. The objects sparkled in the sun with different colors, like the feathers of a magpie. Lincoln tore one of them open. Inside the thin, sparkling cover was a brown object resembling an auroch's dropping.

Lincoln offered it to Veenah. "Try it. It's a protein bar. It's food."

"He says it is food," Skyra said in the Una-Loto language.

Veenah accepted it and took a bite. As she chewed, she continued staring at the blue flames.

Lincoln tore the skin from another and gave it to Skyra. She sniffed it then took a bite. Whatever it was, there was no animal flesh in it. She held her hand out toward Lincoln's bag. "Crayfish."

He pulled one out and handed it to her. She bit off the tail and chewed a few times before putting another bite of Lincoln's auroch dropping in her mouth. Much better.

Lincoln used a shining blade he'd pulled from his bag to stab the boiling crayfish and move them from the water to a flat rock. Then he dropped more live ones into the hot water.

Skyra held out a hand until he gave her one of the cooked crayfish. She gave it to Veenah and demanded another. She didn't mind eating crayfish raw, but her birthmother had taught her and Veenah that piercing them with a stick and cooking them over a fire made them tastier. She would gladly eat the creatures boiled.

Soon all the crayfish were gone, and Skyra was too full to consider catching more.

Lincoln put out his campfire by touching something on

the side of the object beneath the bowl. "How much farther is your tribe's camp?" he asked.

Skyra thought about this for a few breaths. "If Veenah is strong, we might get there tomorrow."

He looked at the black strap on his wrist. "It's getting late. Maybe we should find a place to camp."

Skyra looked at the sun. Then she growled. This stop had taken longer than she had hoped. "You go back to your people. I will take Veenah to Una-Loto camp."

Lincoln's face twisted into one of his strange frowns. "It's too late for that. I don't know that I could find my way back. I guess you're stuck with me."

"You cannot go to Una-Loto camp, bolup. My people will kill you."

He shrugged his shoulders once. "I'm just doing what Ripple suggested. Coming with you may have been a mistake, but that's what I decided to do. You didn't give me much time to think about it."

As SKYRA LED the group away from the stream, she searched for a defensible shelter. The area was mostly rolling hills, with fewer exposed rocks than the Dofusofu river plain and no outcrops or caves. Darkness was approaching, so she chose a low area between hills. There was no stream here to attract predators, and the area was dotted with scrubby trees that would provide enough sticks to keep a campfire burning until morning.

Veenah joined in the effort to collect wood, which surprised and pleased Skyra. Veenah's eyes now looked more alive, and she had even started to speak more than simple responses.

As the sun touched the hilltop, Lincoln pulled yet another object from his green bag. He held it to his nose and wrinkled his brows. "Well, this smells like wet crayfish now, but it's better than nothing." He loosened a cord on the bundle and removed a thin skin that had covered it. As Skyra watched, he unrolled it, pieced together some gray sticks that had been hidden inside the roll, and transformed the object, which had started out smaller than his head, into a shelter that was waist-high and longer than his body.

"It's a tent," he said, standing beside the green shelter. "It's, um, not very big, but I think we can all fit inside."

Skyra touched the shelter. The green skin was so thin she could see through it. She pushed open a flap that was obviously a cover for the entry hole and peered inside. "This shelter stinks," she said to Lincoln.

"The smell should go away after a while. I thought maybe you and Veenah would want to sleep where you're not lying in the dirt."

"Lincoln is making a generous offer, and you should accept it," said Ripple.

Skyra looked inside the shelter again. Her mind overflowed with reasons why she should not do this. No. She wouldn't get inside a small shelter and sleep beside a bolup man, and neither would Veenah. She stepped back. "Your shelter is not safe. If wolves or cave lions come for us, you will not see them."

He seemed to think about this. "Okay. I guess we should stay out by our campfire. That'll make it easier to keep the fire burning. I'll leave the tent up in case you change your mind."

Skyra arranged twigs and a few sticks for burning. Her

birthmother had taught her how to start a fire, but the process was difficult and did not always work, so she waited for Lincoln to use his fire stick.

Ripple said, "I will make myself useful tonight. The three of you should get the sleep that your bodies need. I will monitor the fire and add fuel as needed. I will also watch for signs of danger."

"You can add wood to the fire?" Lincoln asked.

Ripple put out a foreleg and knocked a stick from the pile. The creature then stepped forward and tapped the stick until one end was in the flames. "My fine motor skills are quite good, Lincoln. You said I was able to etch a detailed message into my own shell, as well as into a femur, did you not?"

Skyra was tired of hearing Lincoln and Ripple speak words she didn't understand, so she settled in beside the campfire with Veenah. If they would ever stop talking, perhaps she might even get a few stretches of sleep. She moved closer and rested her head on her birthmate's shoulder to share body heat. Veenah let out a long breath and put an arm around Skyra, the way she used to.

Skyra blinked and snapped her head up. She had almost fallen asleep. Perhaps her body was more tired than she thought. She put another stick on the fire and turned to her birthmate. Veenah gazed back at her with clear eyes. Skyra put her hand out, with her palm flat and her thumb up.

Veenah stared at the hand for a few breaths then held her own hand beside it, with her palm facing Skyra's. Her eyes narrowed slightly as she watched Skyra's face.

Skyra slapped her hand.

Veenah grunted and held her hand out again, only to be slapped a second time.

Skyra put her hand back into place and spoke firmly.

"Lotup-aibul-batas-fekho." *Watch my eyes, sister.* She waited two breaths and then swiped to the side. This time Veenah's hand was gone.

Veenah's lips parted slightly as if she were trying to smile.

"That's a good sign," Lincoln said. "I think she's feeling better."

"Yes, indeed," Ripple added. "Perhaps now, Skyra, you will change your mind about returning to your tribe."

Skyra didn't want to think about what she would do in the morning. She just wanted to sit beside some good weapons and a pile of firewood she knew would last the entire night. She wanted to rest with Veenah, believing her birthmate would live to see many more warm seasons. Also, for some reason, she now wanted to talk to this strange bolup who followed her around like an unweaned auroch followed its birthmother.

She turned to Lincoln. "In the cave, you asked me what my people do for laughing. I told you we tell stories. Now I will tell you a story."

He sat up straight. "Really? I mean, I would like that."

"I will tell you a story about Skyra and Veenah hunting pikas. This story happened last cold season. Skyra and Veenah went to a hillside of rocks where we like to hunt for pikas."

Ripple said, "Lincoln, Pikas are small, mountain-dwelling mammals. They are lagomorphs although somewhat smaller than most rabbits."

"I am telling a story, Ripple! Do not talk now."

"It's okay," said Lincoln. "I know what a pika is."

Ripple turned away from the fire, perhaps to watch for predators.

Skyra continued. "Pikas hide in the rocks. Skyra and

Veenah make skinny spears—spears just for killing pikas hiding in the rocks." She made a small circle with her finger and thumb to show how skinny the spears were. "On that day we hunted until we wanted water and food in our bellies, but we did not find pikas. Skyra wanted to go back to Una-Loto camp, but Veenah said, 'No, we will not go back. We will find a pika, and we will make a fire here and Skyra and Veenah will eat the pika without sharing with our tribemates.' Skyra laughed at Veenah's words. 'Yes, Veenah, we will kill a pika and fill our bellies. Then we will make a camp here, and we will not go back to our tribemates until the sun shows us the way in the morning.'"

Skyra paused her story and turned to her birthmate. Again, Veenah was trying to smile, although she did not understand Skyra's English words.

"Skyra and Veenah kept looking for a pika. We looked until the sun touched the hilltops. Then Skyra heard Veenah shout. Skyra watched Veenah. Veenah pushed her pika spear into a crack between the rocks. She pulled her spear out, and a pika was on her spear. Veenah said, 'I see another pika here, Skyra!' Veenah did not have time to pull the first pika from the end of her spear, and she pushed the spear into another crack. Veenah pulled her spear out and two pikas were on her spear. Veenah said, 'I see another pika, Skyra!' Veenah then had another pika on her spear. Veenah said, 'I see a rat under this rock, Skyra!' Veenah held up her spear to show Skyra three pikas and a rat. Veenah said, "Skyra, I see a badger under this rock!' Veenah pushed her spear under the rock and held it up for Skyra to see—three pikas, a rat, and a badger on her spear."

Before going on, Skyra gazed at Lincoln for a few breaths.

"Okay, I see what you're doing," he said. "This is one of those stories you told me about that cannot be true. Your sister did *not* have three pikas, a rat, and a badger on her spear at the same time."

Skyra let out a laugh. "*Aheeee... at-at-at-at-at... at-at-at-at.*"

Lincoln nodded. "Yeah, you got me. I was actually believing your story."

Skyra tried getting her laughter under control. "You have to say when! When was my story not true?"

He wrinkled his brows. "Um, I'd have to say when Veenah got the third pika on her spear. I could believe two pikas at once, but three? I don't think so."

Skyra laughed again. "No! Veenah *did* get three pikas on her spear. Three pikas, Lincoln. I saw her do that! She did not get a rat and badger on her spear."

He twisted his face into one of his strange bolup smiles. "I guess I lose the game, huh?"

"Yes, you lose the game."

"So, if your people like to scare each other and tell stories that aren't true, how do you ever know whether someone is lying or telling the truth?"

Skyra felt her smile fade away. "We scare the children and tell stories when the sun has gone away for the day and we sit by the campfire. That is the time for stories. Una-Loto tribe will punish tribemates who say things that are not true when it is not time for stories. Sometimes they even kill."

Lincoln's smile faded also. "That's... kind of harsh."

They sat in silence for many breaths. Skyra watched the flames, but her eyes seemed to want to glance over at the strange bolup. Each time she looked, he was gazing back at her.

Lincoln suddenly began speaking in a way Skyra had not heard him speak before. "*I stood with my bottle in the pouring rain, I told myself I didn't feel no pain. Oh, baby I miss you. I searched my pockets for the money I owed, I found I've done been bought and sold. Oh, baby I miss you."*

He stopped and bared his teeth. "That's a song I used to like. I realize it's kind of silly now. I'm not a very good singer, but now you've heard me sing. Will you sing for me, Skyra?"

Skyra glanced at her birthmate. Veenah had gone back to staring at the fire as if she hadn't even heard the strange sounds from Lincoln's mouth. Skyra had learned to sing from her birthmother. Her birthmother would only sing when she was away from the other tribemates of Una-Loto. She had told Skyra and Veenah that the other tribemates would not understand singing, but Skyra and Veenah were young then, and they did not believe their birthmother. They started singing while sitting by the campfire at the end of the day. Their birthmother was right, the men and women of Una-Loto did not understand. Skyra and Veenah were already different from other nandups, and when they sang, the men and women became angry. Two of the men, Vall and Gelrut, beat Veenah and chased Skyra into the hills. Skyra stayed alone for three days before finally returning to Una-Loto camp.

Since then, Skyra had only sung alone, or when she was with Ripple. Why should she sing for this strange bolup? Lincoln's singing was just a different way of talking—it sounded nothing like Skyra's singing, so he would probably not like the way she sang.

Lincoln watched her intently, as if he were willing to wait all night for her to decide. There was no anger in his words and no threat in the way he moved his skinny arms and legs. He probably couldn't—and now Skyra believed he *wouldn't*—hurt her if she refused to do what he asked.

For that reason, she opened her mouth and began singing.

12

HOMOTHERIUM

47,659 YEARS ago - Day 2

LINCOLN STARED, fascinated, as Skyra began singing. Her song consisted of single, drawn-out syllables, each followed by a sharp click then another drawn-out syllable with a different vowel at a different pitch. At first the arrangement of syllables seemed random, but soon a pattern began to emerge.

"*Ooooaah-miiiiay-rhaaaaaaaaaa-ooooaah-draaaaaah-ooooaah.*"

The longer Skyra sang, the more it became apparent she was singing each syllable at an intentional and remarkably precise pitch. The cumulative effect of the pattern was mesmerizing.

During the months leading up to this jump, Lincoln had read numerous paleontological, archaeological, and speculative behavioral studies regarding the possible habits and cognitive abilities of Neanderthals. Some researchers had suggested the beings had musical abilities, perhaps even possessing perfect pitch. However, those articles and books had been dry, scientific analyses, supported only by diagrams and photos of ancient skeletal remains and dig sites. Now Lincoln was staring at a live, singing Neanderthal woman, and all previous academic learning went out the window.

Illuminated by the campfire, Skyra's appearance was striking. She obviously possessed human-like intelligence. She was a vicious and skilled fighter, and she was probably just as skilled at hunting. Now it seemed she possessed highly-evolved artistic abilities. Lincoln had never made time in his busy life to develop musical skills, but he knew a gifted voice when he heard one—regardless of the style of music. Skyra's singing was confident, unwavering, and downright beautiful.

After about two minutes she abruptly stopped. She glanced at Veenah, who had watched Skyra's performance without expression.

"Thank you for singing for me," Lincoln said.

She gave him a sidelong look. "I thought *thank you* is what to say when a person saves your life," she gestured toward Veenah, "or saves your birthmate's life."

Ripple turned from staring out into the darkness. "*Thank you* should be used whenever someone does something nice for you. You were being nice to Lincoln by singing for him, so he said thank you."

She seemed to think about this.

"I have a question," Lincoln said. "In fact, I have many questions, but you never ask questions of me. You don't ask where I came from, or what my life was like before coming here. Aren't you curious?"

"You did not come from the place I came from, so I do not ask about such a place. Your life before coming here was not my life, so why would I ask about it?"

Lincoln shook his head, struggling to understand. "I know you just learned the word *curious*, but don't you ever feel curious? Don't you ever want to know about things?"

"I want to know about many things, but why would I ask about things that do not matter to me?"

"Well, that's what curiosity is. Besides, how will you know if something matters to you if you don't learn more about it?"

She chewed on her thick lower lip for a moment. "Maybe if I ask you a question, you will speak the answer, then you will stop talking."

Lincoln couldn't suppress a chuckle. "Okay, that seems fair."

"How are you and your tribemates still alive?"

"Well, I guess we're lucky to be alive after all we've been through since coming here."

She picked a stick from the pile and placed it into the fire. "You are all skinny, and you came here with no spears or khuls. Your tribemate Derek believes he is an animal and attacks you. Your tribemate Jazzlyn has lost her arm, but instead of killing her, her tribemates gave her a weapon in place of her hand."

"This is going to be hard to explain," he said, "but I am a leader of a team, which is like a tribe. I get to choose who is on my team. Years ago, I decided to choose people who have some kind of disability."

"Disability," Skyra said.

"Yes. A disability is a problem a person has to overcome. I believe these problems make people stronger in certain ways."

"Your tribemate Virgil—I think he is afraid of many things. Is that his disability?"

Lincoln hesitated, almost shocked by Skyra's perception. "Yes, but that's just a part of his issue." He considered trying to explain what had happened to Virgil, but he decided against it, particularly considering the horrors Veenah had just experienced. "It's hard to explain."

Skyra stared at him, her visage disarmingly intense. "What is your disability, Lincoln?"

This caught him off guard. "Uh, I guess that's a good question. Maybe this won't make sense to you, but my problem started when I was a child. When I was young, I believed my life was really difficult. People didn't understand me, and many of them were cruel to me. Even more people were cruel to me when I got older, because I was smarter than they were, and because I created things they couldn't understand." Lincoln realized he wasn't making sense. He hadn't described anything that would be traumatic enough to cause someone permanent psychological damage.

He decided to quit while he was ahead. "Okay, maybe I don't actually have a serious problem, but my experiences have allowed me to understand people who have to deal with their own problems. I'm comfortable around those people." He let out a sigh, deciding to give up. "Does any of that make sense?"

Her intense stare didn't let up. "I know enough of your words."

Day 3

Something sharp pressed against Lincoln's cheek near his mouth. He grunted and opened his eyes. The darkness had subsided, replaced by the gray light of early dawn.

He felt the sharp jab again and raised his head.

Skyra was standing over him, holding her spear with its stone tip centimeters from his face. She lowered the spear and put a palm over her mouth, signaling him to be silent. She pointed past the now-smoldering campfire.

Adrenaline surged through Lincoln's body, making him fully alert. He looked where she was pointing. Nothing. He turned back to her and mouthed, "What?"

Veenah was sitting up beside Skyra, her battered face turning one way then the other as she scanned the brush beyond the camp, apparently watching for something.

Lincoln looked again. This time he saw movement. Some kind of creature was pacing from left to right, almost hidden by the vegetation. It was tan in color, and it moved purposefully, more like a stalking predator than a browsing herbivore. Whatever the creature was, it was big, perhaps two hundred kilograms, with shoulders over a meter high.

He got to his knees, grabbed the bow he'd taken from the bolup camp, and pulled an arrow from the quiver. His fingers were now trembling as he tried nocking the arrow. Why in the hell hadn't he practiced with the bow yesterday? Years ago he had made an indoor archery range in one wing of his main lab back home, and he'd even used it every few weeks as a way to clear his head. However, he had used an ultralight compound bow with precision sights and cables and cams allowing a 94% let-off on the draw. This primitive longbow was an entirely different ballgame. The arrow's nock was only a slight indentation in the end of the shaft, and his own knuckle would have to serve as the arrow rest.

Ripple stepped closer to Lincoln and spoke softly. "It appears we are being sized up for attack by two *Homotherium*—scimitar-toothed cats, in case you are not familiar with the genus name. Fossil evidence indicates this creature is built for speed and power, specializing in brute-force attacks, slamming its two-hundred-kilogram body into its prey, then slashing ruthlessly with its ten-centimeter, serrated canine teeth."

"Scaring the hell out of me is *not* helpful," Lincoln hissed.

"I'm making the point that if the scimitar-toothed cats decide to attack, shooting one of them with that bow will have little effect. A better strategy would be to persuade them not to attack in the first place."

"Will your siren scare them off?"

"Possibly, but there is a chance it could enrage them."

Lincoln glanced at the smoldering fire. The pile of sticks he and the Neanderthals had collected was now depleted. "We're out of firewood."

"Yes, we are. Our options are limited."

"The cats are coming closer," Skyra said, no longer whispering.

Lincoln saw both of them now, one approaching from the left, the other from the right. The predators were enormous, at least the size of African lions. Their hind legs were oddly shortened, giving them a hyena-like appearance that somehow made them seem more aggressive.

"Veenah," Skyra said, waving to her sister to come closer. She then grabbed Lincoln's elbow and pulled him to her side. "Stand close—we will look like a larger animal. Raise your arms." She lifted her spear over her head. Veenah held both arms high, and Lincoln raised his bow.

The cats kept approaching, holding their heads low even though they now had no vegetation in which to conceal themselves. Lincoln could see their curved, elongated canines protruding over their lower jaws. Their eyes seemed to be the size of tennis balls. Even armed with a bow, he felt more vulnerable now than when he and the others had attacked the human camp.

At fifteen meters out, the cats slowed their approach and began circling.

"Attack is probable at this point," Ripple said. "We must act before the creatures overcome their last remnants of fear." The drone activated its vision lights and skittered directly toward one of the cats. The cat froze, and Lincoln could see Ripple's light reflected in the creature's eyes.

Ripple didn't slow down. The drone was three meters and closing when it turned on its siren. Instead of backing off, the *Homotherium* rushed forward, knocking the drone onto its side. The second cat sprinted around Lincoln, Skyra, and Veenah and joined in the attack. Ripple's legs retracted into its belly as both cats bit down, their teeth raking the drone's shell loudly enough to be heard above its siren.

Skyra rushed forward, screaming and waving her spear.

One of the cats gave up on Ripple and turned, snarling to face Skyra.

There was no time to think about what to do next. Lincoln ran to Skyra's side and drew back his bow. The bow was stiffer than he'd expected, perhaps fifty pounds of draw weight. It had no sights—he'd have to shoot instinctively. He stared at the creature's eyes for a split second then released.

The arrow struck the cat's face with a dull *chuck*. The creature leapt straight up, its paws clearing the ground by almost a meter. It then scrambled away several meters before plunging its chin onto the ground and spinning in a circle, pawing at the arrow, which appeared to be embedded in one of its eye sockets.

Still standing over Ripple, the second cat stared at its companion for a moment then sprinted off, disappearing among the low trees and scrub brush.

Ripple's siren fell silent.

Growling fiercely, the injured cat rolled on the ground, kicking and scattering rocks in every direction in its attempts to rid itself of the arrow. It suddenly got up and ran, stumbling over its own feet every few strides. Soon it was out of sight, although Lincoln could still hear it thrashing through the weeds for several more seconds.

Ripple kicked its legs out, rolled over, and stood up. "Lincoln, I must apologize for all the times I have complained about the added weight you have given me in the form of a reinforced shell."

Skyra kneeled beside the drone. "You are hurt, Ripple. Why did you do that?"

"Perhaps someday you will decide to thank me for risking my own life to save yours. After all, it is becoming a daily occurrence."

Lincoln's heart was still pounding, and he had to swallow several times to keep from throwing up. He inspected Ripple's shell. It had numerous dents and scratches from the cats' teeth, but the shell material was not punctured. Watching the surrounding area in case the predators came back, he stepped over to where the injured cat had ground its chin into the gravel. Among the splatters of blood was half of his arrow, including the fletching. He picked it up and went back to Skyra, Veenah, and Ripple.

Skyra snatched the broken arrow from his fingers and studied it. She shifted her gaze to the bow in his other hand then back to the arrow. Lincoln could almost see the reasoning taking place behind her eyes. Apparently, her people had not yet developed the use of bows as weapons. Now, though, she understood. Lincoln realized he was witnessing a profoundly significant historical moment. The problem was, Skyra's revelation was the result of his actions. There could now be no doubt that Lincoln's team had impacted the timeline enough to result in a drastically different future. If Skyra and her sister survived to rejoin their tribe.

13

STRENGTH

47,659 years ago - Day 3

SKYRA WATCHED for the long-tooth cats to return while Lincoln folded up his shelter—which no one had used—and put it back into his green bag.

"Show me how to use the bolup weapon," she said after he put the bag on his back.

He twisted his mouth to the side as if he were thinking. Then he shrugged off his bag again and held up the weapon. "The concept is simple. The humans bent this piece of wood before tying the string to each end, so the string is pulled tight by the wood. The string is what throws the arrow forward." He put one of the tiny spears across the weapon then showed how to hold the weapon in one hand and pull the string and spear back with the other hand. Then, instead of letting go, he slowly let the string go back to its original position. "I'm not going to shoot this because I only have five arrows left, and I have no idea how to make more." He held it out to her. "It's called a bow, and it can be deadly if you practice to learn how to hit what you're aiming at."

She took the weapon and the arrow and studied them carefully. The string appeared to be made of thin leather strips twisted together then covered in animal fat, or maybe tree sap. The string would be the most difficult part of this weapon to make, but she was sure she could figure it out. The wood of the bow would have to bend without breaking, and the wood of the arrows would have to be without bends or bumps. Again, she was sure she could find such wood.

She handed the weapon back to Lincoln. "I will make this weapon."

"Yeah, I thought you might say that."

Skyra turned to watch Veenah, who had stepped away and was squatting beside a twisted old scrub tree, relieving herself. Skyra heard Veenah whimper, so she went to her birthmate and helped her up. Veenah wiped away tears that had streaked her face.

Skyra spoke in her tribe's language. "Sister, how long have you had pain when you urinate?"

"Many days," Veenah replied. "The bolup men have tainted my insides. I cannot go back to Una-Loto camp."

Skyra gripped Veenah's shoulder. "This is the very reason you must go back to Una-Loto camp. Odnus will know what medicines you need. We will arrive at Una-Loto camp today before the sun falls below the hills."

Veenah adjusted her waist-skin and fell silent as they walked back to Lincoln.

Skyra slid her two khuls into the sling on her back, shoved her two hand blades firmly into her wrist sheath, and picked up her spear. "Let's go."

She led the group away from the rising sun, heading deeper into the foothills of the Kapolsek mountains. Progress became slower as the hills became taller, but by the middle of the day Skyra began to recognize valleys and hillsides where she had hunted and explored, often with Ripple at her side.

As they moved closer to Una-Loto camp, Skyra could not force her growing doubts from her mind. Veenah needed medicine, and Odnus would know what herbs or berries to give her. Lincoln, however, had said that his medicines would be better for Veenah. The men of Una-Loto tribe knew Veenah had been taken by bolups. They might not let her rejoin the tribe. If they did, they might taunt and beat her even more than before. Another nandup tribe might let Skyra and Veenah join them, but they would demand to know why the sisters had been forced to leave Una-Loto, then the taunting and beatings might be even worse. Perhaps they would even kill Skyra and Veenah.

As the group crossed a nearly flat hilltop, Skyra stopped. She rested the butt of her spear on the ground and turned to Lincoln. "Lincoln Woodhouse, what are you going to do?"

He and Veenah stopped beside her. He shook his head. "What do you mean?"

"You cannot go to Una-Loto camp. What are you going to do?"

"I haven't thought that far ahead. Right now I'm just helping you get back to your camp safely. After that, I guess I'll try to find my way back to Derek, Jazzlyn, and Virgil. Then we'll return to our home."

She looked out over the distant hilltops, thinking.

Ripple spoke up. "Skyra and Veenah will not be safe at Una-Loto camp, Lincoln."

"What would you suggest I do?" he asked.

Ripple said, "Apparently I left you a message so you would come here and save Skyra's life. I must have determined there was no other option at the time. Such is the importance of Skyra and her twin sister. Saving them was important when you arrived two days ago, and it is still important today, as it will be tomorrow, and for many days to come."

Lincoln stared at Ripple for a few breaths. "What are you saying, that we have to stay here indefinitely? For what? To protect these two Neanderthals? Hell, Skyra could probably kill all of us. It seems to me she can take care of herself. In fact, she'd probably be even safer if we weren't here."

Skyra lifted her spear and jammed it into the dirt. "Stop talking like I am not here!" She did not really want Lincoln to go, but she eyed him and said, "You go back to your people and your camp. I will take Veenah to Una-Loto camp."

"You should come with us," he said. He glanced at Veenah then back at Skyra. "We have a way to get you and your sister to a place where you will be safe. You won't have to worry about being attacked by predators or by bolup men. There will be good medicine there for Veenah. In fact, the help she gets there might save her life. We can turn back now, then you and Veenah can be in this safe place by the end of the day tomorrow."

Skyra felt a strange tingling rush over her skin. Could this bolup really take her and her birthmate to such a place, or was he trying to trick her?

"That is not the solution, Lincoln," Ripple said, its voice more forceful than usual. "Skyra and Veenah must stay in this timeline."

"Timeline!" Lincoln said with just as much force. "You tried to convince me we were in the same timeline as the one we left behind."

Skyra spun around, turning her back on Lincoln and Ripple. She heard something—a muffled grunt. She heard it again. Something was moving beyond the edge of the hilltop. She gestured to the others to stop talking then made her way closer to the slope. A breeze was gently blowing her hair from behind, carrying her scent directly to the source of the grunts. She waved to the others then started moving to one side to alter the path of her scent in the wind. The grunts continued as she reached the edge of the hilltop and peered over the edge.

Halfway down the slope was a woolly rhino, lifting its head high and sniffing the air. It was obviously grunting in anger at the smell of Skyra and her group.

Lincoln and the others came up to Skyra's side. "Holy crap," Lincoln said. "I didn't know they got that big."

A whimper escaped from Veenah's mouth, and Skyra turned to her birthmate. Veenah was staring down at the rhino, her eyes wide. "Skyra-Una-Loto," she said, loud enough for the rhino to hear.

The creature grunted again and shifted its stance, turning toward Veenah's voice.

Even though Veenah was still suffering from the bolups' abuse, she should have known better. Something was very wrong. Skyra's chest began to tighten as she watched her sister's face. Then she followed Veenah's gaze to the woolly rhino. The rhino was a male, with a shoulder hump much taller than Skyra's head. Its main snout horn was almost as long as Skyra's body, with a piece broken off, leaving a jagged tip.

Skyra's chest pressed in on itself so hard she could barely breathe. She knew this woolly rhino. This was the old male that had killed her birthmother three cold seasons past. As she stared at the creature, she tightened her grip on her spear until her fingers hurt. Skyra had dreamed of this day, although she never believed she would actually see the rhino again. Woolly rhinos roamed over vast areas of the foothills and river plain, and males traveled far in search of females. Skyra could hardly believe her luck. Today, finally, she would take the strength from the creature that had taken her birthmother.

She pulled one of the khuls from the sling on her back and tossed it by Veenah's feet. Then she rose to her full height and faced the rhino. She spoke aloud, "Kami-fu-menga. Mumanati-de-lé-melu-rha aibul-khulo-tekne-té." *Listen to me speak, woolly rhino. Today I will not submit to you, and I will take all your strength.*

The creature could not see her, as woolly rhinos were nearly blind, but it heard her words. It snorted again and trotted several steps in her direction.

Lincoln grabbed her wrist. "What are you doing?"

She shook his hand off. "Stay here. If the rhino kills me, take Veenah with you, please, to the place where she will not be hunted by predators or bolup men. Tell me you will take her to that place, Lincoln!"

He stared at her with his tiny eyes. "You can't be serious. Look how big that thing is. There is no way—"

The rhino grunted and charged. Its thick feet pounded the sand and gravel as it raced up the hillside, picking up speed with every breath.

Skyra turned and ran down the slope, angling away from the creature and shouting to draw the rhino's attention. She looked over her shoulder—it was changing course, coming straight at her.

Skyra gripped her spear tightly as she ran, knowing the weapon was the only way she could kill her birthmother's killer. She focused on four trees growing beside the dry stream bed at the bottom of the hill. They were the only trees she could see in the area, the only shelters strong enough to block the rhino's charge.

She glanced back again. The creature was gaining speed, and the trees were too far away. She wasn't going to make it. She had to change her plans now and hope that her bolup-made spear was strong enough to save her life. With the rhino only a few breaths away, she scanned the ground and spotted a protruding stone that appeared to be firmly embedded. She dropped to her knees, jammed the spear against the protruding rock, and slapped one hand against the spear's butt to hold it in place. Skyra actually felt the ground shaking through her knees as she positioned the spear's tip toward the charging rhino.

The creature ran headlong into the spear. The stone tip grazed its snout just below its main horn and entered its meaty shoulder. The impact rolled the rhino onto its side, and its massive body tumbled past Skyra in a cloud of spewing sand and gravel.

Skyra's spear was yanked from her hand, but then it came loose from the creature's shoulder as the rhino fought to stop its own momentum. She lunged for the spear, rolled over it, and was back on her feet just as the rhino stopped tumbling. Surprisingly, the spear was still in one piece, so she clenched the shaft in both hands and threw her entire weight at the creature's exposed belly. The spear's tip punctured the hide but only went in half the length of Skyra's arm. She threw herself backwards to pull the spear free and keep the struggling animal from snapping it in half. This sent her tumbling back onto the rocks.

She jumped up just as the rhino got to its feet. It swung its enormous horn toward her and charged again. She had no time to plant the spear this time, so she ran down the slope for the trees. The woolly rhino could outrun her, but its massive body required more time to get up to full speed, and she made it to the first tree with the creature still several breaths behind.

Skyra heard shouts and then Ripple's piercing scream as she circled to the back of the tree's low branches, which split from the trunk just above the ground. The rhino came straight at the tree then skidded to one side at the last moment. As it passed by, Skyra thrust her spear into its ribs just behind its foreleg. The rhino spun around, again wrenching the spear from her grip, and came back at the tree. Tossing its horn from side to side, it crashed into the branches as Skyra scrambled around to the tree's opposite side.

"Hey, Woolly, over here!" The voice was Lincoln's. He was now standing in front of one of the other trees, waving his arms over his head with his bow in one hand and an arrow in the other.

The rhino turned toward Lincoln and charged.

Ripple came flying in from the side, screeching like an angry eagle. The rhino changed its path slightly and threw its head to the side, striking Ripple's shell with its horn's jagged tip. Ripple flipped upside down, hit the ground, and rolled across the rocks.

Without even slowing down, the rhino corrected its path and hurtled toward Lincoln.

"The tree!" Skyra shouted.

Lincoln circled to the other side of the low branches. Instead of circling around after him, the rhino crashed straight into the branching limbs, cracking some in two and wedging itself between the others.

Lincoln backed away from the tree but tripped and fell onto the gravel, dropping his bow.

The thrashing rhino pushed its way through the cracked limbs, tearing Skyra's spear from its side. She rushed forward and snatched up the weapon. "Lincoln!" she cried. The human had picked up his bow and was trying to get the arrow into place, not realizing the rhino was now turning toward him.

The creature charged again. Skyra sprinted around the broken tree, and as Lincoln drew his bow back, she slid to the ground in front of him and quickly jammed the butt of her spear into the rocks at his feet. Skyra heard him release the bow then saw the arrow bounce harmlessly off the rhino's horn as the creature came thundering toward both of them. Skyra mashed her knee onto the base of her spear to hold it in place then wrenched the shaft upward just after the rhino's chin passed over the weapon's stone point.

This time the spear's tip plunged directly into the creature's throat. It threw its head back, apparently intending to impale Skyra and Lincoln, but the spear's tip hit something solid, stopping the creature's forward motion. It stumbled to the side, once again ripping the spear from Skyra's grip.

She felt Lincoln's hands grasping her armpits.

"This way," he said, dragging her back toward the broken tree.

Skyra refused to take her eyes off the rhino, which was still stumbling as it tried to spot its attackers. A figure darted in from the edge of her vision. "No!" Skyra cried. She pulled away from Lincoln's grip, got to her feet, and ran.

Veenah came to a stop only an arm's length from the rhino and hacked its neck with the khul Skyra had left on the hilltop. The rhino swung around, slashing at her with its horn, but Veenah managed to dart out of its reach. She then stepped in and hacked its neck a second time. The rhino let out a fierce grunt as it swung around again, this time striking Veenah and sending her flying onto her back. The rhino immediately charged after her.

Skyra slid onto her back under the rhino's chin and thrust out her foot, kicking the spear protruding from the creature's throat and wrenching the shaft to one side.

The rhino's front feet, each larger than Skyra's head, sprayed sand and gravel into her face as they came to a stop only a hand's width from her chest. Skyra screamed, grabbed the spear shaft, and wrenched it again. Then she jammed it in as far as it would go.

A hand shot in from the side, grabbed Skyra's wrist, and dragged her from beneath the rhino's chin. A breath later the beast's legs gave out. It collapsed onto its belly then rolled to its side.

Veenah was back on her feet. She stepped up beside the creature with her khul held ready to strike. Even lying on its side, the rhino's body was the height of Veenah's shoulders. She struck the creature's neck once, but the rhino didn't move. It was dead.

Skyra heard a low buzzing behind her. Ripple flew in and hovered over the woolly rhino, turning from side to side to examine its entire length. Ripple then extended its four legs from its belly and settled onto the gravel. "I am finding it difficult, Skyra, to avoid the conclusion that you do not care whether you live or die. Is there a particular reason why you felt compelled to attempt suicide by attacking this creature?"

Skyra realized Lincoln was still holding her wrist, so she allowed him to help her up. "Use words I know, Ripple."

"Why did you risk your life to kill this woolly rhinoceros?"

Skyra turned to Veenah, and their eyes met. For the first time since before the bolup men had taken Veenah, Skyra saw her birthmate expose her teeth in a real smile. Skyra turned back to Ripple. "This woolly rhino took my strength when it killed my birthmother. It took Veenah's strength. Three cold seasons ago. Today I take back my strength from this rhino, and Veenah takes back her strength. Today is a good day for Skyra and Veenah."

Ripple's red ring around its orb flashed then spun in a circle. "I have been nearly destroyed on two occasions already today. I do not—"

"Oh, shit," Lincoln said. "I think we have another problem."

Skyra spun around and followed Lincoln's gaze along the valley between hills. Nandups. Many of them, carrying spears and khuls but nothing else—a hunting party. The nandups were approaching cautiously, holding their weapons ready. Skyra took a step toward the hunters and squinted. The two in the lead were men Skyra knew, Gelrut and Vall. She felt a growl growing in her chest.

The hunters were her own people—Una-Loto tribe.

14

GELRUT

47,659 years ago - Day 3

Lincoln's heart was still racing from nearly being killed by a three-ton rhinoceros, and now the situation wasn't getting any better. The approaching figures were more robust than the humans he'd fought at the bolup camp. He could tell even from this distance these people were Neanderthals—short, muscular legs, thick necks, and large, intense eyes like Skyra's. The group—maybe fifteen—continued approaching warily, about sixty meters out.

"Una-Loto," Veenah said, barely loud enough for Lincoln to hear.

He shot a glance at Skyra. "Una-Loto? These are your people?"

"Yes," she replied quietly. "They must not hear me speak your language."

Lincoln heard scuffling and turned to see Ripple darting off toward a stand of high weeds, apparently to hide.

He turned back to Skyra and whispered, "But this is good, right?"

"No, it is not good."

He cursed silently. "Should I run?"

"You cannot outrun nandups."

Actually, Lincoln was confident he *could* outrun Neanderthals, but only over a long distance. Their bodies were built for sprinting, and they were now only fifty meters away. He decided to stay put.

Two of the men were walking ahead of the others, and one of them spoke. "Skyra-Una-Loto. Veenah-Una-Loto."

"Gelrut-Una-Loto," Skyra called back.

The two men stopped about twenty meters away, which also stopped the others behind them. The group included both men and women—Lincoln could see some of the women's breasts through gaps in their fur capes. They all wore clothing and footwraps similar to Skyra's and Veenah's, with no discernible differences between the women's and men's garments. In general, though, the men were slightly taller, with broader shoulders and faces. They had no facial hair that Lincoln could see.

The man named Gelrut stared at the dead rhinoceros for several long seconds. Some of the others were doing the same, some were staring directly at Lincoln.

The man beside Gelrut pointed his spear at Lincoln and spoke. "Khala-kho-bolup-kho-mesendop. Banap!" The man punctuated his words with sharp clicks, as Skyra and Veenah often did.

Skyra said, "Mesendop-kho-Lincoln-nokho." She continued with a long string of words in her language.

The two men in the lead moved closer, followed by the

others. Their eyes repeatedly shifted between Lincoln, the two sisters, and the woolly rhinoceros.

"Mesendop-kho-Lincoln-nokho!" Skyra repeated. This time her words sounded more frantic, as if she saw something in her tribemates' intent that Lincoln hadn't detected. She stepped in front of Lincoln as if to guard him.

Lincoln felt a heavy pit forming in his stomach as he stared over Skyra's shoulder at Gelrut, whose mannerisms seemed more aggressive than those of the others. The Neanderthal stepped to the side to see around Skyra and looked Lincoln up and down for a few seconds. He then focused intently on Lincoln's face, as if already dismissing the strange appearance of his fleece shirt, denim jeans, and hiking shoes. Lincoln had lost his bow and even his daypack during the battle with the rhinoceros. Once again, he felt vulnerable.

Gelrut and the man beside him stepped closer, and Skyra lifted a hand to the back of her neck. Lincoln saw her fingers inching toward the blade of her khul, which was still hanging in the sling on her back. She spoke again in her language as her tribemates approached and converged in a semicircle around her, Lincoln, and Veenah.

Veenah let out a soft whimper then began walking away. Several of the Neanderthals darted in front of her and blocked her path.

Both lead men stepped around Skyra and stood on either side of Lincoln. They studied his face and his clothing. Lincoln focused on Gelrut's eyes, ignoring the other man.

The right side of the Neanderthal's mouth twitched slightly—he was about to swing out his right arm.

With no time to process alternatives, Lincoln assumed he was about to get hit, so he threw out his right hand, knocking

Gelrut's arm back just as the man was starting to swing it forward.

The Neanderthal blinked at him, then widened his eyes and cried, "El-de-né! Mesendop-kho-kilelo!"

Some of Gelrut's companions rushed forward, and Lincoln was overwhelmed by a half dozen men and women at once. They slammed him to the rocky ground. Something struck his face from the side, nearly knocking him senseless. Another blow came to his throat. As he gagged and coughed, hands gripped his arms and legs and pulled at his clothing. His shoes were torn from his feet. Someone grabbed the cuffs of his jeans and pulled, lifting most of his body off the ground. The jeans slid down from his waist, over his knees, then over his feet, and he dropped back onto the jagged gravel. His attackers ripped his underwear from his body then peeled off his socks. Gelrut grabbed a fistful of Lincoln's shirt and yanked on it, obviously trying to tear it from his body. When the fleece fabric didn't split, the Neanderthal put his knee on Lincoln's groin and shoved the shirt up over his face. Lincoln was temporarily blinded until someone jerked the shirt off over his head and arms.

He lay naked on the sand and rocks while the Neanderthals stared down at his body. While exchanging words he couldn't understand, they prodded and pinched his skin. He gasped in pain as someone roughly prodded his scrotum. Completely surrounded by his attackers, he couldn't even see Skyra or Veenah.

Skyra's voice rose above the noise. "Khamu-Veenah-rha!"

The Neanderthals crouching over Lincoln turned to look. Several of them got up and moved away, opening the view for Lincoln to see.

"Khamu-Veenah-rha!" Skyra shouted again. She was on

her stomach, pinned to the ground by two men and a woman. She was yelling at Veenah, or perhaps at the three women who were holding Veenah to the ground and yanking at the skin garment around her waist.

Gelrut was still kneeling with his knee pressed to Lincoln's gut, but now he got up and stepped over to Veenah and the women. He exchanged words with the women for at least half a minute. The women got up and pulled Veenah to her feet, then Gelrut grabbed Veenah's throat.

Skyra grunted and fought to get up. "Rha. Rha!"

Gelrut yelled at Veenah, his voice snarling with aggression.

She struggled and whimpered, but she didn't speak back.

The man spoke again, but still he didn't get a reply. He got to his knees, pulled up Veenah's waist-skin, and plunged his hand between her legs.

Veenah cried out. Her knees buckled, but the women held her up.

Gelrut got to his feet. He put his hand to his nose, sniffing it, then he held it up for the others to see. Blood had stained two of his fingers red.

Low grumbles came from the other Neanderthals, including those who were still holding Lincoln down.

"Rha," Skyra screamed. "Rha!"

Gelrut wiped his fingers on Veenah's hair. Moving deliberately, he reached behind his head and pulled out his khul.

Skyra began thrashing wildly. She got her left leg free and kicked one of her captors. She pulled her right arm free and began pummeling the woman holding her left arm. The man who had lost his grip on her arm grabbed her by the hair and quickly regained control.

"Rha, Gelrut-Una-Loto!" Skyra screamed.

Gelrut shot a glance at Skyra then turned his attention back to Veenah. He hesitated for a few seconds then swung the khul. The stone blade crushed Veenah's skull with a sickening *crack*.

The women holding Veenah stepped away, and her body collapsed into a heap.

"Motherfucking savages!" Lincoln growled. He fought to pull free, earning himself a sharp blow to his temple. Dazed, he lifted his head and turned to Skyra.

No longer struggling, Skyra stared vacantly at her birthmate's body.

15

ILMEKHO

47,659 years ago - Day 3

Skyra's birthmother's skin was warm and smelled like gentleness and security. Skyra loved suckling her mother's breasts, even though she now had teeth and could eat berries and mashed reindeer flesh. She wanted to keep suckling forever, but her birthmother had told her and Veenah they would have to stop when the cold season came.

Skyra sighed and drew up closer to her birthmother's belly and breast. Without turning her head, she looked over at her birthmate. Veenah was eagerly suckling the other breast as if she were starving. That was the way Veenah always ate, and Skyra had found it fun to tease her about it.

Veenah gazed back at her with sleepy eyes, then she held out a finger and poked Skyra's bulging cheek, causing a trickle of milk to run down their birthmother's belly.

Skyra grabbed her twin's hand to make her stop. Skyra

and Veenah intertwined their fingers, finding the same comfort in each other that they found in their birthmother's skin. Skyra waited for Veenah to close her eyes, then she let her own eyelids droop shut. Veenah's fingers clenched her hand, and Skyra never wanted to let go.

Something slapped Skyra's forehead. The blow hurt, so she clamped her eyes shut. Something hit her again, this time even harder. She whimpered and slowly opened her eyes. One side of her face was in the gravel. There was no soft skin here, no gentleness or security. She felt her waist-skin being shoved up, then rough hands groping her groin. Another whimper escaped from her throat.

A voice said, "Skyra-rha-wakhum-bolup-mafeem." *Skyra is not tainted by bolup men.*

Other voices spoke, some arguing about what to do, others asking questions about the dead woolly rhino. Skyra stopped listening. She just gazed at Veenah. Her birthmate was not suckling a warm, full breast. Her fingers were not intertwined with Skyra's. She was dead, her face no longer the shape it had been only a few breaths past.

Skyra felt like a part of her own body was missing.

A familiar humming sound interrupted Skyra's thoughts. A scream came from someone nearby as the humming grew louder. Skyra knew that sound. Amlun, Durnin, and Thoka were still holding her down, but she managed to lift her head and saw the sound was coming from Ripple. The creature had come out of hiding and flown into the midst of the Una-Loto hunters. It was hovering within arm's reach of Gelrut.

"I warned you about this," Ripple said in the Una-Loto language. "I warned you never to harm Skyra or Veenah. I told you I would return if you harmed them. I told you I would punish the Una-Loto tribe. Now I am angry. I am going to take Skyra and the bolup away from this place. If you interfere, I will destroy all of you. Do you understand me?"

Skyra had taught Ripple a few words of the Una-Loto language, only a few. How had the creature learned to speak so many words?

Ripple switched to English. "Skyra, get up. Lincoln, get up. We are leaving now."

Skyra's attention was drawn to Vall, one of the men who had often beaten her and Veenah. He was shifting his eyes slightly, as if watching Ripple but thinking of something else. He raised his hand to his neck. Skyra knew then what he was going to do, but she couldn't find her voice. She could only stare as Vall pulled his khul from its sling, grabbed the handle with his other hand, and swung it at Ripple. Vall's stone blade struck Ripple's shell with a *clack*. Ripple wobbled in the air for a breath, and Vall struck again. This time, Ripple flipped over and dropped to the ground. The creature's feet didn't even pull up into its shell—it just lay there, not moving.

Vall lifted his khul again and landed another fierce blow. He stood over Ripple's body. "I do not know what you are, creature, but I have taken your strength. You will not destroy Una-Loto tribe. I should have killed you before when you came to our camp."

The other Una-Loto hunters began talking at once, praising Vall for his fearless attack on the creature.

Gelrut's voice rose above the others. "Silence!" He waited for the hunters to stop speaking. "Vall has killed the strange creature, and we will not fear it again. I will kill the strange bolup, then there will be nothing for us to fear. We will take food, bones, and skin from the woolly rhino and carry them to

Una-Loto camp. Our hunt is over. Skyra has returned to us, and she has killed this woolly rhino. After our work is finished, Skyra will tell stories of what she has done in the days since she left Una-Loto camp. We will eat and celebrate for six sunrises before we hunt again. Today is a good day for Una-Loto tribe."

Vall's voice then said, "Yes, this is a good day for Una-Loto. We have lost Veenah, but Skyra is back, and she is in her ilmekho. This, too, is good for Una-Loto tribe. I will take Skyra to my shelter, and I will be the first to honor her ilmekho."

"No, Vall, it is I, Gelrut, who will be the first to honor her ilmekho. It is I who will take her to my shelter. If you wish to challenge me for Skyra, I will accept your challenge. I will even allow you to choose the terms of your challenge."

"*Aheeee... at-at-at-at-at,*" Vall laughed. "Yes, Gelrut, I will challenge you, and it will be a festive day of challenge, after many festive days of eating and telling stories. Kill the strange bolup so we may begin our work."

Skyra heard Gelrut chuckle. "*At-at-at-at.*" Leather footwraps crunched the gravel as he stepped closer to Lincoln.

Skyra stared at her birthmate's fractured face. Veenah had known she couldn't return to Una-Loto tribe. Skyra should have known too. She and Veenah should have gone with Lincoln to the place where they would not have to fear being killed. Maybe there really was such a place, but it was too late now.

Lincoln's voice interrupted her thoughts. "You going to kill me while I'm being held down, you ugly bastard? You're a goddamn coward!"

Skyra pushed herself up to her hands and knees. Amlun,

Durnin, and Thoka, now barely restraining her, allowed her to shrug free from their grip. "Rha, Gelrut!" she said. "This strange bolup can teach us. He has a weapon that throws tiny spears with great force. You have seen these tiny spears, Gelrut. You know they can kill. He calls this weapon a *bow*. This weapon will help Una-Loto tribe hunt and fight raiding bolups. You must allow him to show us how the weapon works. We can learn to make these weapons. You must allow him to show us."

Gelrut, his khul stained with Veenah's blood, gazed at Lincoln then turned to Skyra. "He is a bolup. I must kill him."

She got to her feet. "He must die, but I will kill him myself. It is my right to do so, as he intended to take me to his tribe to bear bolup children. First you must let him show us how to make and use this weapon called a bow." Skyra had never told a lie to her tribemates, other than in her campfire stories. When they found out, they might not kill her because she was now in ilmekho, but they would push her face into a campfire until her skin burned off.

Gelrut seemed to think about this. Then he shoved Tamlil out of the way and stepped to Lincoln's side. He grabbed Lincoln's arm with one hand and yanked him to his feet.

"Skyra, what's going on?" Lincoln asked. "Are they going to kill me next?"

Skyra ignored him. "Do not kill him," she said in her own language. "I will get the weapon." She stepped over to where Lincoln had dropped his bow then held it up for him to see. "Lotup-afu-nabul?" *Where are your tiny spears?*

Lincoln just shook his head, so Skyra held the bow up and pretended to pull the string back.

He looked around, then pointed. The leather sheath of

arrows was near the tree the rhino had destroyed. Skyra picked it up then handed the bow and sheath to Lincoln. "Makhol-Una-Loto-melu-fusa." *Show Una-Loto tribe how you kill.*

"What do you want me to do?" he asked.

She pointed to the arrows and again pretended to pull back the bow string.

Lincoln took out an arrow then put the sheath over his shoulder. He positioned the arrow on the bow. "You want me to pull it back?"

Skyra pointed to the dead rhino and went through the shooting motion yet again.

Lincoln let out a long breath. "Okay." He pulled the arrow and string back then released. *Thonk.* The arrow hit the rhino's haunch, penetrating the creature's thick hide almost to the arrow's blunt end.

Gelrut and some of the others stepped over to the rhino. Gelrut tapped the arrow with his finger then pulled it out. He stared at the blood-stained shaft and stone tip. "Yes, this strange bolup will show us how to make this weapon and these tiny spears."

Skyra said, "You are wise, Gelrut. Skyra will go with you to your shelter for my ilmekho."

Gelrut bared his teeth with pleasure.

"My challenge will determine who is first," Vall said.

"I will also challenge Gelrut," said Durnin.

Gelrut bared his teeth even more and let out another chuckle.

Skyra turned to Lincoln and spoke in English. "You do not have footwraps upon your feet, but we are going to run. Now, use your bow to kill Gelrut, then we will run."

"El-de-né!" cried one of her tribemates.

"What language are you speaking?" Gelrut demanded.

Lincoln said, "Skyra, are you serious?"

She kept her gaze leveled at Gelrut but spoke to Lincoln. "You must kill Gelrut now!"

From the corner of her eye, she saw Lincoln reach over his shoulder and take out another arrow.

Gelrut took a step toward Skyra, lifting his khul slightly. "What language are you speaking?" he asked again.

"Why do you talk like the strange bolup?" Vall added.

Lincoln's hand moved again, putting the arrow into its place on the bow.

Someone grabbed Skyra's arm from behind. "You must stop speaking, birthchild of Sayleeh."

Skyra did not turn around, but she knew the voice to be that of Bolyu, one of the few Una-Loto women who had been kind to Skyra's birthmother even after the rest of the tribe knew that Skyra and Veenah were different from other nandups.

Bolyu said, "Soon you can tell us how the bolup made you talk this way, then we will understand. But now you must stop, or you will join your birthmate in death."

Lincoln started lifting his bow.

Skyra saw Gelrut's eye twitch. He was about to turn and look at Lincoln. "Gelrut!" she shouted. "Tekne-té-Veenah-fofiyu-meleen." *Veenah's strength now lives in me.*

Gelrut's head snapped to the side. Skyra glimpsed the arrow passing through his face then embedding itself in Vall's throat. Vall staggered back, choking. He pulled the arrow from his neck then fell onto his back.

Gelrut was still standing, so Skyra pulled away from Bolyu's grip and reached behind her head for her khul. The weapon was gone.

"Skyra, let's go!" Lincoln shouted.

She looked at Gelrut's face, aware that her other tribemates were now shouting and moving steadily toward Lincoln. Gelrut seemed confused. Blood was gushing from holes on either side of his face just below each eye. He coughed, and blood spewed from his nose. Still, he remained on his feet. Skyra lunged forward to grab Gelrut's khul from his hand, intending to kill him with his own weapon. He growled and pushed her away, then he raised his khul to strike.

Skyra hesitated. As much as she wanted to kill Gelrut herself, now was not the time. He would surely die soon anyway. She turned to Lincoln. "Run now!"

He was trying to place another arrow on his bow, but he gave up and started fleeing for the hillside, pausing only to grab one of his strange footwraps.

Skyra turned to her other tribemates. They were confused now, but in a few breaths they would pursue and kill Lincoln. She shouted in the Una-Loto language, "I will kill the bolup! He took me and forced me to speak his language, so it is my right to kill him myself." She pointed to the dead rhino. "I killed this creature for Una-Loto tribe. This is the same rhino that took the strength of my birthmother Sayleeh. Take the rhino's food, bones, and skin. I will return to you and celebrate this kill and my ilmekho. Una-Loto!"

They stared at her, obviously wary. "Una-Loto!" several of them replied.

Skyra glanced at Gelrut. He was still on his feet, glaring at her. He tried to speak, but his words turned into bubbling, animal-like utterances as blood ran down his chin onto the furs of his cape.

She turned away from her tribemates to follow Lincoln.

Then she hesitated. Ripple was still lying motionless a few paces away, perhaps dead. Skyra darted over, grabbed Ripple by one leg, and ran after Lincoln with the creature dangling over her shoulder, its body slamming against her back with every stride.

16

RUNNING

47,659 years ago - Day 3

Lincoln's feet were killing him by the time he was halfway up the hillside. He kept going anyway. He tried stepping on the sand between rocks and found that it was impossible. Each step was becoming more painful than the last. He had managed to grab one of his shoes, though he'd been too terrified to stop to put it on. As he was picking up the shoe, he'd dropped his loose arrow, leaving him with the bow, quiver, and only two arrows.

Finally, he stopped and glanced over his shoulder. Skyra was now running up the hillside after him. So far, the murderous tribesmen weren't following. He looked down at the shoe in his hand. It was the left. Glancing down the hillside every few seconds, he fumbled with the double knot until it came loose then shoved his foot into the shoe and hastily tied the laces.

He glanced at Skyra—she was carrying something heavy

over her shoulder. Lincoln squinted. "What the hell?" he muttered. Skyra was carrying Ripple.

He considered descending the hillside to help her, or at least convince her to leave the drone behind, but the thought of taking extra steps with even one bare foot made him change his mind. Besides, she was making surprisingly steady progress on her own.

As he waited for her to catch up, Lincoln considered what he would do if the other Neanderthals came after him. His bow and two arrows wouldn't do him much good. He would have to run. If he had his clothing, he could wrap his shirt around his foot. Even a sock would be better than nothing. However, he was naked other than his left shoe.

As Skyra drew nearer, Lincoln watched her tribemates far below. Some were staring up the hill toward him, others appeared to be exchanging words. Lincoln could still see one of the men he'd shot lying motionless on the ground. He hadn't intended to kill two tribesmen. It had been an accident, not that it mattered—it wasn't like he could apologize to the tribe for killing two of them instead of only one. They would come after him, and the chase would surely be brief. It wasn't fair that almost a decade of running sixty kilometers per week wouldn't help him when he needed it most. Missing a shoe, he wouldn't make it another half kilometer.

"You must keep running," Skyra said when she was twenty meters from Lincoln. "My tribemates must see you running. Run!"

The urgency in her voice convinced him to turn and hobble the rest of the way up the slope. Near the hill's summit he felt a jagged rock slice into the skin of his right sole. He grunted and paused.

"Run!" Skyra ordered. She was now ten meters behind him.

Lincoln had no choice but to trust her, so he gritted his teeth and continued up the slope and onto the relatively flat hilltop. When he was halfway across the plateau, he glanced back. He and Skyra were well out of sight of the other Neanderthals now, so he paused to inspect the bottom of his foot. The skin was split and bleeding in two places. He cursed under his breath.

Skyra came to a stop beside him. She lowered Ripple to the ground and put her hands on her knees, her chest heaving.

"I assume they're going to come after me and kill me now," Lincoln said. "Why did you follow me?"

Skyra spoke in spurts between breaths. "It is my right to kill you myself."

He stared at her. "Is that what you intend to do?"

She shot him a glance. "That is what I wish my tribemates to know. They know that now, but when I do not return they will know I did not kill you. We must keep running." She hefted Ripple back onto her shoulder. The drone was only slightly smaller than Maddy, but Skyra lifted it as if it were no heavier than a bag of potatoes.

"I'm sorry about your sister," he said.

She stared at him for a moment, and Lincoln saw in her large eyes a hollowness that wasn't there before. She glanced back again as if making sure her tribemates weren't coming over the hill's edge. When she turned back to him, the hollowness looked more like raw determination. "Veenah's strength is within me now."

As he watched her eyes, Lincoln realized he had no right to complain about his bleeding foot. "Well, I don't really want you to kill me, so I guess we need to get as far away as possible. Which direction should we go?"

"I want to go to your home land, where I will not worry about being killed by creatures or taken by bolup men."

A surge of emotion swelled in Lincoln's chest, momentarily throwing him off guard. This strange, deadly, magnificent nandup was beyond anything he had imagined encountering in this place. He was now naked and almost completely vulnerable, but Skyra saw in him a way to start a new life. At this moment, under her fervent gaze, he wanted nothing more than to possess the strength to make that happen.

"I will take you to that place," he said. He turned and began hobbling to the east, to where he hoped to find his team and the T3 waiting.

Skyra walked beside him. Soon she started jogging, the drone's shell thumping awkwardly against her back.

Lincoln picked up his pace to keep up. Every step was excruciating, but he pushed the pain from his mind. After all, what the hell did he know about suffering?

When Skyra stopped to rest on the broad summit of the third hill, Lincoln found a flat rock that wouldn't cut into his bare butt and sat down to catch his breath. He put his bow and quiver on the ground then looked back over the hills. Still no sign that the hunters were in pursuit.

Skyra lowered Ripple to the ground and pointed to Lincoln's bleeding foot. "You are leaving a trail my tribemates will follow."

He folded his leg to inspect his foot. The sole was covered

with too many punctures and gashes to count. "Not much I can do about it."

She pulled her cape up over her head then sat beside him with the garment in her lap. Her exposed breasts somehow made Lincoln feel less self-conscious about his own nudity.

She began pulling at a cord that apparently had been used to attach the pieces of fur together. "Skin of the lynx," she said. "It is soft and easy to wrap. I will make for you a dayun—a footwrap." She got the end of the cord loose and began pulling it out through holes in the hide.

"I don't want you to destroy your own cape for the sake of my foot."

She shot him a sidelong look. "This is a nandup cape. We put extra furs on our capes to use when we need them. You need a footwrap."

Lincoln let out a silent sigh of relief. The agony of running on the rocks had become almost too much for him. Assuming Skyra would need at least a few minutes to separate the skins, he crawled over to Ripple. "You risked your life to bring this drone," he said. "Why?"

She didn't lift her eyes from her work. "I do not know *drone*."

"I mean Ripple. We call these things drones."

"Ripple is my friend."

Lincoln stared at the drone. Did Skyra even realize this was a machine and not a living being? Was her mind even capable of understanding that a non-living thing could think and talk? He had noticed she seemed almost oblivious to technological devices like his watch and the butane camping stove. In fact, her tribemates had even ignored his watch even though they'd torn everything else from his body.

It occurred to Lincoln that he had long ago allowed

himself to consider Maddy a friend, although he knew full well that everything Maddy did and said was a result of her coding. It was certainly possible Skyra could believe Ripple was really her friend.

He grabbed Ripple's leg and turned the drone so its ventral side faced him. "What the hell?" he muttered. The drone was far lighter than he had expected. He positioned his knees carefully in the sand between rocks and picked up Ripple. No wonder Skyra had been able to carry the drone so effortlessly. Ripple weighed no more than ten kilograms, perhaps only a quarter of Maddy's mass.

He laid the machine back on its side. At some point in his future, for some reason, Lincoln became determined to give his drones the ability to levitate and fly. The drone's minimal weight made sense—the levitation problem couldn't be solved without drastically reducing the weight. He sighed. It all seemed so impossible. How could he have accomplished all this in only fourteen years?

On Ripple's belly was an access panel, similar to Maddy's. This panel even had the same four locking knobs, each with six possible positions. He put his fingers on one of the knobs. Was it possible he still used the same four knob positions fourteen years later? He was certainly a creature of habit, so maybe. He turned all four knobs to the positions for the combination he currently used.

The panel popped open.

He blinked. "Seriously?"

The control touchscreen was slightly larger, but the hard button arrangement hadn't changed. He powered the screen on and scrolled through the main menu. The menu contained several items he'd never seen before, such as *Maglev Settings*,

Charging Options, Power Management, and *Autonomy Settings.*

He felt an almost overwhelming urge to explore these, particularly the last one, but there wasn't time. He found *Reboot Options* at the bottom of the list, tapped it, and worked his way through the same set of choices he was already accustomed to. Finally, he tapped *Reboot.*

The screen flashed a series of updates, each appearing for only a few seconds: *System Check... Data Integrity Check... Damage Assessment... Sensory Mods Check... Cognitive State Analysis...* and finally, *Unit Integrity Confirmed Following Blunt Force Attack From Indigenous Environmental Constituent.*

Lincoln started to smile at this last one, but Ripple spoke up. "I was less than four minutes from an auto-reboot, but I wish to express my thanks to whomever accelerated the process manually. I sense I am over two kilometers from where I was attacked. May I ask how I arrived at this location?"

Lincoln lifted the drone to its feet. Ripple turned until its vision lens faced him. "Ah, there you are, Lincoln. I am pleased you are still alive. May I ask how I arrived at this location?"

Lincoln nodded toward Skyra. "You need to thank Skyra for that. She carried you."

Ripple turned and stepped closer to Skyra, who had paid little attention to Lincoln's efforts to reboot the drone and was still working on the skins of her cape. "Thank you for carrying me," Ripple said. "The loss of your sister is a regrettable tragedy. You must be experiencing emotional turmoil. However, your survival is even more important than before.

Where are your tribemates? How were you able to leave them behind and come this far?"

Skyra pulled a piece of fur loose from her cape and gestured for Lincoln to give her his foot. He sat his bare butt on the gravel and placed his right foot in her lap, then he gritted his teeth as she brushed away sand and rocks that were stuck to the blood. She positioned the skin against his foot one way, then tried several other arrangements until she apparently found one she liked. She plucked up the cord she'd removed from her cape and twisted her mouth to one side, perhaps considering how best to secure the skin to his foot.

"Skyra, you are ignoring me," Ripple said. "I am sorry about Veenah's death. I tried to—"

"I know what you tried to do, Ripple! I told you many times to never show yourself to Una-Loto tribe. When did you go to Una-Loto camp?"

Lincoln looked from Skyra to Ripple then back to Skyra. What was she talking about?

Ripple hesitated, probably calculating the most placating response. "It was sixty-one days ago. I understood your importance. I understood Veenah's importance. I thought I could frighten your people and convince them they should never harm you or Veenah."

"Sixty-one days ago?" she almost shouted. "My tribemates have become even more cruel to me and to Veenah. Some of my tribemates have said they want to kill me and Veenah. These things have happened more. Do you know how many days these things have happened more?"

Ripple hesitated again. "I am sorry, Skyra. I made a mistake."

Skyra laid the lynx skin flat on the ground. She pulled one of her stone knives from the sheath on her wrist, placed the sharpened tip against the skin, and repeatedly twisted the knife to drill a small hole. Lincoln and Ripple watched her silently as she drilled two more holes. She wrapped the skin around Lincoln's foot again and began threading the cord through the new holes.

Lincoln considered what he'd just heard, and he was even more curious now to explore the drone's *Autonomy Settings*. Presumably, Ripple had devised its own plan to frighten Skyra's tribe—without Skyra's knowledge or permission. Lincoln had routinely coded his drones with some level of autonomy. This was essential for carrying on coherent, engaging conversations as well as for making quick decisions while evaluating environments during jumps into the past. This drone, though, consistently displayed an almost disturbing level of autonomy. It had been hatching complex schemes that might not even work. Lincoln racked his brain to imagine why he would code his future drones with this level of independence.

"Did your tribemates let you and Lincoln go?" Ripple asked.

"Yes," Skyra said, focusing intently on the footwrap. "They let us go so that I could kill Lincoln."

"But you haven't killed Lincoln."

She ignored this.

"Are they coming for you?"

"Yes, probably."

"Then we must go," Ripple said. "We are only two kilometers ahead of them."

Skyra finished threading the cord through the holes and pulled the cord tight. She deftly tied a knot of some kind then jiggled the entire wrap, apparently to see if it was tight enough. A slight growl emerged from her throat.

Lincoln handed her his quiver. "Maybe you can use this strap."

She sawed through each end of the leather shoulder strap and tied the strap around Lincoln's ankle, firmly securing the loose lynx hide to his leg. This time the footwrap hardly moved when she tugged on it. She shoved Lincoln's foot from her lap, got to her feet, and replaced the cape around her neck and shoulders. The skins again concealed her breasts and belly, which again increased Lincoln's awareness of his own nudity.

"Your foot will hurt, but this dayun will help you," she said to Lincoln. "Soon you will have to run, or you will be killed by Una-Loto khuls."

Lincoln got up and tried putting pressure on his foot. Yeah, it definitely hurt, but the wrap would at least prevent additional cuts. "How do you know your people are coming after us?" he asked.

"They are coming, Lincoln. I told the Una-Loto hunters I would kill you and return. I have not returned. Some of the hunters will stay with the woolly rhino to take its food and its fur and bones. Hyenas and cats will steal it if they leave it. The other hunters will come for us. They will take me back because I am in my ilmekho. They will kill you because you killed Gelrut and Vall. Then they will kill you again because you are a bolup."

He sighed and looked out over the hilltops to the east. "Ripple, how far is it to where we left Maddy and the others?"

"Approximately twenty-four kilometers, based upon magnetic pole triangulation. Based upon visual data from the last two days, my estimate is closer to twenty-seven. We must take into account, however, that two kilometers of this estimate are dependent on magnetic pole triangulation of our present position relative to where I was brutally attacked, resulting in—"

"That's okay," Lincoln said. "It's close enough." He closed his eyes and rubbed his eyelids. Twenty-four kilometers, naked to the elements, with an injured foot, running from murderous Neanderthals. Shit. He ran his hand over his scalp and down the back of his neck, realizing for the first time that his ponytail was no longer braided. He sighed and opened his eyes then took several steps back to the west, eyeing the sand and gravel at his feet. In addition to the blood trail he'd left, even his untrained eyes were able to pick out several of his and Skyra's footprints. Now that Ripple would be walking, a third set of prints would help reveal the group's trail to the Neanderthal hunters, who were no doubt skilled at tracking.

On top of all this, there was the uncertainty of using the T_3 a second time. Was it even possible to jump forward instead of back? The equations had told him yes, but jumping forward had never been tested. He shoved these doubts to the back of his mind—no point in tackling more than one impossible problem at a time. He turned back to Skyra. "I guess we better get going."

She lifted a hand and pointed over his shoulder. "Una-Loto."

He spun around. Four hunters—little more than specks at this distance—were crossing a hilltop two hills back.

SPEED WAS GOING to be their biggest issue. Lincoln could see this by the time his group had ascended and descended three more hills while fleeing to the east. At the top of the second hill, he had turned back to see that the pursuing hunters had closed the gap substantially.

His makeshift footwrap was holding up, and he had found a steady running rhythm despite the searing pain he felt every time his right foot hit the gravel. Skyra, on the other hand, was slowing down. This was partly because she was reaching exhaustion and partly, Lincoln suspected, because Ripple was slowing down.

The drone had started out by levitating at shoulder height, moving ahead faster than Lincoln and Skyra could run. Not surprisingly, this energy-intensive mode of travel could not be sustained farther than the top of the first hill. The drone had proven in the last two days that it could walk at a steady pace for many kilometers, but apparently running was a different matter.

Lincoln almost suggested they leave the drone behind but decided not to bother. Skyra had already demonstrated she would carry Ripple if she had to.

"We have to do something different," Lincoln said between breaths as they started up yet another hill. "If we keep this pace, they'll catch up."

"The sun will soon hide itself," Skyra replied.

Lincoln glanced at the sky. He hadn't realized it was getting so late. "Will your people stop chasing us then?"

"No, but the sun will no longer show them our tracks."

He hadn't even thought of this. Neanderthals, of course, didn't have flashlights. Once it was dark, he and Skyra and Ripple could keep moving, leaving the hunters far behind. Lincoln figured he was incapable of finding his way back to his team in the daylight, let alone in the dark, but perhaps Skyra could. If not, maybe Ripple could. Apparently,

Lincoln's future self had equipped the drone with some kind of magnetic pole positioning sensors.

When they reached the hill's summit, Lincoln saw that the sun was still about half an hour above the horizon, which meant it would be an hour before the growing darkness would hide their tracks. They would have to outrun the hunters for another hour, maybe longer if Neanderthal night vision was better than that of his species.

Still running, although at a slow jog, the group moved over the hilltop, into the next valley, then over the next hill. Skyra had stopped talking, evidently focusing all her energy on moving steadily forward.

They crossed two more hills as the sun moved with excruciating deliberation toward the horizon. The light was definitely fading, and it seemed to Lincoln that the hills were becoming shorter. He figured soon they would be out of the hills and on the wide river plain. As they ascended yet another hill, Skyra slowed to a walk, obviously too fatigued to continue running. Lincoln grabbed her hand and pulled her along, hoping she would understand he was just trying to help her keep moving.

"I am at five percent power," Ripple announced as they crossed the hill's plateau. "Soon I will insist the two of you leave me behind."

Lincoln didn't bother formulating a response. His ongoing struggle to suck in enough air would make his words incomprehensible anyway. As they started down the far slope, he spotted a stream in the valley below. He almost shouted with relief. Perhaps it was the same stream where they had eaten crayfish the day before. If so, they had covered more distance than he thought. If not, the stream would still provide much-needed water and perhaps a chance to throw off their pursuers.

Without slowing down, Skyra plunged into the stream and threw herself face first into the clear water. Lincoln was hesitant to get his makeshift footwrap wet, but there was no avoiding it, so he dropped his bow and the two arrows and followed her in. He stretched out beside her and allowed the cool water to run over his entire body. He looked back toward the shore. Ripple was inserting one of its temperature probes into the water. Unfortunately, the group wouldn't be staying here long enough for the drone to substantially increase its power level.

Lincoln drank deeply, rejuvenating his senses and reacquainting his sandpaper-dry throat with cool moisture.

Skyra got to her feet and helped him up. She pointed downstream. "We will walk in the water. The hunters will know this, but they will not know how far. They will search the sand until they find where we left the water. The search will slow them down. When they find our tracks, the sun will not be in the sky to show them the way."

He nodded. "Just what I was thinking. Let's get moving."

"Ripple, come into the water," Skyra said.

"No," the drone said. "I will not."

Lincoln and Skyra exchanged a glance.

"We have a plan," Lincoln said. "We'll—"

"No. My power level is critical. I am slowing you down. I will slow you down even further if you carry me. I will not allow it. I will find a safe place to replenish my power, then I will catch up to you at the hill of rocks where you left the others of your team. Skyra and Lincoln, you must stay alive, and you must take care of each other. You are both important." Without another word, Ripple retracted both its temperature probes, backed away from the stream, and took off at a gallop, running upstream parallel to the water.

"Ripple!" Skyra shouted. She started for the stream bank.

Lincoln caught her arm. "Maybe we should go on. Ripple can catch up."

She hesitated and let out a deep growl.

"It's what Ripple wants us to do," he added. "Please, Skyra, we have to keep moving."

"Skyra-Una-Loto!"

Lincoln snapped his head up. The voice had come from the hillside. In the growing darkness, it took him a moment to spot the four approaching Neanderthals. They were less than two hundred meters away. The stream would not throw the hunters off their trail after all.

Skyra growled again, this time more menacingly. Then she screamed a string of words in her own language at the approaching hunters.

As they ran down the hillside, one of the men shouted words back.

"What did he say?" Lincoln asked.

"Durnin does not believe I intend to kill you. He comes to kill you himself. You must run, Lincoln. I will stop the hunters."

Panic gripped Lincoln's already-constricted chest. "No! You're coming with me, remember? That's what we agreed." He started pulling her across the stream.

Lincoln heard feet pounding the gravel. He turned and saw Ripple running back toward them. "Skyra, Lincoln, you must not be here. Hyenas are approaching. They are hunting, making their way this direction along the stream. You must go."

Lincoln's eyes were drawn to something moving to his right. Dark shapes were emerging from the brush beside the stream. The hyenas were already here, at least four that Lincoln could see. They appeared mostly as silhouettes in the fading light, but Lincoln could tell they were larger than modern hyenas, appearing to weigh well over a hundred kilograms each. Two more emerged behind the first four. The creatures were creeping forward, as if they were sizing up Ripple, Lincoln, and Skyra.

"If we run now, the hyenas will chase and kill us," Skyra whispered.

Not running was easier said than done—Lincoln's instincts were commanding him to flee. He forced his legs to stay still and glanced at the Neanderthal hunters. They were at the hill's base fifty meters away and still approaching, oblivious to the pack of hyenas.

"Skyra-efop-epalap-lup-bolup," shouted one of the hunters.

The hyenas stopped in their tracks and turned to look at the hunters.

Lincoln, sensing that Skyra was about to shout, put a finger to her lips. "*Shhh.*" There was no point in drawing back the hyenas' attention.

The Neanderthals stopped. "El-de-né!" one of them said. Finally they had spotted the hyena pack.

Ripple's feet scuffled in the gravel as the drone turned and saw the hunters for the first time. The drone spoke with a subdued voice. "Skyra, you have a disturbing talent for attracting mayhem."

For several long seconds the hunters, hyenas, and Lincoln's group engaged in a silent, three-way stand-off.

Ripple took off running straight for the Neanderthal

hunters. At about twenty meters, the drone emitted a cry like a mewling calf.

This was just too tempting for the hyenas—they charged after Ripple.

Still running and crying, the drone abruptly activated its vision light, illuminating the four Neanderthals against the darkness behind them.

"We must run now," Skyra hissed. She pushed Lincoln toward the opposite stream bank.

He considered going back to the other shore for his bow but decided it wasn't worth the risk.

As they jumped from the water onto the gravel, the scene behind them erupted with hyenas' growling barks and men's shouts. A hyena began howling in pain. A man screamed. Ripple's mewling cry was drowned out by the chaos of a life-and-death struggle.

Lincoln and Skyra ran hard. He was vaguely aware that his right foot throbbed with every step, but adrenaline and raw fear drove him to keep up with Skyra's sprint. His footwrap was now wet, but that only made it cling to his ankle more tightly than before.

They cleared the first hill, ran across a narrow valley, and over the next hill before Skyra showed signs of slowing down. Lincoln could hear her panting beside him, but she kept running.

They ran and ran, kilometer after kilometer. After a while, the hills were no more than gradual rises. Several kilometers after that, the two runners began making their way across the relatively flat river plain, avoiding treacherous rocks only by the faint light from stars and a sliver of moon.

Skyra began to stumble, showing signs of extreme fatigue. Lincoln was hardly surprised—he estimated they had run nonstop for at least ten kilometers since leaving Ripple and the stream. Neither of them had tried to speak during the last half hour.

"Okay, we need to rest," Lincoln said, grabbing Skyra's arm to slow her down.

She stopped then dropped to her hands and knees.

Lincoln kneeled beside her. "Maybe they're not even coming... the hyenas attacked. And it's so dark... our tracks."

She continued gasping for air.

He put a hand on her back. The furs of her cape had parted, and his fingers pressed against her skin, which was warm to the touch and slick with sweat. "Are you okay?"

"I have never run so far before," she replied between gasps. "Veenah's strength is truly within me."

Lincoln wasn't sure how to respond to this, so he said, "I have to admit I'm lost. Do you know where we are?"

She pushed herself up onto her knees and scanned the dark, rocky expanse before them. She pointed. "Your tribemates are that way."

"Are you sure? It all looks the same to me."

"No, I am not sure. I will need the sun's light to be sure."

He tapped his watch, which indicated the local time was 10:31 PM. On the previous two mornings the sun hadn't appeared until about 5:30 AM. A lot of hours of darkness were ahead. "If your tribemates survived the hyenas, they would have to wait until morning to track us, right?"

Skyra grunted and got to her feet. She took a few wobbly steps with her eyes on the ground. "This night is too dark for them to follow our tracks."

He got up. "We can't keep going like this. Our bodies need to rest."

She turned and scanned the area again. After a few

moments of silence she sat on the ground and crossed her legs. "We will rest here."

"Here? Don't we need to make a fire? You know, to keep predators away?"

"If my tribemates are coming for us in the dark, they will see our fire. We are not near water, and we are not near trees or caves. Predators do not have a reason to come to a place like this. This night has no wind to carry our scent. We will be safe here, maybe."

He sighed and sat down beside her then shifted back and forth to find a spot with fewer jagged rocks pressing against his bare skin. He was dehydrated and hungry. His core temperature was returning to normal, and despite the lack of wind, his sweat was evaporating, cooling his naked body even faster. He would start shivering soon. It was going to be a long night.

Skyra stretched out on her side and rested her head on a portion of her fur cape.

"I should have stopped you," Lincoln said. "Ripple told me to stop you from taking Veenah to your people. Ripple was right, but I didn't listen. I'm sorry, Skyra."

She lay motionless without responding. Even in the darkness, he could see her large eyes gazing at him.

"What did you mean when you said your people will take you back because you are in your ilmekho? What is *ilmekho?*"

She didn't reply for many seconds. Finally, she said, "Nandup women are of breeding age after they have lived through twelve cold seasons. But Una-Loto men will not put a child in a woman's belly until she has lived through twenty cold seasons." She paused, thinking. "When a man puts a child into a younger nandup woman, the child might die. Sometimes the young woman will die also."

Lincoln knew Skyra was about twenty years old, but he

certainly didn't want to tell her *how* he knew. "So, you have lived through twenty cold seasons, and that means you are now in ilmekho?"

"Yes."

This meant she was now fair game for the men of her tribe. Lincoln felt a strange, illogical sense of relief that Skyra was no longer among her own people. "Do your people get married?"

"I do not know *married*."

"Do your people become a couple—one woman and one man—and live together? Have children together."

"One woman and one man?"

He took this as a *no* but decided to persist. "My people form pair bonds—usually one woman and one man. Often the couple will stay with each other for the rest of their lives."

She raised up onto one elbow. "You know who your birth-father is?"

"Yes, I know my father. My mother and father have been married for forty-six years."

"El-de-né! Has your birthfather put children in the bellies of other women?"

"Only in my mother. Nine children, actually. I have seven brothers. Do you remember me telling you about my sister? I used to have a sister, but she died when I was young."

She seemed to think for a few seconds. "Your sister died, and my sister died."

Lincoln wasn't sure how to respond to this. "Yes."

"When a woman of my tribe is in ilmekho, the Una-Loto people have a celebration for many days. The celebration begins when the tribe kills a woolly rhino or a mammoth. That is how important the celebration is. After the work is done, my people eat and eat and eat even more. They tell stories, and they laugh. The dominant men challenge each other to see which man will be the first to take the woman to his shelter to honor her ilmekho. In his shelter, the man tries to put a child in her belly. After he tries to put a child in her belly, the other men challenge to be the next man to try. Then they challenge to be the next, and then the next after that. It is a time of much celebration."

Except for the woman who happens to be in ilmekho, Lincoln thought to himself. Then he thought he might be making an unfair assumption, so he asked, "Skyra, did you enjoy your ilmekho celebration?"

She lowered her head back down onto her cape. "Skyra and Veenah were in ilmekho before the bolup men raided Una-Loto camp, but our hunters had not yet killed a woolly rhino or a mammoth. The woolly rhino and mammoth do not easily give up their meat and fur and bones."

"I see. So, you haven't had your celebration. Then today you returned, and you killed a woolly rhino, which should have started your ilmekho celebration."

"Yes. Some of my tribemates do not care if I live or die, and they did not care if Veenah lived or died. But the men of Una-Loto wish to start my ilmekho celebration. Veenah was tainted by the bolup men, Skyra was not tainted."

Lincoln was beginning to see why the hunters were being so persistent in their pursuit.

"The Una-Loto men will kill you, and they will take me back," she added, as if this weren't already clear enough.

"Yeah," Lincoln said. He curled up on his side on the gravel. The ground was still warmer than the air, which helped a little, but sleeping this way was going to be impossible. He thought about the pursuing hunters. Could they have escaped the attacking hyenas? Even if they had, the hunters were now far behind. Lincoln fully intended to return with Skyra to his team then to the T3 long before the hunters could catch up. If everything went well, they would jump back to Lincoln's lab, arriving a few minutes after they had left.

Deep within his consciousness, though, Lincoln did not believe this was possible. Perhaps he was simply too stubborn and prideful to admit his Temporal Bridge Theorem was flawed, even though Ripple had said it was, and even though Ripple's and Skyra's remains had somehow existed in the same timeline Ripple had jumped from. It defied logic and mathematics. By their intrusive actions, Lincoln and his team had now significantly impacted this timeline. Hell, even if their actions were not significant, random events during the next 47,000 years would result in a future drastically different from their own. There was no telling what they'd find when they jumped back to the future, if they even could.

Still, they had to try. Whatever they might find, it would surely be better than this place of savagery and death.

Her voice broke the silence. "Skyra and Veenah used to sleep together to stay warm on cold nights."

"I'm really sorry about your sister."

"This is a cold night, and Veenah is gone."

He lifted his head slightly and gazed at her dark form.

"My people took away your skins," she said. "On this night, Skyra and Lincoln must sleep together to stay warm."

Lincoln felt his heart accelerating. Was she serious? Should he be a gentleman and refuse? Skyra probably had no idea how suggestive such words would be in his world. Clearly she meant nothing more than what she had said—they must simply stay warm. Why in the hell was he overthinking this?

Skyra shifted closer to him, and he moved closer to her.

She grabbed his arm and pulled him against her, then lay on her side facing away from him. He pressed his body to her back, already feeling her substantial warmth. A few seconds later she sat up and pulled her cape off over her head. Then she lay back down, positioning the furs over both of them.

Lincoln put his arm around her chest and pulled her closer so her bare skin was against his. Gradually, his heart slowed until he no longer felt it pounding against his ribs. Her skin was softer than he'd thought it would be. Her hair smelled slightly of sweat, but it wasn't an unpleasant smell at all. As they lay together in silence, Lincoln's apprehension and confusion slowly transformed into contentment. Maybe he'd be able to sleep after all. He shifted his body slightly, finding a position with fewer rocks poking into his skin.

"You must not move during the night," Skyra said, her voice hushed.

"Why?"

"The vipers. The scorpions. They like our warmth. They come to us and rest against our skin as we sleep. If you move, they become angry."

Lincoln lifted his head. "They rest against our skin?"

She remained silent for a few seconds, then her chest shook. "*at-at-at-at-at.*"

17

CORNERED

47,659 years ago - Day 4

WHILE TRYING NOT TO MOVE, Skyra watched the sky turn orange as the sun finally began to show itself. What would this new day bring? Would it be her last? Skyra knew she could never return to Una-Loto tribe. On her own, she might live until the cold season if she could avoid bolup camps, but she would surely die before the hills turned green again. She had little choice but to stay with the strange bolup who now lay against her body with his skinny arms around her neck and chest.

Skyra knew Lincoln was awake. His breathing had changed, and he had been shifting his weight every few breaths. He was not used to sleeping on rocks without his skins, which made Skyra wonder about the place he was from. Did he have a sturdy shelter, with furs on which he slept in secure comfort? How was it possible that the place he was from did not have predators or men to fear? Skyra had never known of such a place. If Lincoln was lying to her, she would have to kill him then find another nandup tribe willing to accept her. She hoped his words were true—she did not want to kill him.

He gently squeezed her chest then pulled away. The cold air rushed in against her back. She growled her displeasure, sat up, and pulled her cape on over her head. She scanned the wide river plain around them and saw no sign of her tribemates. Then she turned to watch Lincoln as he brushed his hand over his body, wiping away sand and rocks that had stuck to his skin. She did not understand many things about this strange bolup, but she was glad she had found him. Skyra's chest hurt for many days after the woolly rhino had killed her birthmother. When Gelrut had killed Veenah, the hurting started all over again. While lying with Lincoln, though, the hurting was not so bad. Again, she hoped she did not have to kill the strange bolup.

"Thank you for sharing your warmth with me," he said.

"*Thank you* is a strange word."

He bared his teeth. "It's actually two words. Why is it strange?"

"It is strange because I do not know when to say it."

"You say it whenever you like what someone has done for you."

She grunted as she got to her feet. "That does not make sense. It also does not make sense when you say *I'm sorry*. You and Ripple say these words, and the words do not make sense to me. Stop saying them, please."

He looked up at her for several breaths. "Yet you like to say *please*. Okay, I'll try to remember." He got up and looked out across the plain. "Speaking of Ripple, I thought maybe we'd see the sneaky little bastard by now."

She stared at him. "What does that mean?"

"It just means I thought Ripple might catch up to us during the night."

"Ripple planned to meet us at the hill of rocks."

"Yeah, I know." He wrapped his skinny arms around his own belly. "Are you ready to go? I'm not looking forward to walking on my foot, but I need to get moving to warm myself."

She secured the two knives in her wrist sheath. These were now the only weapons she and Lincoln had, which made her feel vulnerable. The hunters from her tribe—at least some of them—were probably alive, and they would be coming soon. Cave hyenas could certainly kill nandups, but the creatures were easier to frighten than lions or long-tooth cats. She gazed toward the rising sun, studying the faint shapes of the distant hills, then she pointed. "The hill of rocks is that way. If we do not find water before we get there, we will fill our bellies when we cross the river. We will also make weapons at the river."

Lincoln said, "If we go straight to my team then get to the T_3, we won't need weapons."

"What is the T_3?"

"It's the object we were hiding behind when you first saw us days ago. I'm not even going to try to explain it, but the object will help us get to the place where I am from."

"You do not need weapons in this place?"

He seemed to think about this for a few breaths. "No, not really. Not very often."

Again, Skyra tried to imagine such a place.

They had no belongings to gather, so they started walking toward the rising sun. Lincoln limped on his hurt foot, mumbling several words Skyra did not know. Soon, though, he began to run, and Skyra ran beside him.

They ran until the flat river plain became dotted with mounds of boulders. When Skyra was sure they were far ahead of any Una-Loto hunters that might be tracking them, she slowed to a walk.

They continued walking until the sun was high above before coming upon a small stream. After filling their bellies with water, Skyra caught four crayfish and gave two to Lincoln. He made strange faces and noises, but this time he ate them raw. Skyra was still hungry, but she didn't want to risk staying any longer. They moved on.

The boulder mounds became larger, and Skyra soon realized she had not been to this area before. She had led Lincoln to the wrong place. She left Lincoln on the ground, climbed atop one of the mounds, and looked out over the plain. In the distance was a line of trees and a river. Several low, rocky hills rose up beside the river, and Skyra immediately recognized them. The burned forest and bolup camp would be beyond those rocky hills. She followed the line of trees with her eyes as the river wound its way nearer to her and Lincoln. Then she spotted what she was looking for. The hill of rocks was just there, beyond the river, only a short walk away.

"We are almost there!" she shouted down to Lincoln.

"Good," he replied. "I was starting to think we were lost."

She looked back the way they had come and scanned the horizon. There was movement—three figures, running steadily toward her between the scattered mounds of rocks. A growl rose from Skyra's chest.

One of the figures stopped. Skyra couldn't be sure, but she thought the figure was pointing at her. The other two stopped and stared. Then they all started running again.

Skyra dropped to her butt and slid down the rock to the next boulder, then the next below that, until she was on the ground beside Lincoln. "Una-Loto hunters!" she said. "They are coming." She turned and pointed. Now she could actually see the approaching hunters from the ground. They were getting closer with every breath.

"Shit," Lincoln said. "We have to get my team and get to the T3."

Skyra started running. When he caught up to her, she said, "We must keep running, or we must stop and fight."

"We won't have to fight if we can just get to the T3."

This didn't make sense to Skyra, but there was no time to ask questions now. She spotted the tree-lined river as they rounded another boulder pile, so she grabbed Lincoln's arm and changed direction, heading for the trees.

She looked back over her shoulder as they neared the river. For now, the hunters were beyond the trees lining the river and were not in sight, which meant they could not see her and Lincoln either.

"Into the water," she said.

They plunged in. Lincoln took her hand in his, and she held on tight. They began walking upstream as fast as they could. Lincoln fell to his knees, but she pulled him back up to his feet.

"They will know we are in the river," she said, "but they will not know if we are walking upstream or downstream."

He glanced back. "Let's hope they choose the wrong direction."

They kept moving, but Skyra did not like how slow they were forced to walk in the water. Her tribemates could catch up to them by running along the riverbank. She headed to the far side, pulling Lincoln with her. They stepped from the water and began running again. As they emerged from the narrow strip of trees, Skyra spotted the hill of rocks in the distance and pointed.

"It's wide open between here and there," Lincoln said, still running. "We'll be visible, but we have no choice."

Skyra still did not understand, but she remained silent and continued running. By the time they had crossed the open rocky field between the river and the hill of rocks, she was struggling to keep up with Lincoln. It seemed as if the skinny bolup could run forever without slowing down.

She looked back—still no sign of her tribemates. Maybe they were still searching along the river.

As they stopped at the base of the hill of boulders, Lincoln cupped his hands to his face and shouted, "Jazzlyn, Derek, Virgil!"

Skyra threw a hand over his mouth. "My tribemates will hear you!"

"I'm sorry," he said, pulling her hand away. "I thought it'd be faster than climbing up there. We all need to get to the T_3."

She growled. "The T_3 is at the river. My tribemates are probably at the river. They want to kill you. Why do you want to go to the T_3?"

"I don't know if I can explain it to you. The T_3 will take us to where I'm from. We'll be safe there." He turned and stared up the hill of boulders. "They must not have heard me."

Skyra took Lincoln's hand and began making her way up one of the sloped rocks at the foot of the hill. "Your tribemates are in a cave we can defend. They have the spears we made. If we are not going to keep running, that is where we need to go."

He let go of her hand but continued following. "The last thing I want is to be cornered in a tiny cave. I can't imagine that ending well." After several more breaths he said, "I wonder why they didn't hear me."

As they climbed, Skyra paused atop each boulder and rock slab to gaze out toward the river. She did not see the hunters.

When they were nearing the cave, Skyra thought she heard something—a voice. It was faint, as if from a great distance. She snapped her head around and scanned the scene below. She could see nothing there. The voice came again. "Listen!" she hissed to Lincoln.

He froze.

The voice continued, this time swelling and fading away then swelling again.

"It's music," he said. "Maddy must be playing music."

"What is *music*?"

Instead of answering her, he put his hands to his face again and called out, "Hey! Can you hear me?"

The sound stopped. Several breaths later, a face appeared over a ledge above. It was the dark-faced woman, Jazzlyn. "Lincoln, it's you!"

The other two bolups, Derek and Virgil, appeared beside Jazzlyn. "Hot damn!" Derek said. "We were getting seriously worried."

Jazzlyn said, "You don't look so good, sir. What happened to your clothes?"

"Listen up," Lincoln said. "We've got a problem. We need to get to the T3 now, then jump the hell out of here."

They fell silent and glanced at each other.

"Now! We have to go."

"Our gear is scattered all over," Derek said. "It'll take us a while to pack it up."

Lincoln muttered something Skyra couldn't understand.

He closed his eyes for a few breaths as if thinking. "Just leave the stuff. Get down here now."

Virgil spoke for the first time. "We can't leave our gear. It's all we've got in case—"

"Oh shit, Lincoln!" Jazzlyn said. She pointed down the boulder slope past Lincoln and Skyra. "Does our problem have anything to do with those men?"

Skyra spun around and stepped closer to the edge. She saw nothing but boulders. Then movement caught her eye as two nandup men came into view, crawling up a sloped rock on their way up the hill of boulders. Skyra knew them—Durnin and Brillir. Both were dominant men in Una-Loto tribe.

A third man appeared on the rock behind them. Skyra squinted and stared, shocked. The man was Gelrut. His face was still smeared with his own blood, and even from this distance Skyra could see the two holes in his face where Lincoln's arrow had passed through. How was Gelrut still alive, and how could he have traveled so far with such a wound?

Gelrut paused and looked up. His eyes met Skyra's. He tried to speak, but nothing came from his mouth but garbled, bubbling sounds. He wiped blood from his chin and resumed climbing.

Skyra stepped back from the edge and turned to Lincoln. "Durnin and Brillir and Gelrut. These men are skilled hunters and fighters. They have chased us very far, so I know they will not return to Una-Loto without killing you and taking me."

He looked at the climbing men below then at his tribemates above. "They'll kill my team, too, won't they?"

"Yes, your tribemates are bolups. We must fight."

His lips trembled as he took a deep breath. "I thought we

were far enough ahead. Jesus Christ, I can't believe this! We aren't fighters. We're just—"

She struck him in the chest, knocking him back a step. His eyes widened.

She stepped closer to his face. "Your fear will kill you! Push your fear out of your head and into your arms and legs, then it will save you."

"You guys are scaring the hell out of me," Virgil said from above. "Are those men coming to kill us?"

Lincoln continued staring at Skyra for another breath, then he nodded. "Okay, we can do this. We can do it. We need to get in the cave, right?"

"Yes, we can defend the cave." She stepped away from Lincoln and turned to the others looking down from above. "Do you still have the two spears?"

Derek said, "Yeah, and we made a third one so we'd each have one. We also collected a bunch of rocks. There's been a big-ass bear climbing around on these boulders—we wanted to be able to defend ourselves."

She peered over the edge again. Durnin, Brillir, and Gelrut were now halfway up the hill of boulders.

Lincoln moved to her side. "Maybe we can hit them with rocks before they even get to the cave."

"Maybe," she said, although she did not believe Una-Loto hunters would be so easily stopped. She stepped back from the edge. "We must go to the cave now."

Skyra did not see any loose rocks as they made their way up—Lincoln's tribemates must have collected them all.

The easiest access to the rock ledge in front of the cave was a narrow, sloped boulder leading to a gap between rocks at one end of the ledge. Skyra considered killing her tribemates as they crawled up the boulder. She dismissed this idea quickly, though, because she would be exposed at the top of the slope. Una-Loto hunters were skilled at throwing their spears, khuls, and hand blades, and once they knew Skyra wanted to kill them, they would kill her on the ledge. No, the ledge was not the place to reveal her intentions.

When Skyra had told Lincoln to use his bow to kill Gelrut, her tribemates could not have understood her words, so she assumed Durnin, Brillir, and Gelrut did not know she was planning to kill them. Maybe they thought Lincoln had somehow tricked her into running away with him. Maybe they still intended to take her back to Una-Loto camp to celebrate her ilmekho. If so, she might be able to surprise them.

Skyra scrambled up the sloped boulder, followed by Lincoln, and they made their way along the ledge to the cave. Lincoln's tribemates each held a spear, and they glanced up and down Lincoln's body as if they thought it was very strange for him to be without his skins.

"Those are hunters from Skyra's tribe," Lincoln said. "Yes, they intend to attack, but I want you to remember what we did to the humans who took Skyra's sister."

"We were lucky then," Virgil said, his voice trembling and showing his fear. "I can't believe this is happening again. Our luck can't—"

"Into the cave!" Skyra ordered.

One at a time, the bolups ducked into the cave opening. Skyra took another look over the ledge. She glimpsed one of her tribemates coming around a boulder, almost to the ledge where she and Lincoln had stood only a few breaths past. She crouched and followed the others inside.

Maddy was standing to one side, the red dots encircling her ruined orb glowing softly. Beside Maddy was a pile of loose rocks that were small enough to throw.

Skyra pointed to the pile and eyed the gray-bearded bolup Derek. "You. Take rocks out of the cave please and try to kill the hunters. Do not let them throw their weapons at you. You must do this now." She held her hand out. "Spear."

Derek glanced at Lincoln.

"Just do what she says," Lincoln said.

Derek nodded. He handed Skyra his spear, gathered an armful of the rocks, and ducked out of the cave and onto the ledge.

Skyra scanned the inside of the cave. The cave opening was nothing more than a gap between boulders that had fallen against each other, and there was only room on one side of the opening for someone to stand without being seen from outside. Skyra positioned herself there, then turned to Lincoln, Jazzlyn, and Virgil. "The hunters know you will kill them if they come into the cave slow, so they will come in fast. When the hunters come in, I will use my spear like this." She drove her spear's sharpened tip straight down from above. She pointed to the rock floor beside her. "Lincoln, you will stand here. You will use your spear like this." She stepped into his spot, lowered her spear, and drove it forward at the height where the entering attacker's head would be. She pointed to Jazzlyn. "Give Lincoln your spear."

Jazzlyn silently handed him the spear.

Derek scuttled in through the cave opening. "Goddammit, I tried. I hit one guy's leg, but I don't think it hurt him much. Then they made it impossible for me to get a clear shot. They'll be at the cave soon." He moved away from the opening.

Skyra positioned Derek and Jazzlyn beside the collected pile of rocks and told them to be ready to throw them at the hunters' heads. Then she put Virgil beside Lincoln and instructed him to use his spear to kill any man who made it all the way into the cave.

That was the plan, and there was no time to change it. Skyra could hear her tribemates just outside the cave, speaking softly to each other. As long as the men were talking, they would remain outside. To calm her fears, she rubbed the tip of her spear against the boulder beside her, rotating the shaft to sharpen the tip evenly on all sides.

Gripping her spear tightly, she raised it into position. She closed her eyes and considered asking the woolly rhino and cave lion to give her strength. She opened her eyes. She had already taken the woolly rhino's strength, and now she possessed Veenah's strength. If Skyra lived until the sun hid among the hills at the end of this day, perhaps she would never again ask for what was already within her.

The men outside fell silent.

Skyra spoke in the Una-Loto language. "Gelrut! There are many bolup men in this cave. They will kill you and Durnin and Brillir if you come in. You must leave me with these men. They have already celebrated my ilmekho and have put a child in my belly. You are my tribemates, and I do not want you to die today. Go back to Una-Loto camp."

The men remained silent, and several long breaths passed.

A snarling growl came from the cave entrance. A stone-tipped spear appeared then began striking the rock sides, slamming back and forth, up and down, attempting to clear the path of anything that might be in the way.

"God almighty," Virgil said as the spear whacked against the stones so fast that Skyra's eyes couldn't follow it.

A body dove into the cave beneath the striking spear. Skyra drove her spear downward, but the body was already past her, and the spear's tip hit the rock floor between the man's legs. She stabbed again, barely missing an ankle. In less than a breath, Brillir was on his feet, drawing back his khul. He swung wildly without seeing what he was swinging at, then Lincoln thrust his spear into Brillir's chest, driving the hunter back into the boulder wall.

Skyra turned back to the opening. A second hunter was already diving in under the striking spear. She thrust downward again, but her spear's tip caught the hunter's waist-skin and could not penetrate the thick rhino hide. She struck again, this time hitting the man's leg below the knee.

The spear that had been striking the rock entrance disappeared. Skyra knew the third hunter would be coming through next, so she ignored the screaming and fighting behind her and raised her spear again.

The entrance darkened. Instead of waiting, Skyra thrust her spear downward. The tip struck the man's head just as he appeared, but it bounced off the side of his skull and hit the rock floor. The weapon cracked in half from the force.

The man came to a stop and rolled over. It was Gelrut. He looked up at Skyra and let out a garbled cry of anger, spitting blood from his mouth and nose. She raised her broken spear to strike again, but he swung out his arm and swept her feet from beneath her. As she started to fall, something hit her from the side, throwing her head and shoulder against the cave wall, and she landed hard on Gelrut's chest with another body on top of her.

Skyra's vision was blocked by thrashing bodies. Gelrut shoved her off, and her face hit the stone floor. The body on top of her scrambled over her head. She looked up and realized it was Durnin. Gelrut started backing out of the cave. Durnin lunged toward the opening, and Gelrut dragged him the rest of the way out.

Skyra got to her hands and knees and saw that Brillir was still in the cave, fighting for his life as Lincoln and the others hit him with rocks and jabbed at him with their spears.

By the time Skyra got to her feet, Brillir was trying to crawl to the cave opening. She kicked him onto his side. As Lincoln and Virgil thrust their spears into his legs and torso, Brillir seemed to realize he wasn't going to make it out of the cave. He stared up at Skyra, wincing every time a spear punctured his body.

"Wakhatum," he grunted. It was a word Una-Loto men called women who were taken by bolups but never tried to escape to return to their own people.

The word hit Skyra like a blow from a khul. She stared at Brillir as his strength poured out of his body, forming a puddle on the rock slab. She gestured to Lincoln and Virgil to stop stabbing the man. Then she kneeled, grabbed Brillir's hair, and forced him to look at her. She spoke in the Una-Loto language. "You were cruel to my birthmother Sayleeh. You were cruel to Veenah. You were cruel to Skyra. You will not be cruel again."

His eyes remained fixed on her for a few more breaths, then his face relaxed. Skyra released his hair, and his head thumped against the stone slab.

Skyra heard a rock hitting the cave floor behind her, followed by a drawn-out moan. She turned to see Derek collapsing to his knees.

"Ahhh... this place is a goddamn nightmare," Derek said, rubbing his face with his hands. He then let out another long moan.

Lincoln dropped his spear and kneeled beside his tribemate. "Focus, Derek! Listen to my voice."

Skyra growled, picked up Brillir's dropped khul, and turned back to the cave entrance. This was no time to think about the strange bolup who sometimes believed he was an animal. She crouched and peered out the cave opening. Gelrut and Durnin had left blood streaks on the rock slab, and the streaks disappeared to one side just outside the opening. The two men were hurt. They were probably still assessing their wounds. Within a few breaths they would decide what to do next.

Skyra shifted her grip on the khul, finding the best spot on its handle for her fingers. She sucked in a chestful of air and tensed her muscles, preparing to lunge through the opening. It was time to kill.

"Derek, stop!" Jazzlyn's voice shouted. "Hold on to him, you guys!"

Skyra blew out her breath and spun around. Derek was grunting and thrashing out at Lincoln and Virgil, who were struggling to hold him against the stone floor. Derek arched his back and threw out an arm, tossing Virgil against the cave wall. He then bit into Lincoln's shoulder.

"Ow! Dammit, Derek, stop!"

Snarling like a cornered cave lion, Derek pushed Lincoln aside, got to his feet, and charged Skyra. She started to swing her khul at him, but the crazed bolup knocked her out of his way and scuttled through the opening. Growls and shouts came from outside the cave.

"Oh, crap!" Lincoln said, and he started for the opening.

Skyra dove through before him and rolled to her feet. Derek was locked in a vicious fight with Durnin, and the two were rolling across the ledge. Derek got too close to the edge and started to tumble. Just before going over the edge, he grabbed Durnin's hair, pulling the nandup with him, and they both disappeared.

A breath later, Skyra heard the two bodies thumping and rolling on the boulders below.

A movement to her side drew Skyra's attention. Gelrut was getting to his feet and pulling his khul from the sling on his back. Lincoln was just coming out through the cave opening, and Gelrut flicked his eyes toward the bolup. Gelrut grabbed his khul's handle with his other hand and raised the weapon as he stepped toward Lincoln.

Skyra lunged at her tribemate and swung her khul. This was a true nandup khul, with a heavier blade than a bolup's khul. Skyra heard her blade break the bones in Gelrut's arm. He grunted and dropped his own khul. She raised her khul to kill him but then hesitated. Gelrut was staring at his arm as if he didn't understand it was now ruined. He lifted the arm and watched his hand and wrist dangle loosely. Then he turned his eyes to Skyra. He tried to speak, but only bubbling grunts came out—Lincoln's arrow the day before had destroyed the inside of Gelrut's face.

Lincoln stepped up beside her and grabbed her raised arm. "Look at him, Skyra. You don't really need to kill him. I know he took Veenah from you, but… you don't really need to kill him, do you?"

No, Skyra realized, she didn't need to kill him, but she wanted to. She wanted to feel her khul take away the stinking nandup's strength.

"If you want him to suffer, maybe you could just let him go," Lincoln said. He released her arm and looked around. "Where's Derek?"

Skyra stared at Gelrut's face—his slack, blood-covered lips, the holes on either side of his nose, now starting to turn black, and the hatred in his eyes. He had always hated Skyra and Veenah. That hadn't stopped him, though, from challenging the other dominant men to be the first to honor Skyra's ilmekho.

"Oh God, Lincoln, he's down there," Jazzlyn said. She and Virgil were now out of the cave, looking over the edge.

Skyra lowered her khul.

Gelrut tried to speak again and only choked, spraying blood at Skyra's face.

She grabbed him by his fur cape and dragged him, stumbling, to the end of the ledge. Lincoln and his tribemates were already climbing down through the narrow gap there, so she waited until they were clear of the slope, then she shoved Gelrut over the edge. He slid and rolled over the rocks to the rock slab below. While Lincoln, Jazzlyn, and Virgil made their way toward Derek's body, Gelrut headed the other way, crawling over boulders and sliding down slopes on his belly. Skyra watched him descend the hill until he disappeared around the edge of a jumble of rocks.

She leapt from boulder to boulder and caught up with Lincoln and the others as they arrived at Derek's body. Between two rounded rocks, the bolup was face-down on top of Durnin.

Virgil and Jazzlyn grabbed Derek's legs, dragged him out from between the rocks, then rolled him over.

Derek moaned and squinted against the sun's glare. "What the hell happened?" He raised his head and looked up. "Oh no. What did I do this time?"

While the others kneeled and started talking to him, Skyra slid between the two rocks. With her knees on Durnin's belly, she pulled his head up by his hair. His eyes were closed, but his lids twitched a few times. She felt the back of his head—his skull was cracked, and the fragments moved when she pressed on them. "I have smelled a cave bear on this hill of rocks," she said in the Una-Loto language, although she doubted Durnin could hear. "Soon the cave bear will find you. I would like to watch the cave bear take your strength, but I will be far away. I will go with my bolup friends to a place where I will not have to fear predators or men."

She released Durnin's head and backed out of the space between the rocks. She got to her feet and gazed toward the base of the hill of boulders. Gelrut was there, just sliding down a rock onto the sand below. She watched him as he began walking slowly over the rocky plain. Maybe he would die before he made it back to Una-Loto camp, or maybe he would live. Skyra no longer cared one way or the other.

18

WHO MADE WHO

47,659 YEARS *ago* - *Day 4*

WHILE HE CHECKED Derek for injuries, Lincoln summarized for his team what had happened to him and Skyra since they'd left. When he finally finished, he stood back and shook his head, surprised he'd found nothing more serious than bruises and scraped skin. The Neanderthal's body had been quite effective at cushioning Derek's fall.

Jazzlyn was staring at the tribesman's body, which was wedged between two massive boulders. "Uh, I think that guy's still alive. Should we, you know... do something?"

"Do not kill him," Skyra said.

Jazzlyn frowned. "I wasn't really thinking about killing him."

Skyra stepped between Jazzlyn and the body. "Leave Durnin as he is."

Derek spoke while gingerly prodding a nasty rock burn on his forearm. "A few days ago I was all gung-ho about this adventure. I'm over it now." He glanced at Skyra and then at Lincoln. "Should we be expecting more attacks?"

"More Una-Loto hunters may come," Skyra said. "We should go."

Derek, Jazzlyn, and Virgil all turned to Lincoln. "We?" Virgil asked.

Lincoln nodded. "She's coming with us."

After several seconds, Virgil said, "Um... is that a good idea?"

Lincoln didn't feel like trying to explain. He wasn't even sure he *could* explain. "She's coming. I suggest we gather the gear and get our asses to the T3."

After a round of exchanged glances, Virgil, Jazzlyn, and Derek headed back to the gap to climb back up. Derek was limping but not complaining.

"I am going with you," Skyra said.

Lincoln wasn't sure if this was meant as a statement or a question. "Yes, you're coming with us."

They followed the others up, and by the time he and Skyra entered the cave, Derek had already dragged the dead Neanderthal onto the ledge. Maddy was now pacing around the chamber, apparently using her memory of previous movements to navigate the space, although this wasn't preventing her from stepping in people's way as they gathered the gear.

"How are you doing, Maddy?" Lincoln asked. "Things were pretty hairy earlier, and I didn't have a chance to speak to you."

Maddy stopped pacing when she heard his voice. "Lincoln, you do know that violence should always be a last resort, do you not?"

"Yeah, I know that. Sometimes there isn't a choice. Especially in this place."

"Yes, in this place. You must leave this place as soon as possible."

"That's the plan."

Maddy remained silent for a moment, and Lincoln glanced at her. The drone's red LEDs were spinning one direction and then the other. "Something on your mind, Maddy?"

"You must leave me here."

Lincoln frowned. His team members quit what they were doing and turned to Maddy.

"You can walk, can't you?" Lincoln asked.

"Not effectively, and you cannot carry me. I will slow you down."

"We'll manage."

"Lincoln, I am insisting."

"The hell you are! Who made who?"

"You coded me to defy your orders if I ascertained it could save your life. I insist you leave me here. Perhaps you will remove my cognitive module and take it with you. It weighs only 233 grams."

Without another word, Maddy scuttled across the rock slab and out the cave opening before Lincoln realized what she was doing. A few seconds later he heard her crashing onto the rocks below.

"Maddy!" Lincoln ducked out to the ledge. Within seconds the others were at his side. They stared down at Maddy's broken body. She was cracked open, and two of her legs had broken off.

"Shit," Derek said. "She didn't give us a clue she was planning to do that."

Lincoln realized he was holding his breath. He let out a long sigh. He reminded himself again that Maddy was only a drone. However, she was a drone that had systematically learned by speaking to him and to others for over three years. That depth of learning could not be replaced easily.

"Maddy was your friend," Skyra said. "Maddy is now dead."

Lincoln closed his eyes for a moment. Skyra had a way of stating the obvious truth, even when the truth was something he had failed to acknowledge. "Yeah, Maddy was my friend."

Virgil put a hand on Lincoln's shoulder. "You want me to go down there and pull her module?"

"No, I'll do it."

"Well, at least grab some clothes from the gear bag first. You're sunburned and scratched from head to foot. We'll pack up the rest of the stuff and meet you down there."

"Yeah, man," Derek said. "You'd be doing us all a favor to get some clothes on."

Lincoln looked at one of his shoulders and muttered a curse. He hadn't even noticed he was sunburned.

The duffel bag contained an extra set of clothes as well as a pair of lightweight running shoes for each of the four team members—extra hiking shoes had been ruled out as being too bulky. Lincoln removed his remaining hiking shoe, pulled on a set of clothes, and carefully removed his makeshift footwrap. There was no bottled water left to wash the cuts, so he slathered on half a tube of antibiotic cream, pulled on a pair of socks, and put on his running shoes. He shoved the single hiking shoe and footwrap into the duffel bag, just in case he needed them later. He grabbed a multi-tool from the bag and got to his feet.

"You guys okay?" he asked his team. They were silently deflating sleeping pads and stuffing them into tiny bags. The three seemed a little shell-shocked. He couldn't blame them—

the body of a Neanderthal man they'd been forced to kill lay just outside the cave, and another was in a heap on the rocks below. They were also probably weary from being scared shitless for three days straight.

"Sorry, but we ate all the food supplies," Derek said, nodding to a pile of foil wrappers at the rear of the chamber.

"That's okay. You had to eat. We didn't exactly come prepared for a long stay."

Derek nodded. "You go on. We'll catch up."

Jazzlyn looked up from packing a sleeping bag to flash Lincoln a half-smile.

"We'll be back to the T_3 soon," Lincoln said. "Whatever happens then, it has to be an improvement, right?"

They all nodded.

Lincoln left the cave. When he reached Maddy's broken body, Skyra was already there on her knees, examining the drone.

"I do not understand this creature," she said, peering into the wide crack on Maddy's shell. "It does not have blood. It does not have a heart. Does Ripple have blood and a heart?"

He kneeled beside her. He took one look at the drone then stuffed the multi-tool into his pocket—he wasn't going to need it. "Some other time I'll try to explain what Maddy and Ripple really are." He pried the crack open until a large side panel of Maddy's shell popped off, exposing her processors, a few of the high-torque flux motors, and the high-lithium-diffusion battery pack. It took him only a few seconds to reach in and pull Maddy's cognitive module from its port.

The module was the size of a cell phone, and he held it up for Skyra to see. "This is actually Maddy's brain." He tapped his own forehead. "You know, the part that allows us all to think. I hope to put it in another body when we get back to my home." Lincoln had doubts this would ever be possible, but he kept them to himself.

Skyra stared at the module with no expression, again perhaps incapable of understanding that Maddy could be anything other than a living creature.

Lincoln got up and carefully put the module into his pocket that did not contain the multi-tool. The module was in a carbon polymer case, but he didn't want to take a chance of damaging it. He stared down at Maddy's remains. This would be the fifteenth drone he had left in the past, possibly to be found by future archeologists. He had never worried too much about it before because he'd always believed the drones to be in a different timeline from the moment they were sent back. Now he didn't know what to believe.

Looking up, he saw Virgil, Jazzlyn, and Derek making their way down the slope from the cave. In spite of his injuries, Derek was again carrying the duffel bag of gear on his back.

"How's the module look?" Virgil asked as he and the others came to a stop beside Maddy's broken body.

Lincoln patted his pocket to indicate he had successfully removed the module.

"Where do we go now?" Skyra asked.

Lincoln pointed to the river. "Back to the T$_3$. From there, back to the place where I'm from."

She looked out over the scene. "Ripple has not come yet."

"Do you want to wait here a little longer?"

She seemed to think about this. "Ripple has told me many times it would have to leave me someday. Maybe this is the day."

Actually, Lincoln had been thinking about the drone also. Ripple still hadn't fully explained why it had left a message for Lincoln to come to this time and place. It was unthinkable to jump back to the future without even learning why they had come here. "Ripple knows we're going to the T3. Maybe it will be there waiting for us."

She continued gazing toward the river. "Yes, maybe. I am ready to go to the T3."

Lincoln took one more look at Maddy's broken body before starting the descent.

Several minutes later, when the group was at the base of the hill of boulders, Jazzlyn turned and stared back up the slope. "Three nights in a cave. That was not on my bucket list."

"You should try sleeping naked on gravel," Lincoln quipped. He didn't mention that his night on the gravel had also involved holding Skyra against his naked body.

As they headed across the open field of rocks toward the river and the T3, Lincoln's apprehension grew. Would the T3 still be functional? Was it even possible to jump to the future? If so, what would they find there?

The others must have been contemplating similar thoughts—they were unusually quiet as they picked their way through the sage-like brush and jagged rocks.

When the group was only a few hundred meters from the river, Skyra pointed ahead. "Ripple! You were right, Lincoln, Ripple is here."

The drone apparently had left the T3 and was walking out to meet them. It stopped as they approached and said, "Skyra and Lincoln, I am pleased to see that you are alive and healthy."

Derek hoisted the duffel bag from his back and let it drop to the ground. "Yeah, the rest of us are okay, too. Thanks for your concern."

Ripple shifted its vision lens toward Derek. "Your sarcasm is noted, and I apologize. Skyra and Lincoln are of immense importance to my mission. Therefore, the majority of my concern is for their well-being."

"You kind of suck at apologizing," Jazzlyn said. "And what do you mean by *my mission?*"

Skyra kneeled beside the drone and ran her fingers over what appeared to be fresh scratches on the front edges of its shell. "You are hurt, Ripple. Did my tribemates attack you again?"

The drone's red lights pulsed twice. "No. They were intensively occupied with fighting off the hyenas, so I was able to make an escape. I replenished my power level and came here."

Virgil stepped closer to the drone and kneeled. "You have something stuck to your foot." From the traction claws of Ripple's left hind foot, he pulled loose a shred of what appeared to be thin leather. "What is this?" Virgil said as he stood up and examined it. He turned it over in his hand. Then he pulled off his glasses to get a better close-up look. "Oh, crap. Is this what I think it is?" He handed the shred to Lincoln.

It wasn't leather at all. It was brown fabric. Hundreds of thread-like tubes extended from the torn edges, severed at various lengths as if the shred had been violently ripped rather than cut with a sharp tool. Lincoln recognized the fabric. He tried to swallow, but his already-dry mouth refused to cooperate. "This is fabric from one of our body bags," he said to Ripple. "Why was this stuck to your foot?"

The drone's red lights rotated clockwise, then reversed, then reversed again. "It is important that you and Skyra remain here."

Lincoln stared, struggling to comprehend.

"What the hell are you saying?" Derek demanded.

"Forgive me," Ripple said. "I am attempting to carry out my mission."

Lincoln stepped toward the drone. "Just what exactly is your mission?"

"At the moment, I am simply trying to make sure that you and Skyra remain here. I tried to disable your T3, but I discovered I am not well equipped for such destructive endeavors. I was not able to inflict as much damage as I had intended, and my efforts have nearly depleted my power level."

Skyra was still on her knees beside the drone. "What are you talking about, Ripple? I want to go with Lincoln to the place he is from. I do not want to stay here."

Ripple turned toward her. "Please trust me. You must remain here."

Derek picked up the duffel bag and shrugged his arms into the handles. "I'm going on ahead to the T3. If that drone has destroyed our chances of getting out of here, I swear I'm going to smash it so it can't even be used for spare parts." He took off toward the river.

Virgil looked at Lincoln. "I'd better go with him."

Lincoln nodded.

Without saying a word, Jazzlyn followed Derek and Virgil.

"You need to explain," Lincoln said to Ripple. "Now!"

The drone shifted to look at him. "You coded me with sufficient autonomy to make decisions and formulate strategies."

"Evidently that was a bad idea."

"It was a very good idea. You, Lincoln, have a deep concern for the well-being of your fellow humans and for the planet. As you continued developing your fascination for studying Earth's past, you came to realize that your drones might be able to do more than simply gather environmental data."

"Such as?"

"Such as doing helpful things for the indigenous constituents. You decided, considering you had no choice but to leave your drones in the past, they might as well make themselves useful. So, you expanded their physical capabilities, increased their longevity, and coded them with unprecedented cognitive skills and autonomy. Of course, the drones' main purpose was still to gather and transmit data during the nineteen minutes the portal remained open. Once the portal closed, however, the drones were free to do as they pleased, limited only by pre-set parameters."

Lincoln could hardly believe he would ever so willingly embrace the idea of interfering with indigenous life and cultures. Then again, hadn't he done just that during the last four days? He glanced at Skyra, who was watching the conversation intently, then turned back to Ripple. "So you completed your data-collection duties, the portal closed, then you befriended Skyra?"

"That is correct, although I encountered several humans and numerous other Neanderthals before befriending Skyra. I recognized Skyra was extraordinary. You don't know this yet, Lincoln, but you expanded your future drones' analysis capabilities with probes for sampling plant and animal tissue, including cursory DNA analyses of blood samples. In spite of the inherent difficulties of finding, subduing, then sampling and analyzing the blood of an indigenous creature, the probes proved to be revelatory. When I recognized Skyra possessed cognitive and sensory capabilities that in many ways mirrored your own, Lincoln, I sampled her blood."

"Use words I know, Ripple," Skyra said.

Ripple ignored her and continued. "As it turns out, Skyra's genetic material is just as extraordinary as yours, Lincoln. I realized you and Skyra were a perfect match for each other."

Lincoln stared at the drone, not sure what to say. "You're freaking kidding me."

Ripple's red lights pulsed twice. "You have stated I was found along with Skyra's remains. I was found because of a beacon I had set to activate at a particular time. Have you wondered, Lincoln, why I set my beacon for that specific time?"

He shook his head, confused by the apparent change of subject.

"I set my beacon to activate on a specific date. Why? Because I knew you would meet a woman named Lottie Atkins one year after that date. Then, four months after that, you and Lottie would become husband and wife. I needed to contact you before you met Lottie. I needed you to come to this time and place so you would meet Skyra before you met Lottie."

"You're freaking kidding me," Lincoln said again, this time almost in a whisper.

"I don't understand," Skyra said, her voice becoming more urgent.

Lincoln turned to her. "Ripple is saying it wanted me to come to this place so you and I would meet each other."

Her intense gaze didn't falter as she stared back at him.

"You are oversimplifying my mission," Ripple said. "You told me my message stated that all of civilization was at risk.

The message was not an exaggeration. When the two of you combine your genetic material and produce offspring, over ninety-five percent of your offspring will be extraordinary. They will possess keen sensory predictive abilities, as do the two of you. They will have remarkable intelligence in the realms of language, mathematics, and problem solving. Also, they will likely have a highly-expressed sense of compassion for others."

"You want us to have kids together," Lincoln said flatly.

"If you do not, future civilization is truly at risk of not reaching its full potential. If you do, civilization 47,000 years from now could be stronger and more vibrant than any civilization you could imagine. This is the plan I have devised. It is my mission. I did not intend to reveal the details quite yet—I would have preferred to do so after the two of you developed a higher level of affection for each other—but circumstances have forced my hand."

Lincoln began pacing back and forth, focusing on the pain on the bottom of his foot simply because it was something real that he could understand. This whole nightmare was taking place because one of his drones had concocted a far-fetched plan for populating the world with human-Neanderthal hybrids. How could he have thought it was a good idea to code his drones with this absurd level of autonomy? And what about this woman, Lottie? Ripple had effectively destroyed his chances of meeting this woman and possibly living the rest of his life in love. What in the living hell?

He stopped pacing and turned back to Ripple. "What about Veenah? What was your plan for her?"

"I had not actually met Veenah until three days ago when we took her from the human camp, but I already understood her to be Skyra's genetically identical twin. I hoped that

Veenah would survive so you could impregnate her as well as Skyra. Multiple times, ideally."

Lincoln could only shake his head.

Skyra, still crouched beside the drone, was watching him with her large, imposing eyes. Did she even understand enough of the conversation to know what was happening? He stepped over and kneeled before her. "Do you still want to go with me? To the place where I'm from?"

"Yes," she said without hesitating.

He turned to Ripple. "We're not staying here."

"You must stay here, or my plan will not succeed."

"Turn yourself off, Ripple," Lincoln ordered.

The drone remained silent for a few seconds. "My plan will not succeed if you—"

Lincoln grabbed two of the drone's legs and pushed it over onto its side. "Turn yourself off, or I'll go in there and do it myself!"

"Please, you must think about what you are doing."

Lincoln held the struggling drone and started turning the four knobs to their unlock positions.

Something sharp pressed against his throat. "Are you trying to hurt Ripple?" Skyra demanded.

He realized the sharp object was one of her stone knives. "No, I'm just making it go to sleep."

Ripple stopped kicking. "Skyra, do not harm Lincoln. You and Lincoln must take care of each other. I will turn myself off."

Lincoln lifted his hands away from Ripple's access panel. "I'm not touching it. Can you please take the knife from my throat?"

She pulled the knife back, but only a few centimeters.

"I will turn myself off," Ripple repeated. "I only ask that

you please consider what I've said. If you consider the logic of it, I'm sure you will conclude that my plan will result in a better world for everyone." The drone retracted its legs into its shell. "Powering down."

Skyra glanced at the drone then slowly placed her stone knife back in her wrist sheath beside the other one.

The following seconds of silence were perhaps the most awkward Lincoln had ever experienced.

"Ripple wants you to put a child in my belly?" Skyra asked.

That made the situation even more awkward. "Um... more than one child, I think."

She chewed on her lower lip. "Well, I *am* in my ilmekho."

He blinked, struggling to comprehend how the conversation had become surreal so quickly. Yes, he found Skyra to be strangely fascinating, perhaps even attractive, but they were from completely different worlds. Hell, they weren't even the same species. He wouldn't last a month in her world, even with her protecting him with her spears, khuls, and knives. She could definitely exist in his world, though, if they could get there. If she were dressed in modern clothing, most people probably wouldn't even notice she was different. He had to at least try to take her there. He got to his feet and held out his hand.

She accepted it and got up.

"Maybe this is something we should talk about later," he said. "If Ripple hasn't completely destroyed the T_3, we'll soon be at the place where I'm from."

"Are you one of the dominant men in your tribe?"

He considered this. "In spite of my appearance, yes. Actually, I *am* the dominant man."

"That is good," she said. She picked up the drone and

hoisted it onto her shoulder. "We will go with you to the land of your tribe."

He shook his head, still bewildered, and started walking.

When they arrived at the T_3, Lincoln's chest tightened. Shreds of torn body bag fabric were scattered everywhere.

"It's not quite as bad as it looks," Virgil said, eyeing the dormant drone as Skyra lowered it to the ground. "Ripple destroyed nine body bags. The other fifteen appear to be intact, including all three of the larger bags for the T_3. The drone also tried to damage the T_3 itself." He pointed to the boulder, which was now covered in minor dents and scrapes.

"No wonder Ripple didn't meet us at the cave," Lincoln said. "It was too busy being destructive here."

Virgil went on. "I think we'll be okay, assuming the T_3 is still functional. As I said, we're down to fifteen body bags. Not enough for three more jumps, but we never thought we'd really need three more jumps anyway, did we?"

Lincoln stared at the T_3, thinking. There was no way to know for sure how many jumps they'd need. The extra body bags were a precaution, in case they found themselves in a dangerous time and place. It was a precaution he didn't want to lose. "We're going to jump with only five bags," he proclaimed. "That includes one of the T_3 bags."

Virgil frowned. Jazzlyn and Derek stopped what they were doing.

Lincoln stepped over and picked up one of the intact bags Virgil had laid out. "We can do this. These bags are large enough for two people each. We've lost some of our gear, most of the food is gone, and we'll only have ten spare body bags to pack. We'll use one of the large bags on the T_3, then we'll squeeze ourselves and the gear into four body bags. That way we'll still have the option of jumping two more times, using five bags each time."

Virgil's expression betrayed his fear. "We haven't really tested... I mean, it might not—"

"It's going to work!" Lincoln said, more forcefully than he'd intended. "Virgil, it's going to work."

Lincoln and his team connected the cords from four of the body bags to the T_3, made sure the connections were secure, and stuffed most of the gear along with the ten remaining bags into one of the connected bags. Surprisingly, Skyra asked no questions throughout the entire process.

When Lincoln pulled out one of the mini-drones and powered it on, Skyra finally spoke up. "El-de-né! What creature is that? It is Maddy's child?"

Lincoln chuckled. "Yeah, I guess it is. We call it a mini-drone."

While Virgil disconnected the gear-filled bag and two of the empty ones, Lincoln placed the rabbit-sized mini-drone into the remaining connected bag and zipped the bag shut. The T_3 was already programmed for the return jump, having processed the massive placement calculations for jumping to Lincoln's lab at four minutes past the time his team had originally jumped.

He tapped his watch's screen, working through the menus. The T_3 began emitting an almost indiscernible hum. He tapped again, and the lump in the body bag where the mini-drone had been abruptly collapsed.

As Lincoln began counting the seconds in his head, he glanced at Skyra. She was staring at the now-empty bag.

"Please, please, please, please," muttered Jazzlyn.

At about twenty seconds his watch chirped and a green checkmark appeared. He smiled and held his watch up for the others to see. "We're good to go, folks. Destination site is clear."

"Yes!" Jazzlyn exclaimed.

Derek reached over and ruffled Virgil's hair. "We're finally leaving this hellhole, Virg!"

Unfortunately, the mini-drone didn't have the time or capability to send video or still images. It was designed for making a destination viability determination as quickly as possible. So, Lincoln still had no idea what would really greet his team after jumping. At least the mini-drone had sent its signal, which proved that jumping to the future was indeed possible.

Derek helped Virgil position one of the large bags over the T3, lining up the holes on the bag with the T3's connection ports. Virgil then reconnected the bag containing the gear and the two remaining empty bags.

"Okay," Lincoln said, "Three empty bags, five people, and one drone. Choose your partner." He took Skyra's hand and pulled her to his side. "I've got mine."

"Oooooh, damn, you guys," Jazzlyn said. "Our boss found himself a girlfriend."

Derek and Virgil looked at their feet, obviously not feeling like joking at this moment. Virgil stepped closer to Jazzlyn. "I'll be with you. I mean, if you don't mind."

She smiled. "I'd be honored, good sir."

"Well, shit," Derek said. He stepped over and picked up the dormant drone. "Let's get this over with. I'm freaking starving."

Within two minutes, Lincoln had zipped Derek and Ripple into one bag and Jazzlyn and Virgil into the other. Skyra had watched the process without speaking.

He pointed to the last bag. "This one's ours. Are you ready?"

"I do not understand."

"Do you trust me?"

She looked at him without answering.

"Okay, I know this seems strange, but I need for you to trust me. We will get inside this bag together, then the T3 will send us to the place I am from."

Again, she looked at him without speaking.

He sighed. "Just get inside with me, okay?" He sat down in the bag and extended a hand to her.

She took it and squeezed so hard that he winced. Was she frightened? Excited? Angry? He had no way of knowing. She sat beside him. He pulled the zipper up to their waists then reclined onto his back. She positioned herself beside him, and he zipped the bag shut.

"This won't take long," he said as he tapped his watch, working through the menus until the green button appeared, labeled *No Time Like the Present*. He turned to Skyra. She was barely visible in the darkness of the bag, but he could see that she was watching his face. "Are you ready?"

"I do not understand," she said again. This time her voice wavered with what he thought might be fear—from this woman who had been fearless. She moved closer, forcing him to put his arm around her. As he pushed his hand around behind her back, he realized she still had two khuls in her sling. She put her arm across his chest.

Lincoln had to pull her closer to reach his watch with his other hand. He stared at the button, trying to control his rapid breathing. After hovering his finger over the screen for a moment, he tapped.

19

ARIZONA

47,659 YEARS *later* - *Day 1*

SKYRA FELT the ground give way, and for an instant she was falling. She landed on something hard, which drove the two khuls in her sling painfully into her shoulder blade. Lincoln grunted in her ear with the impact.

Skyra raised her head. She and Lincoln were on the ground but were no longer inside the bag. They were in a different place. The jagged rocks were gone. The river was gone. Instead of scattered scrub trees, she was now looking at taller trees with spreading trunks and thin, pale leaves. Standing tall among the trees were strange posts with no leaves at all, but the posts were covered in spines, like tall, green hedgehogs.

The sun was almost directly above, but she could barely see it through a layer of brown haze that seemed to spread from one end of the sky to the other. Skyra sniffed the air and coughed. The air was tainted with some kind of smoke—not pleasant like the smoke from a campfire, but foul like burning hair.

Derek's voice broke the silence. "Where are we? Where's the lab?"

Skyra pulled away from Lincoln and sat up. Lincoln's tribemates were all here, Ripple was here, even the strange boulder was here. She ran her hand over the ground at her side and scooped up a handful of dirt. It was a strange mixture of sand, black soil, and bits of dead leaves.

"Ow," Jazzlyn said. "Damn. They're biting!" She and Virgil were squirming and slapping their legs. They jumped to their feet, still brushing away whatever was crawling under the blue skins covering their bodies. They moved away from the spot and slapped the last of the creatures. "Fire ants," Jazzlyn said. "Lincoln, I think we've had a placement error. I've never seen fire ants near the lab, and the vegetation here is wrong. I'm not sure we're even in Arizona."

Lincoln was now sitting up beside Skyra, scanning the ground as if looking for more ants. "I wish it was only a placement error, but I think we all know better."

"No!" Derek said, getting to his feet. "This is all wrong. There's nothing here!"

Skyra felt sick, and she put her hands on her belly. She hadn't eaten much in the last few days, but her stomach was churning like it wanted to force out its contents. She swallowed, trying to make the feeling go away. "Lincoln, I don't understand. How can we be in this place? We did not walk here." The feeling in her belly surged again, and this time she couldn't stop it. She lunged to the side and retched. Nothing came up from her empty belly but sour-tasting fluid. She retched again, her fingers digging into the dirt that was so different from the dirt she had always known.

Lincoln put a hand on her back. He and the others remained silent until her belly finally decided it had nothing to give up. She got to her feet, feeling unsteady, and Lincoln got up beside her.

"The T_3 sent us here, Skyra," he said. "That's what the T_3 does. It sends people and things to a different place—and to a different time, if that makes any sense at all. The T_3 has sent us to the place I am from."

She looked out at the strange landscape. "This is the place you are from?"

He sighed. "Yeah, I'm pretty sure it is. It just looks very different now."

She wiped the sour fluid from her chin. "I don't understand."

Virgil said, "This is disappointing, but it shouldn't be surprising. We all suspected this would happen. We knew Lincoln's Temporal Bridge Theorem was correct—you can't jump back in time without creating a new timeline."

"There's nothing here!" Derek shouted in his booming voice. He pointed to the brown sky. "Except smog. Why is there even smog here? There are no signs of humans—no power lines, no buildings, no roads, none of that shit."

"Those things may very well exist here," Jazzlyn said. "Remember, we're on Lincoln's property. There could be a city just beyond the horizon."

Virgil said, "This place has been in its own timeline for forty-seven thousand years. You guys know this. We volunteered for the jump knowing we were giving up our lives for whatever cause the sacrifice was supposed to represent." He looked at Derek. "Why are you so surprised?"

For a few breaths, Derek looked as if he wanted to attack someone. He shook his head. "I was hoping for the best, dammit."

"I warned you not to do this, and you did not heed my advice."

Skyra looked over at Ripple. The creature's legs were emerging from its shell. It kicked several times before rolling first to its belly then to its feet.

"I told you to power down," Lincoln said. "I didn't say anything about setting an auto-reboot."

Ripple turned to face Lincoln. "I see that we are back in Arizona, and I assume we have jumped back to your own time. In doing so, you have negated my plan."

Derek said, "What plan?"

"It's a long, screwed-up story," Lincoln said.

Ripple went on. "My plan could have resulted in a global civilization that at this current point in time would have been most impressive. The plan was rather brilliant. Now, in this current setting, the cultural, climatic, and species diversity parameters are almost certainly not suitable for producing the desired civilization, even in the future. You squandered the opportunity due to your misguided desire to return to the comforts of your previous timeline. Of course, that world does not exist in this timeline, does it?"

Everyone remained silent for several long breaths.

"I apologize for such an outburst," Ripple said. "My disappointment must have outweighed my amicability coding."

"What the hell kind of drone is that thing?" Derek asked.

"That's a good question," Lincoln said. He stepped over and kneeled in front of Ripple. "There's something I need to know, and I need a straight answer."

"I agree to be forthcoming," Ripple said.

Skyra was tired of listening to words she did not know, so she turned her back on Ripple and the bolups to gaze at the strange landscape. The trees and shrubs here were not like any she had seen before.

She moved away from the others to take a closer look at one of the tall, prickly posts. It was some kind of tree, she was sure of that, but it had no leaves. Its green trunk was thicker than Skyra's body and even taller than the munopo trees that grew beside the Yagua river.

She carefully touched the tips of several of the spines covering the tree's surface. The spines were stiff and very sharp.

A movement on the tree's trunk caught her eye. It was a brown lizard, the length of Skyra's hand. The creature was somehow crawling across the spines without stabbing its own feet or belly. The lizard jerked its head up and down several times as it stared at her. Skyra shot her hand out to grab the creature but only managed to puncture two of her fingers as it scuttled out of reach. She put her fingers in her mouth one at a time, sucking the droplets of blood.

"You are either very smart or very stupid to live among those spines," she said to the lizard, speaking in the Una-Loto language. She found a fist-sized rock and threw it at the lizard, intending to knock it from the tree. Again, the lizard scuttled to the side before getting hit. "You do not easily give up your meat and blood for my hungry belly," she said then decided the small creature was not worth the effort.

She moved away from the spiny tree to where the ground began to slope downward toward a dry river bed stretching into the distance between low hills. Even though the brown haze partially blocked the sun's light, the plants here were thriving. The hillsides were green—even greener than the

Kapolsek foothills during the first days of the wet, warm season. At several spots on the dry river bed, swarms of yellow butterflies flittered, alighting briefly on the sand then spiraling upward again as if they could not decide what they wanted to do.

The air smelled strange, but the sun's light penetrated the haze enough to warm Skyra's skin. If Lincoln's words were true—if she need not fear being killed by predators or taken by bolup tribes—then Skyra was sure she was going to like this place. She didn't understand how she got here, but that didn't matter. All that mattered was that she was here, and that Lincoln was here with her.

Lincoln stared at Ripple. Every time he thought he was starting to understand the drone, Ripple surprised him all over again. Maddy's general appearance had been similar to Ripple's, but apparently that's where the similarity ended. "How did your remains—your other self—how did it end up in the same timeline it had jumped from?" he asked the drone. "That defies the Temporal Bridge Theorem, and it defies logic."

Ripple's red LEDs pulsed twice. "Lincoln, your Temporal Bridge Theorem is not flawed. It is perfect."

"Then why did you tell me a few days ago that the theorem was flawed?"

"I was not being honest with you. I thought if I could convince you it was within your power to prevent the demise of your original civilization, you would join me in trying to save Skyra and Veenah. After all, you jumped to the past with the intention of saving your own civilization. I needed to convince you it was actually possible."

Lincoln inhaled deeply and let it out slowly. "So, if my theorem is perfect, how did your remains end up in the same timeline? That should not have been possible."

"You constantly underestimate your own abilities, Lincoln. You and Skyra are far more extraordinary than either of you know."

"You're not answering the question."

Ripple waited a few seconds before speaking. "We know jumping back in time creates a new timeline. Your theorem proves that, and empirical evidence confirms it. By its very nature, the process of jumping back in time is intricately tied to the concept of jumping between universes. They are two sides of the same coin, as you are fond of saying. You, Lincoln, knew this, and you figured out a way to give your drones the ability to jump between existing universes."

Lincoln's gut tightened to the point where he actually winced. "I did what?"

"You should not be so surprised. It was a logical connection. Now, to answer your question. You sent me back in time to gather environmental data, just as you had done with hundreds of other drones. I carried out my duty, and the portal closed. As I have said, I eventually befriended Skyra and determined she was genetically extraordinary. That is when I devised my plan. I must have determined at some point that Skyra's life was in jeopardy, and I created a message that survived through the millennia—the very message to which you responded."

Ripple paused and turned slightly as if looking beyond Lincoln. Lincoln turned and saw that Skyra had wandered off and was examining a massive saguaro-like cactus.

"We do not know what dangers Skyra may encounter in this place," Ripple said. "Perhaps she should not explore on her own."

Lincoln turned back to Ripple. "Skyra can take care of herself. Keep talking."

The drone shifted again. "You already know that before powering down for the last time, I set my clock to activate my location beacon on a specific date, but here is the portion of my story you may find most interesting. I set my clock to activate a second function as well. Just before activating my location beacon, I activated my *u-jump module*, as you liked to call it. This instantaneously transferred me and most of Skyra's remains between timelines, back to the timeline I had originally jumped from. Back to your own timeline, Lincoln."

Lincoln sat back on his heels, frowning.

"Wait," Virgil said. "Are you saying you could jump back to our original universe right now?"

Ripple turned to face him. "Yes, if I wanted to do that."

Virgil clapped his hands together once. "And you can take us with you?"

"I could take a portion of you with me, but that would likely kill you. The process transfers matter within a sixty-four-centimeter radius of my u-jump module. Your body would not fit within that space."

"Goddammit!" Derek grunted, rubbing his forehead in frustration.

"That's why Skyra's lower leg bones were never found," Lincoln said.

"Yes, that makes sense," Ripple said. "Logically, I would have positioned myself so Skyra's skull and the femur on which I etched the message would be within the u-jump module's effective radius. It was not possible to transfer her entire body."

"Why would I ever equip drones with something like this u-jump module? What's the point?"

"You designed the module in case one of your drones were to discover something so important that it would need to be communicated back to you after the portal had already closed. It appears that is exactly what I have done."

"So, you can't transfer us to our own timeline," Jazzlyn said. "We're stuck here?"

Ripple turned toward Jazzlyn. "You are not stuck here if you still have the equipment for making another jump. If so, I recommend jumping back to Skyra's time."

"I'm not going back there," Derek said.

"Hell, neither am I," Jazzlyn added.

"It matters little whether you do or do not. What matters is that Lincoln and Skyra jump back to Skyra's time. Then my original plan may still come to fruition."

Lincoln got to his feet. He was tired of feeling overwhelmed by mind-blowing revelations. He looked around at the surrounding landscape. Skyra was now nowhere to be seen, which added to his jangled nerves—he had grown accustomed to being near her during the last several days. He sighed and turned back to his team. "Let's not get ahead of ourselves, okay? We don't know anything about where we are now. It seems obvious we can never return to our home timeline, and we're only capable of two more jumps. Before we make any decisions, we should at least check this place out beyond what we can see from here. Can we all agree on that?"

The others nodded, but they didn't look happy.

Skyra's mind was made up—she definitely liked the landscape of this new place. She could even get used to the strange smell. The land was made up of one rolling hill after another, but the hills were hardly noticeable because they were covered with brush and trees, including the green, spiny trees Lincoln had called cactuses, as well as trees with white, spreading trunks.

Lincoln's tribemates had gone in another direction to explore the land. Skyra had told Ripple to stay behind at the T3. She and Lincoln had walked over three hills toward where the sun would set at the end of the day. They had not seen any large animals, only small birds and lizards. Skyra needed to fill her belly with water, but they had only come across dry river beds. She couldn't be sure, but it seemed like the strange smell was becoming stronger as they walked farther from the T3.

"I like this place, Lincoln," she said as they came to a low area between hills. "It is not like the lands I have seen."

He looked back the way they had come. "Yeah. I recognize certain things about it, but it's so different now."

"Is this the place where we will not be afraid of predators, and where I will not have to kill men who come to take me?"

He twisted his mouth to one side. "I honestly don't know yet. Um, I was thinking about that. I owe you an apology."

"What is *apology*?"

"It's when someone says *I'm sorry*. I know you think saying *I'm sorry* doesn't make sense, but I really need to apologize. I told you I'd take you to the place I am from, but this place is very different from where I came from. It's the same location, but it's different now."

She pulled several tiny leaves from a low bush beside her, crushed them between her fingers, then smelled the juices. The leaves smelled sweet, reminding her of the grapes that grew beside streams at the base of the Kapolsek mountains. "Maybe different is not bad. I like this place."

He bared his teeth in a bolup smile, a smile Skyra was beginning to understand. In fact, whenever he smiled like that she felt a warmness within her chest. She tried to imitate his smile, which made him laugh.

He said, "Well, we may be stuck here. I don't know anything about hunting or living off the land, but maybe you could teach me and my team. Maybe we could start a new life here."

She studied his face—his small eyes and thin lips. "Yes, Lincoln. We will start a new life. Maybe you will put children in my belly."

His tiny eyes widened. "Well, that's... um... I don't know." Then he narrowed his eyes. "You're messing with me. Aren't you?"

Skyra didn't know what *messing* was, but she understood anyway. She bared her teeth. "*At-at-at-at.*"

He nodded. "Yeah, okay. Sure. I'll put children in your belly. Hundreds of them."

Skyra heard a strange sound and froze. It was a low rumble, almost like distant thunder, but it seemed much closer.

"Did you hear that?" Lincoln asked.

Skyra turned and ran up the next hill with Lincoln just behind her. The tall trees didn't allow her to see very far in the direction of the sound, but now she could hear more sounds. Some of them sounded like animals growling. The foul smell was even stronger here.

Lincoln pointed. "That hill's taller. Maybe we can see from there."

They made their way among the cactuses and trees down the slope, across the low valley, and up the taller hill.

Skyra began sensing danger even before they got to the hilltop. She was now sure the sounds beyond the hill included growling creatures, and she thought she heard a man screaming. Her instincts told her to turn back, but Lincoln was now well ahead of her, and he was not slowing down.

Lincoln stopped suddenly at the hill's summit, and she came to a stop beside him. She stared, trying to make sense of what she was seeing. Before her was a vast valley. Brown smoke was rising from countless spots across the valley. Each spot was a mound of something—objects that had been piled upon each other and set on fire. More of the objects were scattered across the ground for as far as Skyra could see.

"Good God," Lincoln said. "Those are bodies. Thousands of bodies."

Skyra looked down the hillside at the nearest of the objects. Lincoln was right, they were the bodies of men, and maybe women too. Scattered among the bodies were strange things made from the wood of trees, some of them blackened and still smoking. A growl drew Skyra's attention. She spotted a pack of wolf-like creatures, tearing at the flesh of several of the bodies and snarling at each other.

She scanned the valley and realized some of the bodies were not men or women, they were creatures the size of aurochs. Many of the bodies—both creatures and people—were being consumed by swirling flocks of birds and more packs of wolves.

"How can there be so many bodies?" Skyra whispered.

She had never seen so many people—alive or dead—during her entire life.

"This is a battlefield," Lincoln replied. "There's a war going on here."

"Difo-kha-melé!"

Skyra dropped to her knees and crawled behind some brush, pulling Lincoln with her. The voice came again, shouting words she did not understand. Another sound became louder—a rumbling, rattling sound. It was coming from the base of the hill, just out of sight around the hill's edge.

Two large creatures came into view, followed by two more. The creatures were tall, with thin, knobby legs and strange humps on their backs. They were tied together with leather straps, and they were dragging a wide, flat object made of wood, which moved upon turning circles of wood. Men and women were walking beside the creatures and beside the wood object dragging behind.

As the creatures approached along the hill's base, Skyra studied the men and women. They were short and broad, with large eyes and thick brows. "Those are nandups," she said.

"Nandups!" Lincoln whispered. "How could nandups be here?"

Skyra stared at the nearest woman walking beside the creatures. The woman wore black garments fastened around her waist with a leather strap. Several weapons hung from the strap, including a strange khul with a broad, shiny blade. Dirt and scars covered her face, but there could be no doubt she was a nandup.

Skyra felt Lincoln grip her arm. She glanced at him then followed his gaze back to the creatures and wooden platform they were dragging. Dead men lay upon the wood, their bodies bloodied and their arms and legs tied down with straps. One of them raised his head, and Skyra realized the men were actually alive. She squinted as they drew nearer. The men tied to the platform were bolups.

Lincoln gripped her arm even tighter. "What the hell have we done?"

THERE'S MORE TO THIS STORY!

Lincoln gripped her arm even tighter. "What the hell have we done?"

Good question! What exactly have Skyra, Lincoln, Virgil, Derek, and Jazzlyn gotten themselves into? They survived their ordeal 47,000 years in the past, but what are they facing now that they've jumped back to the present?

Obsolete Theorem is the first book in the **Across Horizons** seres. If you enjoyed this book, you are definitely going to love the second book in the series, **Foregone Conflict**. After that, you'll want to read **Hostile Emergence** (book 3), and **Binary Existence** (Book 4).

And don't miss the **prequel** to the series, **Genesis Sequence**.

Also, if you haven't read my **Diffusion series**, my **Bridgers series**, and my **Fused series**, be sure to check them out.

AUTHOR'S NOTES

I love science and science fiction, so I spend a lot of time thinking about bizarre questions related to such things as time travel, alternate universes, unusual creatures, and much more. Below are some of my thoughts related the concepts in **Obsolete Theorem**. These are in no particular order, and they may not cover everything you're curious about, but if you're at all interested, here you go.

What the heck is Lincoln's Temporal Bridge Theorem? First, let's look at the logic of time travel (or the illogic, if you prefer). Traveling to the past is one thing. Our past is linear—what happened actually happened. But the moment you arrive in the past, say 47,659 years ago, you start a new sequence of events that will lead to a completely different future. It is simply not possible for the same future to occur again, so it is simply not possible to jump back to the same future you had originally jumped from. Why? Because the future is not predetermined. Things happen randomly every millisecond that change the course of history. Even if you are careful to have minimal impact on the environment while you're in the past, random events will result in a completely different future. So, there are infinite possible futures. If you tried a thousand different times to jump back to the future, each time you would end up in a *different* future, and you could never return to the same future you originally left behind.

Lincoln understood all this. He understood you could never get back to the future you left behind, but he wanted a mathematical model to provide proof. Lincoln is a brilliant scientist and mathematician, and he developed the mathematical theorem that proves that jumping to the past creates an alternate universe. His theorem proves (at least mathematically) that the moment his drones jump into the past, they are in a different timeline (a different universe). Because the drones end up in a different universe when he sends them back in time, obviously there is no way they could have any impact on his own timeline. This is why he is so incredulous when one of his drones is found in his timeline (universe). According to his theorem, such a thing should not be possible. When people discover his drone beside Skyra's skeletal remains, they assume his theorem is flawed. Thus the title *Obsolete Theorem*.

Is Lincoln's theorem really obsolete? That's the real question, isn't it? If his theorem is correct, then Ripple's remains should not exist in his universe (for the reasons explained above). At first, upon discovering Ripple's remains, many people conclude that Lincoln's theorem is incorrect. Even Lincoln himself begins to doubt his own theorem. At one point in the story, Ripple even tells Lincoln the theorem is flawed. But, as

Lincoln is discovering, Ripple is capable of deception. Ripple tells Lincoln his theorem is flawed so that Lincoln will believe he is capable of saving his original world. Ripple knows that if Lincoln believes it is possible to save his original future, he will be willing to help save Skyra (and Veenah). Later, Ripple admits that Lincoln's theorem is, in fact, correct. Perhaps his theorem is not obsolete after all.

So, how did Ripple's ancient remains end up in the same timeline? Again, this question gets at the heart of the entire issue. Remember, when you jump back in time, you instantly create a new timeline (universe) when you arrive in the past. There's only one way someone (or something) could jump back in time and then jump forward to the same universe where they started. This could only be possible if that person (or drone) had the capability of jumping (bridging) at will between alternate universes. Not only would the person have to be able to jump at will to a different universe, the person would also have to be able to jump to a very *specific* universe —the exact same universe they originally left behind. *Sheesh...* that's a tall order. As it turns out, though, Lincoln has developed a way for his drones to do this very thing. Ripple was equipped with a *U-jump Module* (U-jump, a whimsical name Lincoln came up with, stands for *universe-jumping module*), basically a piece of machinery that allows the drone to jump back to its own original universe. Soon after Skyra and Ripple were buried under falling rocks, Skyra died. Ripple then created a message that would survive tens of thousands of years (scratched into Skyra's femur and into Ripple's own shell). Ripple set its internal clock to wait 47,659 years and then activate two functions. First, trigger the U-jump Module to transfer Ripple and most of Skyra's skeletal remains between universes—back to Ripple's own original universe. Second, trigger its location beacon so that it would be found, which would then result in the message eventually being shown to Lincoln (especially since Lincoln's name was included in the message).

Can you give me a brief explanation of Ripple's motivation for doing all this? Lincoln, sometime in the fourteen years after we meet him in Chapter 2, decides to give his drones more autonomy so that they can make their own decisions. Therefore, Ripple was coded with intelligence and the ability to devise and carry out plans that the drone decided were likely to help humanity (regardless of the timeline). Ripple then took these abilities to the extreme (I'll let you decide whether Ripple is a rogue robot or not). Ripple carried out its duties of measuring environmental data and then sending that data back to Lincoln during the 19 minutes the portal remained open. After the portal closed, Ripple was left in the past (which is in a different timeline, as we have discussed) to eventually "die" and decompose, with the ability in the meantime to come up with ways to be helpful. Ripple encountered Skyra and soon recognized that Skyra was genetically remarkable. Ripple already knew Lincoln was genetically remarkable, so the drone hatched an idea—somehow get Lincoln and Skyra together in the past. Ripple's plan is based on the drone's assumption that the two would produce remarkable offspring. Since this was at a time when humans and Neanderthals were already intermixing (mating together), Ripple concluded that infusing the populations with Skyra-Lincoln hybrids would result in a much different future, filled with remarkable beings. According to Ripple's plan, Skyra and Lincoln's offspring would spread their advantageous genetic traits throughout the world, resulting in a global population in which their traits are found throughout all of humanity (I am using the word humanity here to refer to a population of Neanderthal-human hybrids, with the best features of both species).

Why had Lincoln never previously tried to jump to the future? Because jumping to the future is meaningless. As I said above, the past is linear... what happened actually happened. But the future is uncertain. Millions of random events occur every microsecond, and every one of them impacts the future. If you jump one year into the future and then jump back to the present, the future you briefly saw cannot possibly come true because random events will not lead to that particular future. You could jump one year into the future a million different times, and every time you would see a different future. The possibilities are infinite, and therefore each of those million different futures is meaningless because it will not happen again. For this reason, Lincoln has never been interested in jumping to the future. The past, on the other hand, is interesting to Lincoln because those events actually happened, and understanding the past can actually benefit humanity.

Is this why, when Lincoln's team jumped back to the present, they found the present to be nothing like their original world? Exactly. You cannot jump forward in time to the same world you jumped back in time from. It's impossible.

What the heck is going on in this present world they all jumped forward to? That's an excellent question. As expected, the present world is completely different from Lincoln's original present world. They are at the site of Lincoln's research campus in Arizona, but the campus isn't there, and the desert plants look different. Everything is different. This will be the setting for the second book in the series, titled **Foregone Conflict**. Lincoln and Skyra do not know yet what is going on there. What they do know is that Neanderthals did not go extinct in this world, and they know Neanderthals and humans are at war with each other. Hmm... this may be a very unpleasant place to be.

Lincoln's team not only jumped back in time, they jumped from Arizona to Spain. How is that possible? They did it this way because going to Spain would not put the team any closer to their destination. Lincoln explained a bit of this in the book (Chapter 4). Jumping back in time is actually the *least* complex part of time travel. The *most* complex part is placement, or jumping through space. You must understand that Earth is moving really fast. As it rotates on its axis, the surface at the equator is spinning at 460 meters per second (about 1,000 miles per hour). So, even if you jumped back in time *one second*, you would have to jump 460 meters back toward the east in order to appear in the same room you jumped from. But that's only one small part of Earth's movement. The planet is also in orbit around the sun, moving at 30 *kilometers* per second (67,000 miles per hour). Not only that, but our solar system (including Earth) is revolving around the center of the Milky Way galaxy at 220 kilometers per second (490,000 miles per hour). As if that weren't enough, the galaxies in our part of the universe are moving at 1,000 kilometers per second (2.2 million miles per hour) toward a huge, dense region of space called the Great Attractor.

Um... are you starting to see how difficult it is to calculate placement if you are jumping back in time only one second? Now imagine trying to calculate placement for jumping back in time 47,659 years! The calculation is staggering. As Lincoln said, we may someday discover deep space is littered with the frozen bodies of time travelers who failed to properly calculate placement.

So, time travel is only possible if your time machine is capable of instantaneously sending you through space to a very specific location that could be billions, or even trillions, of miles away. In other words, time travel is the same thing as space travel. This is very, very different from jumping between alternate universes, as the characters did in the Bridgers series. Bridging between universes does not require movement through space—you simply bridge to the exact same location but on an alternate version of Earth. Fortunately, Lincoln understands all of this, and he designed his T_3 with the capability of processing immensely-complex placement calculations.

It is worth pointing out that Lincoln has very specific interests. He is interested in sending his drones into the past to learn about Earth's history, but he is not particularly interested in traveling to other planets. Space travel would certainly be possible with the T_3—as I said above, you can't have time travel without the ability to travel through space. At least for now, though, Lincoln is only focused on using the T_3 for time travel on Earth (and at the moment, of course, he is preoccupied with survival). Hmm... I wonder if his interests will broaden later on...?

Would it really be possible for Lincoln to "put a child in Skyra's belly?" We know beyond any doubt that humans and Neanderthals interbred. After all, almost all humans today have Neanderthal DNA in their genetic code. In fact, when I got my DNA results back from the ancestry-analysis service I used, it stated that I have more Neanderthal genetic material than 98% of the population of people who have used the service. So, I myself am proof that Neanderthals and humans mated and produced offspring. In general, non-African modern humans have 1% to 4% Neanderthal DNA. People of direct African descent have less because Neanderthals evolved and lived exclusively in Eurasia—only those humans that migrated north out of Africa could have mated with Neanderthals.

Interestingly, DNA analyses of Neanderthal remains in Siberia show that humans and Neanderthals were already interbreeding as long ago as 100,000 years (Skyra lived 47,000 years ago). This was the first evidence showing human DNA in Neanderthals rather than showing Neanderthal DNA in humans.

There is one interesting factor that might make it difficult for Lincoln and Skyra to produce offspring, but it requires a bit of explanation. First, our DNA includes *nuclear DNA* and *mitochondrial DNA* (mtDNA). The nuclear DNA is found inside the nucleus of the cell, whereas the mtDNA is found only in the mitochondria of the cell. It is important to know that the nuclear DNA is passed to the offspring from both the mother and father, but the mtDNA is passed to the offspring *only from the mother*. Why is this important? Because scientists cannot find any Neanderthal mtDNA in humans. This *could* lead us to conclude that all DNA in humans today came from pairings of Neanderthal males with human females, and that would imply that pairings of Neanderthal females with human males produced sterile offspring or no offspring at all. If that were true, then Skyra and Lincoln could *not* produce offspring. However, there are other things that could explain why modern humans do not have Neanderthal mtDNA. For example, it's possible that Neanderthal females and human males did not mate because of some cultural reason (in other words, they *chose* not to mate because it was a taboo, or something like that). Another possibility is that there actually used to be humans with Neanderthal mtDNA, but their lineages died out at some point. Still there is one other possibility (which I think is likely), that modern humans *actually do* carry at least one Neanderthal mtDNA lineage, but we have not yet sequenced that lineage in humans or in Neanderthals, so we simply do not know about it yet. So, I think it is quite possible that Lincoln and Skyra *could* produce offspring, if they wanted to. We know that Ripple definitely wants them to produce offspring. Maybe Ripple knows something we don't know...?

Did Neanderthals actually sing? We cannot know this for sure, of course, based on fossil remains. Perhaps the question we need to examine first is, *could Neanderthals even talk?* There are two things that make me believe they probably had language and could speak. First, they did complex things that might require language. Neanderthals hunted big, dangerous animals (such as cave bears, woolly mammoths, and woolly rhinos). Successfully hunting these creatures would be much easier if the hunters were able to communicate concisely and quickly with each other. Also, their complex tools could have required language to teach each other how to make them. Second, their bone structure and DNA suggest they may have had language. For example, fossil evidence of Neanderthal hyoid bones suggests that their hyoid bones (and therefore their voice boxes) were very similar to those of modern humans. There is also some genetic evidence as well as brain capacity evidence that they may have had language.

If we conclude that Neanderthals had language, can we also assume they could sing? Not necessarily, but it certainly is possible (and to me seems likely). The oldest musical instruments found are dated at 40,000 years old (Skyra lived 47,000 years ago). But these instruments were complex enough that we can assume that precursors to these instruments were developed much earlier but simply haven't been found. Also, it seems reasonable to assume singing evolved *before* the development of instruments. Overall, it is very reasonable to assume *humans* were singing long before Skyra's time. The question is, did *Neanderthals* sing? Here's something to consider. Many carnivores hunt in packs, live in groups, and are very social. They mark and defend their territories in many ways, including complex vocalizations (such as wolves). This behavior is also seen in many primates (howler monkeys are a great example). Researchers have proposed that the evolution of human music is rooted in these complex territory defense behaviors, particularly the vocalizations. In other words, human singing could have had its roots in the same type of behavior as the howling of wolves. It seems reasonable to assume that this could have also occurred in Neanderthals, don't you think? Anyway, Skyra can definitely sing quite beautifully, although her singing does not involve lyrics, at least not in a way that Lincoln could recognize.

Did Neanderthals have cultural traditions like those in Skyra's Una-Loto tribe? No one knows. We can only assume that they did, particularly if they had language. The tradition of celebrating *ilmekho* of women when they reach the age of twenty is entirely from my imagination. Sometimes it is assumed that Neanderthals had shorter natural life spans than humans, but there is little evidence to support this (although I'm sure they suffered more from predation and conflict). Scientists assume that the females reached sexual maturity at about the same time as modern humans. Also, it seems reasonable to me that, if the females suffered high mortality rates when impregnated at a young age, Neanderthal tribes might have developed a tradition of avoiding pregnancy until a later age, perhaps even twenty.

What about the animals? Did all those creatures really live in Spain 467,000 years ago? Yep, all of them. Woolly rhinos, cave bears, ibex, cave hyenas, cave lions, scimitar-toothed cats (Homotherium), reindeer, giant elk, aurochs, bison, pika, badgers, woolly mammoths, lynx, hedgehogs, and many others not mentioned in the story. Neanderthals hunted many of these creatures, including the largest and most dangerous ones. Neanderthals were kind of badass, don't you agree?

ACKNOWLEDGMENTS

I am not capable of creating a book such as this on my own. I have the following people, among others, to thank for their assistance.

First I wish to thank Monique Agueros for her help with editing. She has a keen eye for typos, poorly structured sentences, misplaced commas, and errors of logic. If you find a sentence or detail in the book that doesn't seem right, it is likely because I failed to implement one of her suggestions.

My wife Trish is always the first to read my work, and therefore she has the burden of seeing my stories in their roughest form. Thankfully, she kindly points out where things are a mess. Her suggestions are what get the editing process started. She also helps with various promotional efforts. And finally, she not only tolerates my obsession with writing, she actually encourages it.

I also owe thanks to those on my Advance Reviewer team. They were able to point out numerous typos and inconsistencies, and they are all-around fabulous people!

Finally, I am thankful to all the independent freelance designers out there who provide quality work for independent authors such as myself. Jake Caleb Clark (www.jcalebdesign.com) created the awesome cover for *Obsolete Theorem*.

ABOUT THE AUTHOR

Stan Smith has lived most of his life in the Midwest United States and currently resides with his wife Trish in a house deep in an Ozark forest in Missouri. He writes adventure novels that have a generous sprinkling of science fiction. His novels and stories are about regular people who find themselves caught up in highly unusual situations. They are designed to stimulate your sense of wonder, get your heart pounding, and keep you reading late into the night, with minimal risk of exposure to spelling and punctuation errors. His books are for anyone who loves adventure, discovery, and mind-bending surprises.

Stan's Author Website
http://www.stancsmith.com

Feel free to email Stan at: stan@stancsmith.com
He loves hearing from readers and will answer every email.

ALSO BY STAN C. SMITH

The DIFFUSION series

Diffusion

Infusion

Profusion

Savage

Blue Arrow

Diffusion Box Set

The BRIDGERS series

Bridgers 1: The Lure of Infinity

Bridgers 2: The Cost of Survival

Bridgers 3: The Voice of Reason

Bridgers 4: The Mind of Many

Bridgers 5: The Trial of Extinction

Bridgers 6: The Bond of Absolution

INFINITY: A Bridger's Origin

Bridgers 1-3 Box Set

Bridgers 4-6 Box Set

The ACROSS HORIZONS series

1: Obsolete Theorem

2. Foregone Conflict

3. Hostile Emergence

4. Binary Existence

Prequel: Genesis Sequence

The FUSED series

Prequel: Training Day

1. Rampage Ridge

2. Primordial Pit

Stand-alone Stories

Parthenium's Year

Printed in Great Britain
by Amazon